Jungle Tales of Tarzan

A Dozen Tales of Tarzan

Edgar Rice Burroughs

WILDSIDE PRESS
Doylestown, Pennsylvania

Based on the 1919 Grosset & Dunlap edition.

Jungle Tales of Tarzan
A publication of
WILDSIDE PRESS
P.O. Box 301
Holicong, PA 18928-0301

www.wildsidepress.com

A Dozen Tales of Tarzan

Table of Contents

Introduction:

Master of Our Imagination

*I*f there is such a thing as a "collective subconscious" as proposed by Jung, then Edgar Rice Burroughs leapt into it and never left in 1917 when *Tarzan of the Apes* was published in England, and Burroughs's first Mars book found readers. That was the year before the end of the "Great War," a year of great trouble, and the aftermath of the terrible Influenza epidemic. Millions died in Europe and around the world, soldiers within the trenches, and civilians due to disease, starvation, and economic upheaval.

Imagine the Lord of Greystoke, raised in the Jungle. A man of honor, courage, and uncompromising principles, who knew nothing of Continental politics, Bolshevism, or anarchists with knives, guns and bombs. Imagine, too, a Mars of wonder, with great lords, Princesses, barbarians, and wondrous new inventions. And imagine them coming into a world of trouble and strife. Dreams do serve a purpose; and Edgar Rice Burroughs was nothing if not a great and powerful dreamer.

Burroughs's aficionados note that during his lifetime, his work "failed to gather critical acclaim, yet
influenced a generation." Like so many beloved writ-
ers, Burroughs followed the well-known path to story-
telling success. Burroughs got a start in writing after
some failed attempts at being a salesman, railroad
policeman, and other professions; according to official
biographies, he even had to pawn his wife's jewelry to
make ends meet. He daydreamed and read pulp maga-
zines, and one day decided that he could write a better
pulp story than the ones he knew, and submitted his
first tale to the *All-Story Magazine* at age 35, using the
pseudonym "Normal Bean," believing that the story
was so far-out and fantastic that no one would be
interested. He shouldn't have worried. From that time
forward, readers were hooked.

What can you say about a writer who created Tarzan
of the Apes, John Carter of Mars, and David Innes of
Pellucidar? A writer who took readers — for the first
time, and for many, the times that they imagine and
dream and remember always — to the African jungles,
to the plains and canals of Mars, and to the magical
world of Pellucidar? Worlds within our own, far more
wondrous than any ever imagined before — Barsoom!
Ray Bradbury fully acknowledges his debt to Edgar
Rice Burroughs, and in this beautiful, childlike, dreaming bard's words can we see the reflection of Burroughs's dreams today. In truth, nearly every fantasy
or science fiction writer, and certainly filmmakers,
have drunk from the well of Edgar Rice Burroughs,
and drunk deeply.

Ray Bradbury never spoke more movingly than at
the Nebula Awards in 2001 in Beverly Hills, California.
There is something of magic in him, just as there is
something of complete wonder and magic in Edgar
Rice Burroughs. Ray Bradbury spoke, as he often does,

of the importance of remaining a child, and this is true: there is something of the child in almost every great writer. Do you remember when you were young? How it seemed that if you only wished hard enough and thought hard enough and dreamed long enough, the magic might become real? Toys were not merely playthings, they were real, real friends, real companions, real comrades. And that boy in the jungle that every child knows, swinging from the trees, he can really talk to the lions and the elephants and the crocodiles and to "Cheetah." Tarzan can even talk to Jane. Now, if that's not magic, what is?

No one much compliments Burroughs on his prose, but here is how he introduces John Carter in *A Princess of Mars*: "I am a very old man; how old I do not know. Possibly I am a hundred, possibly more; but I cannot tell because I have never aged as other men, nor do I remember any childhood. So far as I can recollect I have always been a man, a man of about thirty. I appear today as I did forty years and more ago, and yet I feel that I cannot go on living forever; that some day I shall die the real death from which there is no resurrection." Perhaps the suggestion of Carter's agelessness is what offends "critics," but — John Carter may have feared that he would die the "real death," but the truth is — he'll live forever.

Chieftains, Princesses, Adventurers, Barbarians. Lush jungles, garden worlds, and a world within the Earth itself. This is the imagination of a profound dreamer, full of rich images that have fueled more than fifty Tarzan movies and famous Tarzans from Johnny Weismuller and Buster Crabbe to Ron Ely and Christopher Lambert. Fritz Leiber and Philip Jose Farmer have written Tarzan-inspired novels. It doesn't matter how many NASA probes return from Mars empty-handed: dreamers everywhere know that somewhere, sometime, somehow, Barsoom is real.

At the very Nebula Award ceremony where Ray Bradbury spoke, Philip Jose Farmer was named one of science fiction's "Grand Masters." Farmer came up with the idea that there is some kind of vast genetic "family" of heroes and adventurers, all related, and among these are Tarzan, John Carter, and other beloved Burroughs characters. This all sounds quite insane, but how else to explain this extraordinary combination of heroism, strength, and character?

Just like 1917, we are in a world whose moorings have come loose, a world filled with change, fear, and horrific, cataclysmic events. Perhaps these stories of Edgar Rice Burroughs, filled with wonder, adventure, miracles, heroes and villains as they are, fit the same need today as they did during that long-ago time. A distant jungle, to ponder about and imagine, a hero swinging to the rescue, calling nature itself to his aid. A man of adventure, beyond age and limitations, traversing the magical, mystical land of Mars. Pellucidar, whose very name conjures up images of beauty, mystery and wonder.

We are told that to grow up, we must put aside childish things; but what child ever went to war? What child ever flew a plane into a building which was itself a miracle, killing thousands, like the World Trade Towers? And who was ever too old to breathe in wonder at untold vistas beneath the earth, to think that a Princess of Mars was beautiful, to imagine the gardens of Mars and the deep, green jungles of Africa where a man grew to be a hero untouched by human hand?

Edgar Rice Burroughs himself told everyone that his only aim in writing was to "entertain." He wanted to take people's minds off their troubles for a few moments, give them laughter, pleasure and enjoyment. Few, if any, have ever so entertained. Not just one, but many of his characters are as real to us as if they truly lived, breathed and walked. They are truly immortal:

Tarzan will never die; John Carter still lives.

There is too much pain in this world, and too little wonder. Every so often, we receive gifts. And these, like Edgar Rice Burroughs, we ought not question, but rather, treasure.

Edgar Rice Burroughs created a full, rich panoply of characters and worlds of wonder. His work is timeless, like one of his invented worlds: *The Land That Time Forgot.* Edgar Rice Burroughs made pure, unadulterated magic.

— Amy Sterling Casil
February, 2002
Redlands, California

Tarzan's First Love

TEEKA, STRETCHED AT luxurious ease in the
shade of the tropical forest, presented, unquestionably,
a most alluring picture of young, feminine loveliness.
Or at least so thought Tarzan of the Apes, who squatted
upon a low-swinging branch in a near-by tree and
looked down upon her.

Just to have seen him there, lolling upon the swaying
bough of the jungle-forest giant, his brown skin mottled by the brilliant equatorial sunlight which perco-
lated through the leafy canopy of green above him, his
clean-limbed body relaxed in graceful ease, his shapely
head partly turned in contemplative absorption and
his intelligent, gray eyes dreamily devouring the object
of their devotion, you would have thought him the
reincarnation of some demigod of old.

You would not have guessed that in infancy he had
suckled at the breast of a hideous, hairy she-ape, nor
that in all his conscious past since his parents had
passed away in the little cabin by the landlocked harbor
at the jungle's verge, he had known no other associates
than the sullen bulls and the snarling cows of the tribe
of Kerchak, the great ape.

Nor, could you have read the thoughts which passed through that active, healthy brain, the longings and desires and aspirations which the sight of Teeka inspired, would you have been any more inclined to give credence to the reality of the origin of the ape-man. For, from his thoughts alone, you could never have gleaned the truth — that he had been born to a gentle English lady or that his sire had been an English nobleman of time-honored lineage.

Lost to Tarzan of the Apes was the truth of his origin. That he was John Clayton, Lord Greystoke, with a seat in the House of Lords, he did not know, nor, knowing, would have understood.

Yes, Teeka was indeed beautiful!

Of course Kala had been beautiful — one's mother is always that — but Teeka was beautiful in a way all her own, an indescribable sort of way which Tarzan was just beginning to sense in a rather vague and hazy manner.

For years had Tarzan and Teeka been play-fellows, and Teeka still continued to be playful while the young bulls of her own age were rapidly becoming surly and morose. Tarzan, if he gave the matter much thought at all, probably reasoned that his growing attachment for the young female could be easily accounted for by the fact that of the former playmates she and he alone retained any desire to frolic as of old.

But today, as he sat gazing upon her, he found himself noting the beauties of Teeka's form and features — something he never had done before, since none of them had aught to do with Teeka's ability to race nimbly through the lower terraces of the forest in the primitive games of tag and hide-and-go-seek which Tarzan's fertile brain evolved.

Tarzan scratched his head, running his fingers deep into the shock of black hair which framed his shapely, boyish face — he scratched his head and sighed. Teeka's

new-found beauty became as suddenly his despair. He
envied her the handsome coat of hair which covered
her body. His own smooth, brown hide he hated with
a hatred born of disgust and contempt. Years back he
had harbored a hope that some day he, too, would be
clothed in hair as were all his brothers and sisters; but
of late he had been forced to abandon the delectable
dream.

Then there were Teeka's great teeth, not so large as
the males, of course, but still mighty, handsome things
by comparison with Tarzan's feeble white ones. And
her beetling brows, and broad, flat nose, and her
mouth! Tarzan had often practiced making his mouth
into a little round circle and then puffing out his
cheeks while he winked his eyes rapidly; but he felt that
he could never do it in the same cute and irresistible
way in which Teeka did it.

And as he watched her that afternoon, and wondered, a young bull ape who had been lazily foraging
for food beneath the damp, matted carpet of decaying
vegetation at the roots of a near-by tree lumbered
awkwardly in Teeka's direction. The other apes of the
tribe of Kerchak moved listlessly about or lolled rest-
fully in the midday heat of the equatorial jungle. From
time to time one or another of them had passed close
to Teeka, and Tarzan had been uninterested. Why was
it then that his brows contracted and his muscles
tensed as he saw Taug pause beside the young she and
then squat down close to her?

Tarzan always had liked Taug. Since childhood they
had romped together. Side by side they had squatted
near the water, their quick, strong fingers ready to leap
forth and seize Pisah, the fish, should that wary denizen of the cool depths dart surfaceward to the lure of
the insects Tarzan tossed upon the face of the pool.

Together they had baited Tublat and teased Numa,
the lion. Why, then, should Tarzan feel the rise of the

short hairs at the nape of his neck merely because Taug sat close to Teeka?

It is true that Taug was no longer the frolicsome ape of yesterday. When his snarling-muscles bared his giant fangs no one could longer imagine that Taug was in as playful a mood as when he and Tarzan had rolled upon the turf in mimic battle. The Taug of today was a huge, sullen bull ape, somber and forbidding. Yet he and Tarzan never had quarreled.

For a few minutes the young ape-man watched Taug press closer to Teeka. He saw the rough caress of the huge paw as it stroked the sleek shoulder of the she, and then Tarzan of the Apes slipped catlike to the ground and approached the two.

As he came his upper lip curled into a snarl, exposing his fighting fangs, and a deep growl rumbled from his cavernous chest. Taug looked up, batting his blood-shot eyes. Teeka half raised herself and looked at Tarzan. Did she guess the cause of his perturbation? Who may say? At any rate, she was feminine, and so she reached up and scratched Taug behind one of his small, flat ears.

Tarzan saw, and in the instant that he saw, Teeka was no longer the little playmate of an hour ago; instead she was a wondrous thing — the most wondrous in the world — and a possession for which Tarzan would fight to the death against Taug or any other who dared question his right of proprietorship.

Stooped, his muscles rigid and one great shoulder turned toward the young bull, Tarzan of the Apes sidled nearer and nearer. His face was partly averted, but his keen gray eyes never left those of Taug, and as he came, his growls increased in depth and volume.

Taug rose upon his short legs, bristling. His fighting fangs were bared. He, too, sidled, stiff-legged, and growled.

"Teeka is Tarzan's," said the ape-man, in the low

gutturals of the great anthropoids.

"Teeka is Taug's," replied the bull ape.

Thaka and Numgo and Gunto, disturbed by the growlings of the two young bulls, looked up half apathetic, half interested. They were sleepy, but they sensed a fight. It would break the monotony of the humdrum jungle life they led.

Coiled about his shoulders was Tarzan's long grass rope, in his hand was the hunting knife of the long-dead father he had never known. In Taug's little brain lay a great respect for the shiny bit of sharp metal which the ape-boy knew so well how to use. With it had he slain Tublat, his fierce foster father, and Bolgani, the gorilla. Taug knew these things, and so he came warily, circling about Tarzan in search of an opening. The latter, made cautious because of his lesser bulk and the inferiority of his natural armament, followed similar tactics.

For a time it seemed that the altercation would follow the way of the majority of such differences between members of the tribe and that one of them would finally lose interest and wander off to prosecute some other line of endeavor. Such might have been the end of it had the *casus belli* been other than it was; but Teeka was flattered at the attention that was being drawn to her and by the fact that these two young bulls were contemplating battle on her account. Such a thing never before had occurred in Teeka's brief life. She had seen other bulls battling for other and older shes, and in the depth of her wild little heart she had longed for the day when the jungle grasses would be reddened with the blood of mortal combat for her fair sake.

So now she squatted upon her haunches and insulted both her admirers impartially. She hurled taunts at them for their cowardice, and called them vile names, such as Histah, the snake, and Dango, the hyena. She threatened to call Mumga to chastise them with a stick — Mumga, who was so old that she could no longer climb and so toothless that she was forced to confine her diet almost exclusively to bananas and grub-worms.

The apes who were watching heard and laughed. Taug was infuriated. He made a sudden lunge for Tarzan, but the ape-boy leaped nimbly to one side, eluding him, and with the quickness of a cat wheeled and leaped back again to close quarters. His hunting knife was raised above his head as he came in, and he aimed a vicious blow at Taug's neck. The ape wheeled to dodge the weapon so that the keen blade struck him but a glancing blow upon the shoulder.

The spurt of red blood brought a shrill cry of delight from Teeka. Ah, but this was something worth while! She glanced about to see if others had witnessed this evidence of her popularity. Helen of Troy was never one whit more proud than was Teeka at that moment.

If Teeka had not been so absorbed in her own vaingloriousness she might have noted the rustling of leaves in the tree above her — a rustling which was not caused by any movement of the wind, since there was no wind. And had she looked up she might have seen a sleek body crouching almost directly over her and wicked yellow eyes glaring hungrily down upon her, but Teeka did not look up.

With his wound Taug had backed off growling horribly. Tarzan had followed him, screaming insults at him, and menacing him with his brandishing blade. Teeka moved from beneath the tree in an effort to keep close to the duelists.

The branch above Teeka bent and swayed a trifle with the movement of the body of the watcher stretched along it. Taug had halted now and was preparing to make a new stand. His lips were flecked with foam, and saliva drooled from his jowls. He stood with head lowered and arms outstretched, preparing for a sudden charge to close quarters. Could he but lay his mighty hands upon that soft, brown skin the battle would be his. Taug considered Tarzan's manner of fighting unfair. He would not close. Instead, he leaped nimbly just beyond the reach of Taug's muscular fingers.

The ape-boy had as yet never come to a real trial of strength with a bull ape, other than in play, and so he was not at all sure that it would be safe to put his muscles to the test in a life and death struggle. Not that he was afraid, for Tarzan knew nothing of fear. The instinct of self-preservation gave him caution — that was all. He took risks only when it seemed necessary, and then he would hesitate at nothing.

His own method of fighting seemed best fitted to his build and to his armament. His teeth, while strong and sharp, were, as weapons of offense, pitifully inadequate by comparison with the mighty fighting fangs of the anthropoids. By dancing about, just out of reach of an antagonist, Tarzan could do infinite injury with his long, sharp hunting knife, and at the same time escape many of the painful and dangerous wounds which would be sure to follow his falling into the clutches of a bull ape.

And so Taug charged and bellowed like a bull, and Tarzan of the Apes danced lightly to this side and that, hurling jungle billingsgate at his foe, the while he nicked him now and again with his knife.

There were lulls in the fighting when the two would stand panting for breath, facing each other, mustering their wits and their forces for a new onslaught. It was during a pause such as this that Taug chanced to let his eyes rove beyond his foeman. Instantly the entire aspect of the ape altered. Rage left his countenance to be supplanted by an expression of fear.

With a cry that every ape there recognized, Taug turned and fled. No need to question him — his warning proclaimed the near presence of their ancient enemy.

Tarzan started to seek safety, as did the other members of the tribe, and as he did so he heard a panther's scream mingled with the frightened cry of a she-ape. Taug heard, too; but he did not pause in his flight.

With the ape-boy, however, it was different. He looked back to see if any member of the tribe was close pressed by the beast of prey, and the sight that met his eyes filled them with an expression of horror.

Teeka it was who cried out in terror as she fled across a little clearing toward the trees upon the opposite side, for after her leaped Sheeta, the panther, in easy, graceful bounds. Sheeta appeared to be in no hurry. His meat was assured, since even though the ape reached the trees ahead of him she could not climb beyond his clutches before he could be upon her.

Tarzan saw that Teeka must die. He cried to Taug and the other bulls to hasten to Teeka's assistance, and at the same time he ran toward the pursuing beast, taking down his rope as he came. Tarzan knew that once the great bulls were aroused none of the jungle, not even Numa, the lion, was anxious to measure fangs with them, and that if all those of the tribe who chanced to be present today would charge, Sheeta, the great cat, would doubtless turn tail and run for his life.

Taug heard, as did the others, but no one came to Tarzan's assistance or Teeka's rescue, and Sheeta was rapidly closing up the distance between himself and his prey.

The ape-boy, leaping after the panther, cried aloud to the beast in an effort to turn it from Teeka or otherwise distract its attention until the she-ape could gain the safety of the higher branches where Sheeta dared not go. He called the panther every opprobrious name that fell to his tongue. He dared him to stop and do battle with him; but Sheeta only loped on after the luscious tidbit now almost within his reach.

Tarzan was not far behind and he was gaining, but the distance was so short that he scarce hoped to overhaul the carnivore before it had felled Teeka. In his right hand the boy swung his grass rope above his head as he ran. He hated to chance a miss, for the distance was much greater than he ever had cast before except in practice. It was the full length of his grass rope which separated him from Sheeta, and yet there was no other thing to do. He could not reach the brute's side before it overhauled Teeka. He must chance a throw.

And just as Teeka sprang for the lower limb of a great tree, and Sheeta rose behind her in a long, sinuous leap, the coils of the ape-boy's grass rope shot swiftly through the air, straightening into a long thin line as the open noose hovered for an instant above the savage head and the snarling jaws. Then it settled — clean and true about the tawny neck it settled, and Tarzan, with a quick twist of his rope-hand, drew the noose taut, bracing himself for the shock when Sheeta should have taken up the slack.

Just short of Teeka's glossy rump the cruel talons raked the air as the rope tightened and Sheeta was brought to a sudden stop — a stop that snapped the big beast over upon his back. Instantly Sheeta was up — with glaring eyes, and lashing tail, and gaping jaws, from which issued hideous cries of rage and disappointment.

He saw the ape-boy, the cause of his discomfiture, scarce forty feet before him, and Sheeta charged.

Teeka was safe now; Tarzan saw to that by a quick glance into the tree whose safety she had gained not an instant too soon, and Sheeta was charging. It was useless to risk his life in idle and unequal combat from which no good could come; but could he escape a battle with the enraged cat? And if he was forced to fight, what chance had he to survive? Tarzan was constrained to admit that his position was aught but a desirable one. The trees were too far to hope to reach in time to elude the cat. Tarzan could but stand facing that hideous charge. In his right hand he grasped his hunting knife — a puny, futile thing indeed by comparison with the great rows of mighty teeth which lined Sheeta's powerful jaws, and the sharp talons encased within his padded paws; yet the young Lord Greystoke faced it with the same courageous resignation with which some fearless ancestor went down to defeat and death on Senlac Hill by Hastings.

From safety points in the trees the great apes watched, screaming hatred at Sheeta and advice at Tarzan, for the progenitors of man have, naturally, many human traits. Teeka was frightened. She screamed at the bulls to hasten to Tarzan's assistance; but the bulls were otherwise engaged — principally in giving advice and making faces. Anyway, Tarzan was not a real Mangani, so why should they risk their lives in an effort to protect him?

And now Sheeta was almost upon the lithe, naked body, and — the body was not there. Quick as was the great cat, the ape-boy was quicker, He leaped to one side almost as the panther's talons were closing upon him, and as Sheeta went hurtling to the ground beyond, Tarzan was racing for the safety of the nearest tree.

The panther recovered himself almost immediately and, wheeling, tore after his prey, the ape-boy's rope dragging along the ground behind him. In doubling back after Tarzan, Sheeta had passed around a low bush. It was a mere nothing in the path of any jungle creature of the size and weight of Sheeta — provided it had no trailing rope dangling behind. But Sheeta was handicapped by such a rope, and as he leaped once again after Tarzan of the Apes the rope encircled the small bush, became tangled in it and brought the panther to a sudden stop. An instant later Tarzan was safe among the higher branches of a small tree into which Sheeta could not follow him.

Here he perched, hurling twigs and epithets at the raging feline beneath him. The other members of the tribe now took up the bombardment, using such hard-shelled fruits and dead branches as came within their reach, until Sheeta, goaded to frenzy and snapping at the grass rope, finally succeeded in severing its strands. For a moment the panther stood glaring first at one of his tormentors and then at another, until, with a final scream of rage, he turned and slunk off into the tangled mazes of the jungle.

A half hour later the tribe was again upon the ground, feeding as though naught had occurred to interrupt the somber dullness of their lives. Tarzan had recovered the greater part of his rope and was busy fashioning a new noose, while Teeka squatted close behind him, in evident token that her choice was made.

Taug eyed them sullenly. Once when he came close, Teeka bared her fangs and growled at him, and Tarzan showed his canines in an ugly snarl; but Taug did not provoke a quarrel. He seemed to accept after the manner of his kind the decision of the she as an indication that he had been vanquished in his battle for her favors.

Later in the day, his rope repaired, Tarzan took to the trees in search of game. More than his fellows he required meat, and so, while they were satisfied with fruits and herbs and beetles, which could be discovered without much effort upon their part, Tarzan spent considerable time hunting the game animals whose flesh alone satisfied the cravings of his stomach and furnished sustenance and strength to the mighty thews which, day by day, were building beneath the soft, smooth texture of his brown hide.

Taug saw him depart, and then, quite casually, the big beast hunted closer and closer to Teeka in his search for food. At last he was within a few feet of her, and when he shot a covert glance at her he saw that she was appraising him and that there was no evidence of anger upon her face.

Taug expanded his great chest and rolled about on his short legs, making strange growlings in his throat. He raised his lips, baring his fangs. My, but what great, beautiful fangs he had! Teeka could not but notice them. She also let her eyes rest in admiration upon Taug's beetling brows and his short, powerful neck. What a beautiful creature he was indeed!

Taug, flattered by the unconcealed admiration in her eyes, strutted about, as proud and as vain as a peacock. Presently he began to inventory his assets, mentally, and shortly he found himself comparing them with those of his rival.

Taug grunted, for there was no comparison. How could one compare his beautiful coat with the smooth and naked hideousness of Tarzan's bare hide? Who could see beauty in the stingy nose of the Tarmangani after looking at Taug's broad nostrils? And Tarzan's eyes! Hideous things, showing white about them, and entirely unrimmed with red. Taug knew that his own blood-shot eyes were beautiful, for he had seen them reflected in the glassy surface of many a drinking pool.

The bull drew nearer to Teeka, finally squatting close against her. When Tarzan returned from his hunting a short time later it was to see Teeka contentedly scratching the back of his rival.

Tarzan was disgusted. Neither Taug nor Teeka saw him as he swung through the trees into the glade. He paused a moment, looking at them; then, with a sorrowful grimace, he turned and faded away into the labyrinth of leafy boughs and festooned moss out of which he had come.

Tarzan wished to be as far away from the cause of his heartache as he could. He was suffering the first pangs of blighted love, and he didn't quite know what was the matter with him. He thought that he was angry with Taug, and so he couldn't understand why it was that he had run away instead of rushing into mortal combat with the destroyer of his happiness.

He also thought that he was angry with Teeka, yet a vision of her many beauties persisted in haunting him, so that he could only see her in the light of love as the most desirable thing in the world.

The ape-boy craved affection. From babyhood until the time of her death, when the poisoned arrow of Kulonga had pierced her savage heart, Kala had represented to the English boy the sole object of love which he had known.

In her wild, fierce way Kala had loved her adopted son, and Tarzan had returned that love, though the outward demonstrations of it were no greater than might have been expected from any other beast of the jungle. It was not until he was bereft of her that the boy realized how deep had been his attachment for his mother, for as such he looked upon her.

In Teeka he had seen within the past few hours a substitute for Kala — someone to fight for and to hunt for — someone to caress; but now his dream was shattered. Something hurt within his breast. He placed his hand over his heart and wondered what had happened to him. Vaguely he attributed his pain to Teeka. The more he thought of Teeka as he had last seen her, caressing Taug, the more the thing within his breast hurt him.

Tarzan shook his head and growled; then on and on through the jungle he swung, and the farther he traveled and the more he thought upon his wrongs, the nearer he approached becoming an irreclaimable misogynist.

Two days later he was still hunting alone — very morose and very unhappy; but he was determined never to return to the tribe. He could not bear the thought of seeing Taug and Teeka always together. As he swung upon a great limb Numa, the lion, and Sabor, the lioness, passed beneath him, side by side, and Sabor leaned against the lion and bit playfully at his cheek. It was a half-caress. Tarzan sighed and hurled a nut at them.

Later he came upon several of Mbonga's black warriors. He was upon the point of dropping his noose about the neck of one of them, who was a little distance from his companions, when he became interested in the thing which occupied the savages. They were building a cage in the trail and covering it with leafy branches. When they had completed their work the structure was scarcely visible.

Tarzan wondered what the purpose of the thing might be, and why, when they had built it, they turned away and started back along the trail in the direction of their village.

It had been some time since Tarzan had visited the blacks and looked down from the shelter of the great trees which overhung their palisade upon the activities of his enemies, from among whom had come the slayer of Kala.

Although he hated them, Tarzan derived considerable entertainment in watching them at their daily life within the village, and especially at their dances, when the fires glared against their naked bodies as they leaped and turned and twisted in mimic warfare. It was rather in the hope of witnessing something of the kind that he now followed the warriors back toward their village, but in this he was disappointed, for there was no dance that night.

Instead, from the safe concealment of his tree, Tarzan saw little groups seated about tiny fires discussing the events of the day, and in the darker corners of the village he descried isolated couples talking and laughing together, and always one of each couple was a young man and the other a young woman.

Tarzan cocked his head upon one side and thought, and before he went to sleep that night, curled in the crotch of the great tree above the village, Teeka filled his mind, and afterward she filled his dreams — she and the young black men laughing and talking with the young black women.

Taug, hunting alone, had wandered some distance from the balance of the tribe. He was making his way slowly along an elephant path when he discovered that it was blocked with undergrowth. Now Taug, come into maturity, was an evil-natured brute of an exceeding short temper. When something thwarted him, his sole idea was to overcome it by brute strength and ferocity, and so now when he found his way blocked, he tore angrily into the leafy screen and an instant later found himself within a strange lair, his progress effectually blocked, notwithstanding his most violent efforts to forge ahead.

Biting and striking at the barrier, Taug finally worked him-self into a frightful rage, but all to no avail; and at last he became convinced that he must turn back. But when he would have done so, what was his chagrin to discover that another barrier had dropped behind him while he fought to break down the one before him! Taug was trapped. Until exhaustion overcame him he fought frantically for his freedom; but all for naught.

In the morning a party of blacks set out from the village of Mbonga in the direction of the trap they had constructed the previous day, while among the branches of the trees above them hovered a naked young giant filled with the curiosity of the wild things. Manu, the monkey, chattered and scolded as Tarzan passed, and though he was not afraid of the familiar figure of the ape-boy, he hugged closer to him the little brown body of his life's companion. Tarzan laughed as he saw it; but the laugh was followed by a sudden clouding of his face and a deep sigh.

A little farther on, a gaily feathered bird strutted about before the admiring eyes of his somber-hued mate. It seemed to Tarzan that everything in the jungle was combining to remind him that he had lost Teeka; yet every day of his life he had seen these same things and thought nothing of them.

When the blacks reached the trap, Taug set up a great commotion. Seizing the bars of his prison, he shook them frantically, and all the while he roared and growled terrifically. The blacks were elated, for while they had not built their trap for this hairy tree man, they were delighted with their catch.

Tarzan pricked up his ears when he heard the voice of a great ape and, circling quickly until he was down wind from the trap, he sniffed at the air in search of the scent spoor of the prisoner. Nor was it long before there came to those delicate nostrils the familiar odor that told Tarzan the identity of the captive as unerringly as though he had looked upon Taug with his eyes. Yes, it was Taug, and he was alone.

Tarzan grinned as he approached to discover what the blacks would do to their prisoner. Doubtless they would slay him at once. Again Tarzan grinned. Now he could have Teeka for his own, with none to dispute his right to her. As he watched, he saw the black warriors strip the screen from about the cage, fasten ropes to it and drag it away along the trail in the direction of their village.

Tarzan watched until his rival passed out of sight, still beating upon the bars of his prison and growling out his anger and his threats. Then the ape-boy turned and swung rapidly off in search of the tribe, and Teeka.

Once, upon the journey, he surprised Sheeta and his family in a little overgrown clearing. The great cat lay stretched upon the ground, while his mate, one paw across her lord's savage face, licked at the soft white fur at his throat.

Tarzan increased his speed then until he fairly flew through the forest, nor was it long before he came upon the tribe. He saw them before they saw him, for of all the jungle creatures, none passed more quietly than Tarzan of the Apes. He saw Kamma and her mate feeding side by side, their hairy bodies rubbing against each other. And he saw Teeka feeding by herself. Not for long would she feed thus in loneliness, thought Tarzan, as with a bound he landed amongst them.

There was a startled rush and a chorus of angry and frightened snarls, for Tarzan had surprised them; but there was more, too, than mere nervous shock to account for the bristling neck hair which remained standing long after the apes had discovered the identity of the newcomer.

Tarzan noticed this as he had noticed it many times in the past — that always his sudden coming among them left them nervous and unstrung for a considerable time, and that they one and all found it necessary to satisfy themselves that he was indeed Tarzan by smelling about him a half dozen or more times before they calmed down.

Pushing through them, he made his way toward Teeka; but as he approached her the ape drew away.

"Teeka," he said, "it is Tarzan. You belong to Tarzan. I have come for you."

The ape drew closer, looking him over carefully. Finally she sniffed at him, as though to make assurance doubly sure.

"Where is Taug?" she asked.

"The Gomangani have him," replied Tarzan. "They will kill him."

In the eyes of the she, Tarzan saw a wistful expression and a troubled look of sorrow as he told her of Taug's fate; but she came quite close and snuggled against him, and Tarzan, Lord Greystoke, put his arm about her.

As he did so he noticed, with a start, the strange incongruity of that smooth, brown arm against the black and hairy coat of his lady-love. He recalled the paw of Sheeta's mate across Sheeta's face — no incongruity there. He thought of little Manu hugging his she, and how the one seemed to belong to the other. Even the proud male bird, with his gay plumage, bore a close resemblance to his quieter spouse, while Numa, but for his shaggy mane, was almost a counterpart of Sabor, the lioness. The males and the females differed, it was true; but not with such differences as existed between Tarzan and Teeka.

Tarzan was puzzled. There was something wrong. His arm dropped from the shoulder of Teeka. Very slowly he drew away from her. She looked at him with her head cocked upon one side. Tarzan rose to his full height and beat upon his breast with his fists. He raised his head toward the heavens and opened his mouth. From the depths of his lungs rose the fierce, weird challenge of the victorious bull ape. The tribe turned curiously to eye him. He had killed nothing, nor was there any antagonist to be goaded to madness by the savage scream. No, there was no excuse for it, and they turned back to their feeding, but with an eye upon the ape-man lest he be preparing to suddenly run amuck.

As they watched him they saw him swing into a near-by tree and disappear from sight. Then they forgot him, even Teeka.

Mbonga's black warriors, sweating beneath their strenuous task, and resting often, made slow progress toward their village. Always the savage beast in the primitive cage growled and roared when they moved him. He beat upon the bars and slavered at the mouth. His noise was hideous.

They had almost completed their journey and were making their final rest before forging ahead to gain the clearing in which lay their village. A few more minutes would have taken them out of the forest, and then, doubtless, the thing would not have happened which did happen.

A silent figure moved through the trees above them. Keen eyes inspected the cage and counted the number of warriors. An alert and daring brain figured upon the chances of success when a certain plan should be put to the test.

Tarzan watched the blacks lolling in the shade. They were exhausted. Already several of them slept. He crept closer, pausing just above them. Not a leaf rustled before his stealthy advance. He waited in the infinite patience of the beast of prey. Presently but two of the warriors remained awake, and one of these was dozing.

Tarzan of the Apes gathered himself, and as he did so the black who did not sleep arose and passed around to the rear of the cage. The ape-boy followed just above his head. Taug was eyeing the warrior and emitting low growls. Tarzan feared that the anthropoid would awaken the sleepers.

In a whisper which was inaudible to the ears of the Negro, Tarzan whispered Taug's name, cautioning the ape to silence, and Taug's growling ceased.

The black approached the rear of the cage and examined the fastenings of the door, and as he stood there the beast above him launched itself from the tree full upon his back. Steel fingers circled his throat, choking the cry which sprang to the lips of the terrified man. Strong teeth fastened them-selves in his shoulder, and powerful legs wound themselves about his torso.

The black in a frenzy of terror tried to dislodge the silent thing which clung to him. He threw himself to the ground and rolled about; but still those mighty fingers closed more and more tightly their deadly grip.

The man's mouth gaped wide, his swollen tongue protruded, his eyes started from their sockets; but the relentless fingers only increased their pressure.

Taug was a silent witness of the struggle. In his fierce little brain he doubtless wondered what purpose prompted Tarzan to attack the black. Taug had not forgotten his recent battle with the ape-boy, nor the cause of it. Now he saw the form of the Gomangani suddenly go limp. There was a convulsive shiver and the man lay still.

Tarzan sprang from his prey and ran to the door of the cage. With nimble fingers he worked rapidly at the thongs which held the door in place. Taug could only watch — he could not help. Presently Tarzan pushed the thing up a couple of feet and Taug crawled out. The ape would have turned upon the sleeping blacks that he might wreak his pent vengeance; but Tarzan would not permit it.

Instead, the ape-boy dragged the body of the black within the cage and propped it against the side bars. Then he lowered the door and made fast the thongs as they had been before.

A happy smile lighted his features as he worked, for one of his principal diversions was the baiting of the blacks of Mbonga's village. He could imagine their terror when they awoke and found the dead body of their comrade fast in the cage where they had left the great ape safely secured but a few minutes before.

Tarzan and Taug took to the trees together, the shaggy coat of the fierce ape brushing the sleek skin of the English lordling as they passed through the primeval jungle side by side.

"Go back to Teeka," said Tarzan. "She is yours. Tarzan does not want her."

"Tarzan has found another she?" asked Taug.

The ape-boy shrugged.

"For the Gomangani there is another Gomangani,"

he said; "for Numa, the lion, there is Sabor, the lioness; for Sheeta there is a she of his own kind; for Bara, the deer; for Manu, the monkey; for all the beasts and the birds of the jungle is there a mate. Only for Tarzan of the Apes is there none. Taug is an ape. Teeka is an ape. Go back to Teeka. Tarzan is a man. He will go alone."

The Capture of Tarzan

THE BLACK WARRIORS labored in the humid heat of the jungle's stifling shade. With war spears they loosened the thick, black loam and the deep layers of rotting vegetation. With heavy-nailed fingers they scooped away the disintegrated earth from the center of the age-old game trail. Often they ceased their labors to squat, resting and gossiping, with much laughter, at the edge of the pit they were digging.

Against the boles of near-by trees leaned their long, oval shields of thick buffalo hide, and the spears of those who were doing the scooping. Sweat glistened upon their smooth, ebon skins, beneath which rolled rounded muscles, supple in the perfection of nature's uncontaminated health.

A reed buck, stepping warily along the trail toward water, halted as a burst of laughter broke upon his startled ears. For a moment he stood statuesque but for his sensitively dilating nostrils; then he wheeled and fled noiselessly from the terrifying presence of man.

A hundred yards away, deep in the tangle of impenetrable jungle, Numa, the lion, raised his massive head.

Numa had dined well until almost daybreak and it had required much noise to awaken him. Now he lifted his muzzle and sniffed the air, caught the acrid scent spoor of the reed buck and the heavy scent of man. But Numa was well filled. With a low, disgusted grunt he rose and slunk away.

Brilliantly plumaged birds with raucous voices darted from tree to tree. Little monkeys, chattering and scolding, swung through the swaying limbs above the black warriors. Yet they were alone, for the teeming jungle with all its myriad life, like the swarming streets of a great metropolis, is one of the loneliest spots in God's great universe.

But were they alone?

Above them, lightly balanced upon a leafy tree limb, a gray-eyed youth watched with eager intentness their every move. The fire of hate, restrained, smoldered beneath the lad's evident desire to know the purpose of the black men's labors. Such a one as these it was who had slain his beloved Kala. For them there could be naught but enmity, yet he liked well to watch them, avid as he was for greater knowledge of the ways of man.

He saw the pit grow in depth until a great hole yawned the width of the trail — a hole which was amply large enough to hold at one time all of the six excavators. Tarzan could not guess the purpose of so great a labor. And when they cut long stakes, sharpened at their upper ends, and set them at intervals upright in the bottom of the pit, his wonderment but increased, nor was it satisfied with the placing of the light cross-poles over the pit, or the careful arrangement of leaves and earth which completely hid from view the work the black men had performed.

When they were done they surveyed their handiwork with evident satisfaction, and Tarzan surveyed it, too. Even to his practiced eye there remained scarce a vestige of evidence that the ancient game trail had been tampered with in any way.

So absorbed was the ape-man in speculation as to the purpose of the covered pit that he permitted the blacks to depart in the direction of their village without the usual baiting which had rendered him the terror of Mbonga's people and had afforded Tarzan both a vehicle of revenge and a source of inexhaustible delight.

Puzzle as he would, however, he could not solve the mystery of the concealed pit, for the ways of the blacks were still strange ways to Tarzan. They had entered his jungle but a short time before — the first of their kind to encroach upon the age-old supremacy of the beasts which laired there. To Numa, the lion, to Tantor, the elephant, to the great apes and the lesser apes, to each and all of the myriad creatures of this savage wild, the ways of man were new. They had much to learn of these black, hairless creatures that walked erect upon their hind paws — and they were learning it slowly, and always to their sorrow.

Shortly after the blacks had departed, Tarzan swung easily to the trail. Sniffing suspiciously, he circled the edge of the pit. Squatting upon his haunches, he scraped away a little earth to expose one of the crossbars. He sniffed at this, touched it, cocked his head upon one side, and contemplated it gravely for several minutes. Then he carefully re-covered it, arranging the earth as neatly as had the blacks. This done, he swung himself back among the branches of the trees and moved off in search of his hairy fellows, the great apes of the tribe of Kerchak.

Once he crossed the trail of Numa, the lion, pausing for a moment to hurl a soft fruit at the snarling face of his enemy, and to taunt and insult him, calling him eater of carrion and brother of Dango, the hyena. Numa, his yellow-green eyes round and burning with concentrated hate, glared up at the dancing figure above him. Low growls vibrated his heavy jowls and his great rage transmitted to his sinuous tail a sharp, whiplike motion; but realizing from past experience the futility of long distance argument with the ape-man, he turned presently and struck off into the tangled vegetation which hid him from the view of his tormentor. With a final scream of jungle invective and an apelike grimace at his departing foe, Tarzan continued along his way.

Another mile and a shifting wind brought to his keen nostrils a familiar, pungent odor close at hand, and a moment later there loomed beneath him a huge, gray-black bulk forging steadily along the jungle trail. Tarzan seized and broke a small tree limb, and at the sudden cracking sound the ponderous figure halted. Great ears were thrown forward, and a long, supple trunk rose quickly to wave to and fro in search of the scent of an enemy, while two weak, little eyes peered suspiciously and futilely about in quest of the author of the noise which had disturbed his peaceful way.

Tarzan laughed aloud and came closer above the head of the pachyderm.

"Tantor! Tantor!" he cried. "Bara, the deer, is less fearful than you — you, Tantor, the elephant, greatest of the jungle folk with the strength of as many Numas as I have toes upon my feet and fingers upon my hands. Tantor, who can uproot great trees, trembles with fear at the sound of a broken twig."

A rumbling noise, which might have been either a sign of contempt or a sigh of relief, was Tantor's only reply as the uplifted trunk and ears came down and the beast's tail dropped to normal; but his eyes still roved about in search of Tarzan. He was not long kept in suspense, however, as to the whereabouts of the ape-man, for a second later the youth dropped lightly to the broad head of his old friend. Then stretching himself at full length, he drummed with his bare toes upon the thick hide, and as his fingers scratched the more tender surfaces beneath the great ears, he talked to Tantor of the gossip of the jungle as though the great beast understood every word that he said.

Much there was which Tarzan could make Tantor understand, and though the small talk of the wild was beyond the great, gray dreadnaught of the jungle, he stood with blinking eyes and gently swaying trunk as though drinking in every word of it with keenest appreciation. As a matter of fact it was the pleasant, friendly voice and caressing hands behind his ears which he enjoyed, and the close proximity of him whom he had often borne upon his back since Tarzan, as a little child, had once fearlessly approached the great bull, assuming upon the part of the pachyderm the same friendliness which filled his own heart.

In the years of their association Tarzan had discovered that he possessed an inexplicable power to govern and direct his mighty friend. At his bidding, Tantor would come from a great distance — as far as his keen ears could detect the shrill and piercing summons of the ape-man — and when Tarzan was squatted upon his head, Tantor would lumber through the jungle in any direction which his rider bade him go. It was the power of the man-mind over that of the brute and it was just as effective as though both fully understood its origin, though neither did.

For half an hour Tarzan sprawled there upon Tantor's back. Time had no meaning for either of them. Life, as they saw it, consisted principally in keeping their stomachs filled. To Tarzan this was a less arduous labor than to Tantor, for Tarzan's stomach was smaller, and being omnivorous, food was less difficult to obtain. If one sort did not come readily to hand, there were always many others to satisfy his hunger. He was less particular as to his diet than Tantor, who would eat only the bark of certain trees, and the wood of others, while a third appealed to him only through its leaves, and these, perhaps, just at certain seasons of the year.

Tantor must needs spend the better part of his life in filling his immense stomach against the needs of his mighty thews. It is thus with all the lower orders — their lives are so occupied either with searching for food or with the processes of digestion that they have little time for other considerations. Doubtless it is this handicap which has kept them from advancing as rapidly as man, who has more time to give to thought upon other matters.

However, these questions troubled Tarzan but little, and Tantor not at all. What the former knew was that he was happy in the companionship of the elephant. He did not know why. He did not know that because he was a human being — a normal, healthy human being — he craved some living thing upon which to lavish his affection. His childhood playmates among the apes of Kerchak were now great, sullen brutes. They felt nor inspired but little affection. The younger apes Tarzan still played with occasionally. In his savage way he loved them; but they were far from satisfying or restful companions. Tantor was a great mountain of calm, of poise, of stability. It was restful and satisfying to sprawl upon his rough pate and pour one's vague hopes and aspirations into the great ears which flapped ponderously to and fro in apparent understanding. Of all the jungle folk, Tantor commanded Tarzan's greatest love since Kala had been taken from him. Sometimes Tarzan wondered if Tantor reciprocated his affection. It was difficult to know.

It was the call of the stomach — the most compelling and insistent call which the jungle knows — that took Tarzan finally back to the trees and off in search of food, while Tantor continued his interrupted journey in the opposite direction.

For an hour the ape-man foraged. A lofty nest yielded its fresh, warm harvest. Fruits, berries, and tender plantain found a place upon his menu in the order that he happened upon them, for he did not seek such foods. Meat, meat, meat! It was always meat that Tarzan of the Apes hunted; but sometimes meat eluded him, as today.

And as he roamed the jungle his active mind busied itself not alone with his hunting, but with many other subjects. He had a habit of recalling often the events of the preceding days and hours. He lived over his visit with Tantor; he cogitated upon the digging blacks and the strange, covered pit they had left behind them. He wondered again and again what its purpose might be. He compared perceptions and arrived at judgments. He compared judgments, reaching conclusions – not always correct ones, it is true, but at least he used his brain for the purpose God intended it, which was the less difficult because he was not handicapped by the second-hand, and usually erroneous, judgment of others.

And as he puzzled over the covered pit, there loomed suddenly before his mental vision a huge, gray-black bulk which lumbered ponderously along a jungle trail. Instantly Tarzan tensed to the shock of a sudden fear. Decision and action usually occurred simultaneously in the life of the ape-man, and now he was away through the leafy branches ere the realization of the pit's purpose had scarce formed in his mind.

Swinging from swaying limb to swaying limb, he raced through the middle terraces where the trees grew close together. Again he dropped to the ground and sped, silently and light of foot, over the carpet of decaying vegetation, only to leap again into the trees where the tangled undergrowth precluded rapid advance upon the surface.

In his anxiety he cast discretion to the winds. The caution of the beast was lost in the loyalty of the man, and so it came that he entered a large clearing, denuded of trees, without a thought of what might lie there or upon the farther edge to dispute the way with him.

He was half way across when directly in his path and but a few yards away there rose from a clump of tall grasses a half dozen chattering birds. Instantly Tarzan turned aside, for he knew well enough what manner of creature the presence of these little sentinels proclaimed. Simultaneously Buto, the rhinoceros, scrambled to his short legs and charged furiously. Haphazard charges Buto, the rhinoceros. With his weak eyes he sees but poorly even at short distances, and whether his erratic rushes are due to the panic of fear as he attempts to escape, or to the irascible temper with which he is generally credited, it is difficult to determine. Nor is the matter of little moment to one whom Buto charges, for if he be caught and tossed, the chances are that naught will interest him thereafter.

And today it chanced that Buto bore down straight upon Tarzan, across the few yards of knee-deep grass which separated them. Accident started him in the direction of the ape-man, and then his weak eyes discerned the enemy, and with a series of snorts he charged straight for him. The little rhino birds fluttered and circled about their giant ward. Among the branches of the trees at the edge of the clearing, a score or more monkeys chattered and scolded as the loud snorts of the angry beast sent them scurrying affrightedly to the upper terraces. Tarzan alone appeared indifferent and serene.

Directly in the path of the charge he stood. There had been no time to seek safety in the trees beyond the clearing, nor had Tarzan any mind to delay his journey because of Buto. He had met the stupid beast before and held him in fine contempt.

And now Buto was upon him, the massive head lowered and the long, heavy horn inclined for the frightful work for which nature had designed it; but as he struck upward, his weapon raked only thin air, for the ape-man had sprung lightly aloft with a catlike leap that carried him above the threatening horn to the broad back of the rhinoceros. Another spring and he was on the ground behind the brute and racing like a deer for the trees.

Buto, angered and mystified by the strange disappearance of his prey, wheeled and charged frantically in another direction, which chanced to be not the direction of Tarzan's flight, and so the ape-man came in safety to the trees and continued on his swift way through the forest.

Some distance ahead of him Tantor moved steadily along the well-worn elephant trail, and ahead of Tantor a crouching, black warrior listened intently in the middle of the path. Presently he heard the sound for which he had been hoping — the cracking, snapping sound which heralded the approach of an elephant.

To his right and left in other parts of the jungle other warriors were watching. A low signal, passed from one to another, apprised the most distant that the quarry was afoot. Rapidly they converged toward the trail, taking positions in trees down wind from the point at which Tantor must pass them. Silently they waited and presently were rewarded by the sight of a mighty tusker carrying an amount of ivory in his long tusks that set their greedy hearts to palpitating.

No sooner had he passed their positions than the warriors clambered from their perches. No longer were they silent, but instead clapped their hands and shouted as they reached the ground. For an instant Tantor, the elephant, paused with upraised trunk and tail, with great ears up-pricked, and then he swung on along the trail at a rapid, shuffling pace — straight

toward the covered pit with its sharpened stakes upstanding in the ground.

Behind him came the yelling warriors, urging him
on in the rapid flight which would not permit a careful
examination of the ground before him. Tantor, the
elephant, who could have turned and scattered his
adversaries with a single charge, fled like a frightened
deer — fled toward a hideous, torturing death.

And behind them all came Tarzan of the Apes, racing
through the jungle forest with the speed and agility of
a squirrel, for he had heard the shouts of the warriors
and had interpreted them correctly. Once he uttered a
piercing call that reverberated through the jungle; but
Tantor, in the panic of terror, either failed to hear, or
hearing, dared not pause to heed.

Now the giant pachyderm was but a few yards from
the hidden death lurking in his path, and the blacks,
certain of success, were screaming and dancing in his
wake, waving their war spears and celebrating in advance the acquisition of the splendid ivory carried by
their prey and the surfeit of elephant meat which
would be theirs this night.

So intent were they upon their gratulations that they
entirely failed to note the silent passage of the man-
beast above their heads, nor did Tantor, either, see or
hear him, even though Tarzan called to him to stop.

A few more steps would precipitate Tantor upon the
sharpened stakes; Tarzan fairly flew through the trees
until he had come abreast of the fleeing animal and
then had passed him. At the pit's verge the ape-man
dropped to the ground in the center of the trail. Tantor
was almost upon him before his weak eyes permitted
him to recognize his old friend.

"Stop!" cried Tarzan, and the great beast halted to
the upraised hand.

Tarzan turned and kicked aside some of the brush
which hid the pit. Instantly Tantor saw and under-

stood.

"Fight!" growled Tarzan. "They are coming behind you." But Tantor, the elephant, is a huge bunch of nerves, and now he was half panic-stricken by terror.

Before him yawned the pit, how far he did not know, but to right and left lay the primeval jungle untouched by man. With a squeal the great beast turned suddenly at right angles and burst his noisy way through the solid wall of matted vegetation that would have stopped any but him.

Tarzan, standing upon the edge of the pit, smiled as he watched Tantor's undignified flight. Soon the blacks would come. It was best that Tarzan of the Apes faded from the scene. He essayed a step from the pit's edge, and as he threw the weight of his body upon his left foot, the earth crumbled away. Tarzan made a single Herculean effort to throw himself forward, but it was too late. Backward and downward he went toward the sharpened stakes in the bottom of the pit.

When, a moment later, the blacks came they saw even from a distance that Tantor had eluded them, for the size of the hole in the pit covering was too small to have accommodated the huge bulk of an elephant. At first they thought that their prey had put one great foot through the top and then, warned, drawn back; but when they had come to the pit's verge and peered over, their eyes went wide in astonishment, for, quiet and still, at the bottom lay the naked figure of a white giant.

Some of them there had glimpsed this forest god before and they drew back in terror, awed by the presence which they had for some time believed to possess the miraculous powers of a demon; but others there were who pushed forward, thinking only of the capture of an enemy, and these leaped into the pit and lifted Tarzan out.

There was no scar upon his body. None of the

sharpened stakes had pierced him — only a swollen
spot at the base of the brain indicated the nature of
his injury. In the falling backward his head had struck
upon the side of one of the stakes, rendering him
unconscious. The blacks were quick to discover this,
and equally quick to bind their prisoner's arms and
legs before he should regain consciousness, for they
had learned to harbor a wholesome respect for this
strange man-beast that consorted with the hairy tree
folk.

They had carried him but a short distance toward
their village when the ape-man's eyelids quivered and
raised. He looked about him wonderingly for a moment, and then full consciousness returned and he
realized the seriousness of his predicament. Accustomed almost from birth to relying solely upon his
own resources, he did not cast about for outside aid
now, but devoted his mind to a consideration of the
possibilities for escape which lay within himself and
his own powers.

He did not dare test the strength of his bonds while
the blacks were carrying him, for fear they would
become apprehensive and add to them. Presently his
captors discovered that he was conscious, and as they
had little stomach for carrying a heavy man through
the jungle heat, they set him upon his feet and forced
him forward among them, pricking him now and then
with their spears, yet with every manifestation of the
superstitious awe in which they held him.

When they discovered that their prodding brought
no outward evidence of suffering, their awe increased,
so that they soon desisted, half believing that this
strange white giant was a supernatural being and so
was immune from pain.

As they approached their village, they shouted aloud
the victorious cries of successful warriors, so that by
the time they reached the gate, dancing and waving

their spears, a great crowd of men, women, and children were gathered there to greet them and hear the story of their adventure.

As the eyes of the villagers fell upon the prisoner, they went wild, and heavy jaws fell open in astonishment and incredulity. For months they had lived in perpetual terror of a weird, white demon whom but few had ever glimpsed and lived to describe. Warriors had disappeared from the paths almost within sight of the village and from the midst of their companions as mysteriously and completely as though they had been swallowed by the earth, and later, at night, their dead bodies had fallen, as from the heavens, into the village street.

This fearsome creature had appeared by night in the huts of the village, killed, and disappeared, leaving behind him in the huts with his dead, strange and terrifying evidences of an uncanny sense of humor.

But now he was in their power! No longer could he terrorize them. Slowly the realization of this dawned upon them. A woman, screaming, ran forward and struck the ape-man across the face. Another and another followed her example, until Tarzan of the Apes was surrounded by a fighting, clawing, yelling mob of natives.

And then Mbonga, the chief, came, and laying his spear heavily across the shoulders of his people, drove them from their prey.

"We will save him until night," he said.

Far out in the jungle Tantor, the elephant, his first panic of fear allayed, stood with up-pricked ears and undulating trunk. What was passing through the convolutions of his savage brain? Could he be searching for Tarzan? Could he recall and measure the service the ape-man had performed for him? Of that there can be no doubt. But did he feel gratitude? Would he have risked his own life to have saved Tarzan could he have

known of the danger which confronted his friend? You
will doubt it. Anyone at all familiar with elephants will
doubt it. Englishmen who have hunted much with
elephants in India will tell you that they never have
heard of an instance in which one of these animals has
gone to the aid of a man in danger, even though the
man had often befriended it. And so it is to be doubted
that Tantor would have attempted to overcome his
instinctive fear of the black men in an effort to succor
Tarzan.

The screams of the infuriated villagers came faintly
to his sensitive ears, and he wheeled, as though in
terror, contemplating flight; but something stayed
him, and again he turned about, raised his trunk, and
gave voice to a shrill cry.

Then he stood listening.

In the distant village where Mbonga had restored
quiet and order, the voice of Tantor was scarcely audi-
ble to the blacks, but to the keen ears of Tarzan of the
Apes it bore its message.

His captors were leading him to a hut where he
might be confined and guarded against the coming of
the nocturnal orgy that would mark his torture-laden
death. He halted as he heard the notes of Tantor's call,
and raising his head, gave vent to a terrifying scream
that sent cold chills through the superstitious blacks
and caused the warriors who guarded him to leap back
even though their prisoner's arms were securely bound
behind him.

With raised spears they encircled him as for a moment longer he stood listening. Faintly from the distance came another, an answering cry, and Tarzan of
the Apes, satisfied, turned and quietly pursued his way
toward the hut where he was to be imprisoned.

The afternoon wore on. From the surrounding village the ape-man heard the bustle of preparation for
the feast. Through the doorway of the hut he saw the

women laying the cooking fires and filling their earthen caldrons with water; but above it all his ears were bent across the jungle in eager listening for the coming of Tantor.

Even Tarzan but half believed that he would come. He knew Tantor even better than Tantor knew himself. He knew the timid heart which lay in the giant body. He knew the panic of terror which the scent of the Gomangani inspired within that savage breast, and as night drew on, hope died within his heart and in the stoic calm of the wild beast which he was, he resigned himself to meet the fate which awaited him.

All afternoon he had been working, working, working with the bonds that held his wrists. Very slowly they were giving. He might free his hands before they came to lead him out to be butchered, and if he did — Tarzan licked his lips in anticipation, and smiled a cold, grim smile. He could imagine the feel of soft flesh beneath his fingers and the sinking of his white teeth into the throats of his foe-men. He would let them taste his wrath before they over-powered him!

At last they came — painted, befeathered warriors — even more hideous than nature had intended them. They came and pushed him into the open, where his appearance was greeted by wild shouts from the assembled villagers.

To the stake they led him, and as they pushed him roughly against it preparatory to binding him there securely for the dance of death that would presently encircle him, Tarzan tensed his mighty thews and with a single, powerful wrench parted the loosened thongs which had secured his hands. Like thought, for quickness, he leaped forward among the warriors nearest him. A blow sent one to earth, as, growling and snarling, the beast-man leaped upon the breast of another. His fangs were buried instantly in the jugular of his adversary and then a half hundred black men had leaped upon him and borne him to earth.

Striking, clawing, and snapping, the ape-man fought — fought as his foster people had taught him to fight — fought like a wild beast cornered. His strength, his agility, his courage, and his intelligence rendered him easily a match for half a dozen black men in a hand-to-hand struggle, but not even Tarzan of the Apes could hope to successfully cope with half a hundred.

Slowly they were overpowering him, though a score of them bled from ugly wounds, and two lay very still beneath the trampling feet, and the rolling bodies of the contestants.

Overpower him they might, but could they keep him over-powered while they bound him? A half hour of desperate endeavor convinced them that they could not, and so Mbonga, who, like all good rulers, had circled in the safety of the background, called to one to work his way in and spear the victim. Gradually, through the milling, battling men, the warrior approached the object of his quest.

He stood with poised spear above his head waiting for the instant that would expose a vulnerable part of the ape-man's body and still not endanger one of the blacks. Closer and closer he edged about, following the movements of the twisting, scuffling combatants. The growls of the ape-man sent cold chills up the warrior's spine, causing him to go carefully lest he miss at the first cast and lay himself open to an attack from those merciless teeth and mighty hands.

At last he found an opening. Higher he raised his spear, tensing his muscles, rolling beneath his glistening, ebon hide, and then from the jungle just beyond the palisade came a thunderous crashing. The spear-hand paused, the black cast a quick glance in the direction of the disturbance, as did the others of the blacks who were not occupied with the subjugation of the ape-man.

In the glare of the fires they saw a huge bulk topping the barrier. They saw the palisade belly and sway inward. They saw it burst as though built of straws, and an instant later Tantor, the elephant, thundered down upon them.

To right and left the blacks fled, screaming in terror. Some who hovered upon the verge of the strife with Tarzan heard and made good their escape, but a half dozen there were so wrapt in the blood-madness of battle that they failed to note the approach of the giant tusker.

Upon these Tantor charged, trumpeting furiously. Above them he stopped, his sensitive trunk weaving among them, and there, at the bottom, he found Tarzan, bloody, but still battling.

A warrior turned his eyes upward from the melee. Above him towered the gigantic bulk of the pachyderm, the little eyes flashing with the reflected light of the fires — wicked, frightful, terrifying. The warrior screamed, and as he screamed, the sinuous trunk encircled him, lifted him high above the ground, and hurled him far after the fleeing crowd.

Another and another Tantor wrenched from the body of the ape-man, throwing them to right and to left, where they lay either moaning or very quiet, as death came slowly or at once.

At a distance Mbonga rallied his warriors. His greedy eyes had noted the great ivory tusks of the bull. The first panic of terror relieved, he urged his men forward to attack with their heavy elephant spears; but as they came, Tantor swung Tarzan to his broad head, and, wheeling, lumbered off into the jungle through the great rent he had made in the palisade.

Elephant hunters may be right when they aver that this animal would not have rendered such service to a man, but to Tantor, Tarzan was not a man — he was but a fellow jungle beast.

And so it was that Tantor, the elephant, discharged an obligation to Tarzan of the Apes, cementing even more closely the friendship that had existed between them since Tarzan as a little, brown boy rode upon Tantor's huge back through the moonlit jungle beneath the equatorial stars.

The Fight for the Balu

*T*EEKA HAD BECOME a mother. Tarzan of the Apes was intensely interested, much more so, in fact, than Taug, the father. Tarzan was very fond of Teeka. Even the cares of prospective motherhood had not entirely quenched the fires of carefree youth, and Teeka had remained a good-natured playmate even at an age when other shes of the tribe of Kerchak had assumed the sullen dignity of maturity. She yet retained her childish delight in the primitive games of tag and hide-and-go-seek which Tarzan's fertile man-mind had evolved.

To play tag through the tree tops is an exciting and inspiring pastime. Tarzan delighted in it, but the bulls of his child-hood had long since abandoned such childish practices. Teeka, though, had been keen for it always until shortly before the baby came; but with the advent of her first-born, even Teeka changed.

The evidence of the change surprised and hurt Tarzan immeasurably. One morning he saw Teeka squatted upon a low branch hugging something very close to her hairy breast — a wee something which squirmed and wriggled. Tarzan approached filled with the curiosity which is common to all creatures endowed with brains which have progressed beyond the microscopic stage.

Teeka rolled her eyes in his direction and strained the squirming mite still closer to her. Tarzan came nearer. Teeka drew away and bared her fangs. Tarzan was nonplussed. In all his experiences with Teeka, never before had she bared fangs at him other than in play; but today she did not look playful. Tarzan ran his brown fingers through his thick, black hair, cocked his head upon one side, and stared. Then he edged a bit nearer, craning his neck to have a better look at the thing which Teeka cuddled.

Again Teeka drew back her upper lip in a warning snarl. Tarzan reached forth a hand, cautiously, to touch the thing which Teeka held, and Teeka, with a hideous growl, turned suddenly upon him. Her teeth sank into the flesh of his forearm before the ape-man could snatch it away, and she pursued him for a short distance as he retreated incontinently through the trees; but Teeka, carrying her baby, could not overtake him. At a safe distance Tarzan stopped and turned to regard his erstwhile play-fellow in unconcealed astonishment. What had happened to so alter the gentle Teeka? She had so covered the thing in her arms that Tarzan had not yet been able to recognize it for what it was; but now, as she turned from the pursuit of him, he saw it. Through his pain and chagrin he smiled, for Tarzan had seen young ape mothers before. In a few days she would be less suspicious. Still Tarzan was hurt; it was not right that Teeka, of all others, should fear him. Why, not for the world would he harm her, or her balu, which is the ape word for baby.

And now, above the pain of his injured arm and the hurt to his pride, rose a still stronger desire to come close and inspect the new-born son of Taug. Possibly you will wonder that Tarzan of the Apes, mighty fighter that he was, should have fled before the irritable attack of a she, or that he should hesitate to return for the satisfaction of his curiosity when with ease he might have vanquished the weakened mother of the new-born cub; but you need not wonder. Were you an ape, you would know that only a bull in the throes of madness will turn upon a female other than to gently chastise her, with the occasional exception of the individual whom we find exemplified among our own kind, and who delights in beating up his better half because she happens to be smaller and weaker than he.

Tarzan again came toward the young mother — warily and with his line of retreat safely open. Again Teeka growled ferociously. Tarzan expostulated.

"Tarzan of the Apes will not harm Teeka's balu," he said. "Let me see it."

"Go away!" commanded Teeka. "Go away, or I will kill you."

"Let me see it," urged Tarzan.

"Go away," reiterated the she-ape. "Here comes Taug. He will make you go away. Taug will kill you. This is Taug's balu."

A savage growl close behind him apprised Tarzan of the nearness of Taug, and the fact that the bull had heard the warnings and threats of his mate and was coming to her succor.

Now Taug, as well as Teeka, had been Tarzan's play-fellow while the bull was still young enough to wish to play. Once Tarzan had saved Taug's life; but the memory of an ape is not overlong, nor would gratitude rise above the parental instinct. Tarzan and Taug had once measured strength, and Tarzan had been victorious. That fact Taug could be depended upon still to remember; but even so, he might readily face another defeat for his first-born — if he chanced to be in the proper mood.

From his hideous growls, which now rose in strength

and volume, he seemed to be in quite the mood. Now
Tarzan felt no fear of Taug, nor did the unwritten law
of the jungle demand that he should flee from battle
with any male, unless he cared to from purely personal
reasons. But Tarzan liked Taug. He had no grudge
against him, and his man-mind told him what the
mind of an ape would never have deduced — that
Taug's attitude in no sense indicated hatred. It was but
the instinctive urge of the male to protect its offspring
and its mate.

Tarzan had no desire to battle with Taug, nor did the
blood of his English ancestors relish the thought of
flight, yet when the bull charged, Tarzan leaped nimbly
to one side, and thus encouraged, Taug wheeled and
rushed again madly to the attack. Perhaps the memory
of a past defeat at Tarzan's hands goaded him. Perhaps
the fact that Teeka sat there watching him aroused a
desire to vanquish the ape-man before her eyes, for in
the breast of every jungle male lurks a vast egotism
which finds expression in the performance of deeds of
derring-do before an audience of the opposite sex.

At the ape-man's side swung his long grass rope —
the play-thing of yesterday, the weapon of today — and
as Taug charged the second time, Tarzan slipped the
coils over his head and deftly shook out the sliding
noose as he again nimbly eluded the ungainly beast.
Before the ape could turn again, Tarzan had fled far
aloft among the branches of the upper terrace.

Taug, now wrought to a frenzy of real rage, followed
him. Teeka peered upward at them. It was difficult to
say whether she was interested. Taug could not climb
as rapidly as Tarzan, so the latter reached the high levels
to which the heavy ape dared not follow before the
former overtook him. There he halted and looked
down upon his pursuer, making faces at him and
calling him such choice names as occurred to the fertile
man-brain. Then, when he had worked Taug to such a

pitch of foaming rage that the great bull fairly danced upon the bending limb beneath him, Tarzan's hand shot suddenly outward, a widening noose dropped swiftly through the air, there was a quick jerk as it settled about Taug, falling to his knees, a jerk that tightened it securely about the hairy legs of the anthropoid.

Taug, slow of wit, realized too late the intention of his tormentor. He scrambled to escape, but the ape-man gave the rope a tremendous jerk that pulled Taug from his perch, and a moment later, growling hideously, the ape hung head downward thirty feet above the ground.

Tarzan secured the rope to a stout limb and descended to a point close to Taug.

"Taug," he said, "you are as stupid as Buto, the rhinoceros. Now you may hang here until you get a little sense in your thick head. You may hang here and watch while I go and talk with Teeka."

Taug blustered and threatened, but Tarzan only grinned at him as he dropped lightly to the lower levels. Here he again approached Teeka only to be again greeted with bared fangs and menacing growls. He sought to placate her; he urged his friendly intentions, and craned his neck to have a look at Teeka's balu; but the she-ape was not to be persuaded that he meant other than harm to her little one. Her motherhood was still so new that reason was yet subservient to instinct.

Realizing the futility of attempting to catch and chastise Tarzan, Teeka sought to escape him. She dropped to the ground and lumbered across the little clearing about which the apes of the tribe were disposed in rest or in the search of food, and presently Tarzan abandoned his attempts to persuade her to permit a close examination of the balu. The ape-man would have liked to handle the tiny thing. The very sight of it awakened in his breast a strange yearning.

He wished to cuddle and fondle the grotesque little ape-thing. It was Teeka's balu and Tarzan had once lavished his young affections upon Teeka.

But now his attention was diverted by the voice of Taug. The threats that had filled the ape's mouth had turned to pleas. The tightening noose was stopping the circulation of the blood in his legs — he was beginning to suffer. Several apes sat near him highly interested in his predicament. They made uncomplimentary remarks about him, for each of them had felt the weight of Taug's mighty hands and the strength of his great jaws. They were enjoying revenge.

Teeka, seeing that Tarzan had turned back toward the trees, had halted in the center of the clearing, and there she sat hugging her balu and casting suspicious glances here and there. With the coming of the balu, Teeka's care-free world had suddenly become peopled with innumerable enemies. She saw an implacable foe in Tarzan, always heretofore her best friend. Even poor old Mumga, half blind and almost entirely toothless, searching patiently for grub worms beneath a fallen log, represented to her a malignant spirit thirsting for the blood of little balus.

And while Teeka guarded suspiciously against harm, where there was no harm, she failed to note two baleful, yellow-green eyes staring fixedly at her from behind a clump of bushes at the opposite side of the clearing.

Hollow from hunger, Sheeta, the panther, glared greedily at the tempting meat so close at hand, but the sight of the great bulls beyond gave him pause.

Ah, if the she-ape with her balu would but come just a trifle nearer! A quick spring and he would be upon them and away again with his meat before the bulls could prevent.

The tip of his tawny tail moved in spasmodic little jerks; his lower jaw hung low, exposing a red tongue and yellow fangs. But all this Teeka did not see, nor did any other of the apes who were feeding or resting about her. Nor did Tarzan or the apes in the trees.

Hearing the abuse which the bulls were pouring upon the helpless Taug, Tarzan clambered quickly among them. One was edging closer and leaning far out in an effort to reach the dangling ape. He had worked himself into quite a fury through recollection of the last occasion upon which Taug had mauled him, and now he was bent upon revenge. Once he had grasped the swinging ape, he would quickly have drawn him within reach of his jaws. Tarzan saw and was wroth. He loved a fair fight, but the thing which this ape contemplated revolted him. Already a hairy hand had clutched the helpless Taug when, with an angry growl of protest, Tarzan leaped to the branch at the attacking ape's side, and with a single mighty cuff, swept him from his perch.

Surprised and enraged, the bull clutched madly for support as he toppled sidewise, and then with an agile movement succeeded in projecting himself toward another limb a few feet below. Here he found a handhold, quickly righted him-self, and as quickly clambered upward to be revenged upon Tarzan, but the ape-man was otherwise engaged and did not wish to be interrupted. He was explaining again to Taug the depths of the latter's abysmal ignorance, and pointing out how much greater and mightier was Tarzan of the Apes than Taug or any other ape.

In the end he would release Taug, but not until Taug was fully acquainted with his own inferiority. And then the maddened bull came from beneath, and instantly Tarzan was transformed from a good-natured, teasing youth into a snarling, savage beast. Along his scalp the hair bristled: his upper lip drew back that his fighting fangs might be uncovered and ready. He did not wait for the bull to reach him, for something in the appearance or the voice of the attacker aroused within the ape-man a feeling of belligerent antagonism that would not be denied. With a scream that carried no human note, Tarzan leaped straight at the throat of the attacker.

The impetuosity of this act and the weight and momentum of his body carried the bull backward, clutching and clawing for support, down through the leafy branches of the tree. For fifteen feet the two fell, Tarzan's teeth buried in the jugular of his opponent, when a stout branch stopped their descent. The bull struck full upon the small of his back across the limb, hung there for a moment with the ape-man still upon his breast, and then toppled over toward the ground.

Tarzan had felt the instantaneous relaxation of the body beneath him after the heavy impact with the tree limb, and as the other turned completely over and started again upon its fall toward the ground, he reached forth a hand and caught the branch in time to stay his own descent, while the ape dropped like a plummet to the foot of the tree.

Tarzan looked downward for a moment upon the still form of his late antagonist, then he rose to his full height, swelled his deep chest, smote upon it with his clenched fist and roared out the uncanny challenge of the victorious bull ape.

Even Sheeta, the panther, crouched for a spring at the edge of the little clearing, moved uneasily as the mighty voice sent its weird cry reverberating through the jungle. To right and left, nervously, glanced Sheeta, as though assuring himself that the way of escape lay ready at hand.

"I am Tarzan of the Apes," boasted the ape-man; "mighty hunter, mighty fighter! None in all the jungle so great as Tarzan."

Then he made his way back in the direction of Taug. Teeka had watched the happenings in the tree. She had even placed her precious balu upon the soft grasses and come a little nearer that she might better witness all that was passing in the branches above her. In her heart of hearts did she still esteem the smooth-skinned Tarzan? Did her savage breast swell with pride as she witnessed his victory over the ape? You will have to ask Teeka.

And Sheeta, the panther, saw that the she-ape had left her cub alone among the grasses. He moved his tail again, as though this closest approximation of lashing in which he dared indulge might stimulate his momentarily waned courage. The cry of the victorious ape-man still held his nerves beneath its spell. It would be several minutes before he again could bring himself to the point of charging into view of the giant anthropoids.

And as he regathered his forces, Tarzan reached Taug's side, and then clambering higher up to the point where the end of the grass rope was made fast, he unloosed it and lowered the ape slowly downward, swinging him in until the clutching hands fastened upon a limb.

Quickly Taug drew himself to a position of safety and shook off the noose. In his rage-maddened heart was no room for gratitude to the ape-man. He recalled only the fact that Tarzan had laid this painful indignity upon him. He would be revenged, but just at present his legs were so numb and his head so dizzy that he must postpone the gratification of his vengeance.

Tarzan was coiling his rope the while he lectured Taug on the futility of pitting his poor powers, physical and intellectual, against those of his betters. Teeka had come close beneath the tree and was peering upward. Sheeta was worming his way stealthily forward, his belly close to the ground. In another moment he would be clear of the underbrush and ready for the rapid charge and the quick retreat that would end the brief existence of Teeka's balu.

Then Tarzan chanced to look up and across the clearing. Instantly his attitude of good-natured bantering and pompous boastfulness dropped from him. Silently and swiftly he shot downward toward the ground. Teeka, seeing him coming, and thinking that he was after her or her balu, bristled and prepared to fight. But Tarzan sped by her, and as he went, her eyes followed him and she saw the cause of his sudden descent and his rapid charge across the clearing. There in full sight now was Sheeta, the panther, stalking slowly toward the tiny, wriggling balu which lay among the grasses many yards away.

Teeka gave voice to a shrill scream of terror and of warning as she dashed after the ape-man. Sheeta saw Tarzan coming. He saw the she-ape's cub before him, and he thought that this other was bent upon robbing him of his prey. With an angry growl, he charged.

Taug, warned by Teeka's cry, came lumbering down to her assistance. Several other bulls, growling and barking, closed in toward the clearing, but they were all much farther from the balu and the panther than was Tarzan of the Apes, so it was that Sheeta and the ape-man reached Teeka's little one almost simultaneously; and there they stood, one upon either side of it, baring their fangs and snarling at each other over the little creature.

Sheeta was afraid to seize the balu, for thus he would give the ape-man an opening for attack; and for the same reason Tarzan hesitated to snatch the panther's prey out of harm's way, for had he stooped to accomplish this, the great beast would have been upon him in an instant. Thus they stood while Teeka came across the clearing, going more slowly as she neared the panther, for even her mother love could scarce overcome her instinctive terror of this natural enemy of her kind.

Behind her came Taug, warily and with many pauses and much bluster, and still behind him came other bulls, snarling ferociously and uttering their uncanny challenges. Sheeta's yellow-green eyes glared terribly at Tarzan, and past Tarzan they shot brief glances at the apes of Kerchak advancing upon him. Discretion prompted him to turn and flee, but hunger and the close proximity of the tempting morsel in the grass before him urged him to remain. He reached forth a paw toward Teeka's balu, and as he did so, with a savage guttural, Tarzan of the Apes was upon him.

The panther reared to meet the ape-man's attack. He swung a frightful raking blow for Tarzan that would have wiped his face away had it landed, but it did not land, for Tarzan ducked beneath it and closed, his long knife ready in one strong hand — the knife of his dead father, of the father he never had known.

Instantly the balu was forgotten by Sheeta, the panther. He now thought only of tearing to ribbons with his powerful talons the flesh of his antagonist, of burying his long, yellow fangs in the soft, smooth hide of the ape-man, but Tarzan had fought before with clawed creatures of the jungle. Before now he had battled with fanged monsters, nor always had he come away unscathed. He knew the risk that he ran, but Tarzan of the Apes, inured to the sight of suffering and death, shrank from neither, for he feared neither.

The instant that he dodged beneath Sheeta's blow, he leaped to the beast's rear and then full upon the tawny back, burying his teeth in Sheeta's neck and the fingers of one hand in the fur at the throat, and with the other hand he drove his blade into Sheeta's side.

Over and over upon the grass rolled Sheeta, growling and screaming, clawing and biting, in a mad effort to dislodge his antagonist or get some portion of his body within range of teeth or talons.

As Tarzan leaped to close quarters with the panther, Teeka had run quickly in and snatched up her balu. Now she sat upon a high branch, safe out of harm's way, cuddling the little thing close to her hairy breast, the while her savage little eyes bored down upon the contestants in the clearing, and her ferocious voice urged Taug and the other bulls to leap into the melee.

Thus goaded the bulls came closer, redoubling their hideous clamor; but Sheeta was already sufficiently engaged — he did not even hear them. Once he succeeded in partially dislodging the ape-man from his back, so that Tarzan swung for an instant in front of those awful talons, and in the brief instant before he could regain his former hold, a raking blow from a hind paw laid open one leg from hip to knee.

It was the sight and smell of this blood, possibly, which wrought upon the encircling apes; but it was Taug who really was responsible for the thing they did.

Taug, but a moment before filled with rage toward Tarzan of the Apes, stood close to the battling pair, his red-rimmed, wicked little eyes glaring at them. What was passing in his savage brain? Did he gloat over the unenviable position of his recent tormentor? Did he long to see Sheeta's great fangs sink into the soft throat of the ape-man? Or did he realize the courageous unselfishness that had prompted Tarzan to rush to the rescue and imperil his life for Teeka's balu — for Taug's little balu? Is gratitude a possession of man only, or do the lower orders know it also?

With the spilling of Tarzan's blood, Taug answered these questions. With all the weight of his great body he leaped, hideously growling, upon Sheeta. His long fighting fangs buried themselves in the white throat. His powerful arms beat and clawed at the soft fur until it flew upward in the jungle breeze.

And with Taug's example before them the other bulls charged, burying Sheeta beneath rending fangs and filling all the forest with the wild din of their battle cries.

Ah! but it was a wondrous and inspiring sight — this

battle of the primordial apes and the great, white ape-man with their ancestral foe, Sheeta, the panther.

In frenzied excitement, Teeka fairly danced upon the limb which swayed beneath her great weight as she urged on the males of her people, and Thaka, and Mumga, and Kamma, with the other shes of the tribe of Kerchak, added their shrill cries or fierce barkings to the pandemonium which now reigned within the jungle.

Bitten and biting, tearing and torn, Sheeta battled for his life; but the odds were against him. Even Numa, the lion, would have hesitated to have attacked an equal number of the great bulls of the tribe of Kerchak, and now, a half mile away, hearing the sounds of the terrific battle, the king of beasts rose uneasily from his midday slumber and slunk off farther into the jungle.

Presently Sheeta's torn and bloody body ceased its titanic struggles. It stiffened spasmodically, twitched and was still, yet the bulls continued to lacerate it until the beautiful coat was torn to shreds. At last they desisted from sheer physical weariness, and then from the tangle of bloody bodies rose a crimson giant, straight as an arrow.

He placed a foot upon the dead body of the panther, and lifting his blood-stained face to the blue of the equatorial heavens, gave voice to the horrid victory cry of the bull ape.

One by one his hairy fellows of the tribe of Kerchak followed his example. The shes came down from their perches of safety and struck and reviled the dead body of Sheeta. The young apes refought the battle in mimicry of their mighty elders.

Teeka was quite close to Tarzan. He turned and saw her with the balu hugged close to her hairy breast, and put out his hands to take the little one, expecting that Teeka would bare her fangs and spring upon him; but instead she placed the balu in his arms, and coming nearer, licked his frightful wounds.

And presently Taug, who had escaped with only a few scratches, came and squatted beside Tarzan and watched him as he played with the little balu, and at last he too leaned over and helped Teeka with the cleansing and the healing of the ape-man's hurts.

The God of Tarzan

AMONG THE BOOKS of his dead father in the little cabin by the land-locked harbor, Tarzan of the Apes found many things to puzzle his young head. By much labor and through the medium of infinite patience as well, he had, without assistance, discovered the purpose of the little bugs which ran riot upon the printed pages. He had learned that in the many combinations in which he found them they spoke in a silent language, spoke in a strange tongue, spoke of wonderful things which a little ape-boy could not by any chance fully understand, arousing his curiosity, stimulating his imagination and filling his soul with a mighty longing for further knowledge.

A dictionary had proven itself a wonderful store-house of information, when, after several years of tireless endeavor, he had solved the mystery of its purpose and the manner of its use. He had learned to make a species of game out of it, following up the spoor of a new thought through the mazes of the many definitions which each new word required him to consult. It was like following a quarry through the jungle — it was hunting, and Tarzan of the Apes was an indefatigable huntsman.

There were, of course, certain words which aroused his curiosity to a greater extent than others, words which, for one reason or another, excited his imagination. There was one, for example, the meaning of which was rather difficult to grasp. It was the word *God.* Tarzan first had been attracted to it by the fact that it was very short and that it commenced with a larger g-bug than those about it — a male g-bug it was to Tarzan, the lower-case letters being females. Another fact which attracted him to this word was the number of he-bugs which figured in its definition — Supreme Deity, Creator or Upholder of the Universe. This must be a very important word indeed, he would have to look into it, and he did, though it still baffled him after many months of thought and study.

However, Tarzan counted no time wasted which he devoted to these strange hunting expeditions into the game preserves of knowledge, for each word and each definition led on and on into strange places, into new worlds where, with increasing frequency, he met old, familiar faces. And always he added to his store of knowledge.

But of the meaning of *God* he was yet in doubt. Once he thought he had grasped it — that God was a mighty chieftain, king of all the Mangani. He was not quite sure, however, since that would mean that God was mightier than Tarzan — a point which Tarzan of the Apes, who acknowledged no equal in the jungle, was loath to concede.

But in all the books he had there was no picture of God, though he found much to confirm his belief that God was a great, an all-powerful individual. He saw pictures of places where God was worshiped; but never any sign of God. Finally he began to wonder if God were not of a different form than he, and at last he determined to set out in search of Him.

He commenced by questioning Mumga, who was very old and had seen many strange things in her long life; but Mumga, being an ape, had a faculty for recalling the trivial. That time when Gunto mistook a sting-bug for an edible beetle had made more impression upon Mumga than all the innumerable manifestations of the greatness of God which she had witnessed, and which, of course, she had not understood.

Numgo, overhearing Tarzan's questions, managed to wrest his attention long enough from the diversion of flea hunting to advance the theory that the power which made the lightning and the rain and the thunder came from Goro, the moon. He knew this, he said, because the Dum-Dum always was danced in the light of Goro. This reasoning, though entirely satisfactory to Numgo and Mumga, failed fully to convince Tarzan. However, it gave him a basis for further investigation along a new line. He would investigate the moon.

That night he clambered to the loftiest pinnacle of the tallest jungle giant. The moon was full, a great, glorious, equatorial moon. The ape-man, upright upon a slender, swaying limb, raised his bronzed face to the silver orb. Now that he had clambered to the highest point within his reach, he discovered, to his surprise, that Goro was as far away as when he viewed him from the ground. He thought that Goro was attempting to elude him.

"Come, Goro!" he cried, "Tarzan of the Apes will not harm you!" But still the moon held aloof.

"Tell me," he continued, "if you be the great king who sends Ara, the lightning; who makes the great noise and the mighty winds, and sends the waters down upon the jungle people when the days are dark and it is cold. Tell me, Goro, are you God?"

Of course he did not pronounce God as you or I would pronounce His name, for Tarzan knew naught of the spoken language of his English forbears; but he had a name of his own invention for each of the little bugs which constituted the alphabet. Unlike the apes he was not satisfied merely to have a mental picture of the things he knew, he must have a word descriptive of each. In reading he grasped a word in its entirety; but when he spoke the words he had learned from the books of his father, he pronounced each according to the names he had given the various little bugs which occurred in it, usually giving the gender prefix for each.

Thus it was an imposing word which Tarzan made of *God*. The masculine prefix of the apes is *bu*, the feminine *mu*; g Tarzan had named *la*, o he pronounced *tu*, and d was *mo*. So the word God evolved itself into *Bulamutumumo*, or, in English, he-g-she-o-she-d.

Similarly he had arrived at a strange and wonderful spelling of his own name. Tarzan is derived from the two ape words *tar* and *zan*, meaning white skin. It was given him by his foster mother, Kala, the great she-ape. When Tarzan first put it into the written language of his own people he had not yet chanced upon either *white* or *skin* in the dictionary; but in a primer he had seen the picture of a little white boy and so he wrote his name *bumude-mutomuro*, or he-boy.

To follow Tarzan's strange system of spelling would be laborious as well as futile, and so we shall in the future, as we have in the past, adhere to the more familiar forms of our grammar school copybooks. It would tire you to remember that *do* meant b, *tu* o, and *ro* y, and that to say he-boy you must prefix the ape masculine gender sound *bu* before the entire word and the feminine gender sound *mu* before each of the lower-case letters which go to make up boy — it would tire you and it would bring me to the nineteenth hole several strokes under par.

And so Tarzan harangued the moon, and when Goro did not reply, Tarzan of the Apes waxed wroth. He swelled his giant chest and bared his fighting fangs, and hurled into the teeth of the dead satellite the challenge of the bull ape.

"You are not Bulamutumumo," he cried. "You are not king of the jungle folk. You are not so great as Tarzan, mighty fighter, mighty hunter. None there is so great as Tarzan. If there be a Bulamutumumo, Tarzan can kill him. Come down, Goro, great coward, and fight with Tarzan. Tarzan will kill you. I am Tarzan, the killer."

But the moon made no answer to the boasting of the ape-man, and when a cloud came and obscured her face, Tarzan thought that Goro was indeed afraid, and was hiding from him, so he came down out of the trees and awoke Numgo and told him how great was Tarzan — how he had frightened Goro out of the sky and made him tremble. Tarzan spoke of the moon as *he*, for all things large or awe inspiring are male to the ape folk.

Numgo was not much impressed; but he was very sleepy, so he told Tarzan to go away and leave his betters alone.

"But where shall I find God?" insisted Tarzan. "You are very old; if there is a God you must have seen Him. What does He look like? Where does He live?"

"I am God," replied Numgo. "Now sleep and disturb me no more."

Tarzan looked at Numgo steadily for several minutes, his shapely head sank just a trifle between his great shoulders, his square chin shot forward and his short upper lip drew back, exposing his white teeth. Then, with a low growl he leaped upon the ape and buried his fangs in the other's hairy shoulder, clutching the great neck in his mighty fingers. Twice he shook the old ape, then he released his tooth-hold.

"Are you God?" he demanded.

"No," wailed Numgo. "I am only a poor, old ape. Leave me alone. Go ask the Gomangani where God is.

They are hairless like yourself and very wise, too. They should know."

Tarzan released Numgo and turned away. The suggestion that he consult the blacks appealed to him, and though his relations with the people of Mbonga, the chief, were the antithesis of friendly, he could at least spy upon his hated enemies and discover if they had intercourse with God.

So it was that Tarzan set forth through the trees toward the village of the blacks, all excitement at the prospect of discovering the Supreme Being, the Creator of all things. As he traveled he reviewed, mentally, his armament — the condition of his hunting knife, the number of his arrows, the newness of the gut which strung his bow — he hefted the war spear which had once been the pride of some black warrior of Mbonga's tribe.

If he met God, Tarzan would be prepared. One could never tell whether a grass rope, a war spear, or a poisoned arrow would be most efficacious against an unfamiliar foe. Tarzan of the Apes was quite content — if God wished to fight, the ape-man had no doubt as to the outcome of the struggle. There were many questions Tarzan wished to put to the Creator of the Universe and so he hoped that God would not prove a belligerent God; but his experience of life and the ways of living things had taught him that any creature with the means for offense and defense was quite likely to provoke attack if in the proper mood.

It was dark when Tarzan came to the village of Mbonga. As silently as the silent shadows of the night he sought his accustomed place among the branches of the great tree which overhung the palisade. Below him, in the village street, he saw men and women. The men were hideously painted — more hideously than usual. Among them moved a weird and grotesque figure, a tall figure that went upon the two legs of a man and yet had the head of a buffalo. A tail dangled to his ankles behind him, and in one hand he carried a zebra's tail while the other clutched a bunch of small arrows.

Tarzan was electrified. Could it be that chance had given him thus early an opportunity to look upon God? Surely this thing was neither man nor beast, so what could it be then other than the Creator of the Universe! The ape-man watched the every move of the strange creature. He saw the black men and women fall back at its approach as though they stood in terror of its mysterious powers.

Presently he discovered that the deity was speaking and that all listened in silence to his words. Tarzan was sure that none other than God could inspire such awe in the hearts of the Gomangani, or stop their mouths so effectually without recourse to arrows or spears. Tarzan had come to look with contempt upon the blacks, principally because of their garrulity. The small apes talked a great deal and ran away from an enemy. The big, old bulls of Kerchak talked but little and fought upon the slightest provocation. Numa, the lion, was not given to loquacity, yet of all the jungle folk there were few who fought more often than he.

Tarzan witnessed strange things that night, none of which he understood, and, perhaps because they were strange, he thought that they must have to do with the God he could not understand. He saw three youths receive their first war spears in a weird ceremony which the grotesque witch-doctor strove successfully to render uncanny and awesome.

Hugely interested, he watched the slashing of the three brown arms and the exchange of blood with Mbonga, the chief, in the rites of the ceremony of blood brotherhood. He saw the zebra's tail dipped into a caldron of water above which the witch-doctor had made magical passes the while he danced and leaped

about it, and he saw the breasts and foreheads of each
of the three novitiates sprinkled with the charmed
liquid. Could the ape-man have known the purpose of
this act, that it was intended to render the recipient
invulnerable to the attacks of his enemies and fearless
in the face of any danger, he would doubtless have
leaped into the village street and appropriated the
zebra's tail and a portion of the contents of the caldron.

But he did not know, and so he only wondered, not
alone at what he saw but at the strange sensations
which played up and down his naked spine, sensations
induced, doubtless, by the same hypnotic influence
which held the black spectators in tense awe upon the
verge of a hysteric upheaval.

The longer Tarzan watched, the more convinced he
became that his eyes were upon God, and with the
conviction came determination to have word with the
deity. With Tarzan of the Apes, to think was to act.

The people of Mbonga were keyed to the highest
pitch of hysterical excitement. They needed little to
release the accumulated pressure of static nerve force
which the terrorizing mummery of the witch-doctor
had induced.

A lion roared, suddenly and loud, close without the
palisade. The blacks started nervously, dropping into
utter silence as they listened for a repetition of that
all-too-familiar and always terrorizing voice. Even the
witch-doctor paused in the midst of an intricate step,
remaining momentarily rigid and statuesque as he
plumbed his cunning mind for a suggestion as how
best he might take advantage of the condition of his
audience and the timely interruption.

Already the evening had been vastly profitable to
him. There would be three goats for the initiation of
the three youths into full-fledged warriorship, and
besides these he had received several gifts of grain and

beads, together with a piece of copper wire from admiring and terrified members of his audience.

Numa's roar still reverberated along taut nerves
when a woman's laugh, shrill and piercing, shattered
the silence of the village. It was this moment that
Tarzan chose to drop lightly from his tree into the
village street. Fearless among his blood enemies he
stood, taller by a full head than many of Mbonga's
warriors, straight as their straightest arrow, muscled
like Numa, the lion.

For a moment Tarzan stood looking straight at the
witch-doctor. Every eye was upon him, yet no one had
moved — a paralysis of terror held them, to be broken
a moment later as the ape-man, with a toss of head,
stepped straight toward the hideous figure beneath the
buffalo head.

Then the nerves of the blacks could stand no more.
For months the terror of the strange, white, jungle god
had been upon them. Their arrows had been stolen
from the very center of the village; their warriors had
been silently slain upon the jungle trails and their dead
bodies dropped mysteriously and by night into the
village street as from the heavens above.

One or two there were who had glimpsed the strange
figure of the new demon and it was from their oft-re-
peated descriptions that the entire village now recognized Tarzan as the author of many of their ills. Upon
another occasion and by daylight, the warriors would
doubtless have leaped to attack him, but at night, and
this night of all others, when they were wrought to such
a pitch of nervous dread by the uncanny artistry of
their witch-doctor, they were helpless with terror. As
one man they turned and fled, scattering for their huts,
as Tarzan advanced. For a moment one and one only
held his ground. It was the witch-doctor. More than
half self-hypnotized into a belief in his own charla-
tanry he faced this new demon who threatened to

undermine his ancient and lucrative profession.

"Are you God?" asked Tarzan.

The witch-doctor, having no idea of the meaning of the other's words, danced a few strange steps, leaped high in the air, turning completely around and alighting in a stooping posture with feet far outspread and head thrust out toward the ape-man. Thus he remained for an instant before he uttered a loud "Boo!" which was evidently intended to frighten Tarzan away; but in reality had no such effect.

Tarzan did not pause. He had set out to approach and examine God and nothing upon earth might now stay his feet. Seeing that his antics had no potency with the visitor, the witch-doctor tried some new medicine. Spitting upon the zebra's tail, which he still clutched in one hand, he made circles above it with the arrows in the other hand, meanwhile backing cautiously away from Tarzan and speaking confidentially to the bushy end of the tail.

This medicine must be short medicine, however, for the creature, god or demon, was steadily closing up the distance which had separated them. The circles therefore were few and rapid, and when they were completed, the witch-doctor struck an attitude which was intended to be awe inspiring and waving the zebra's tail before him, drew an imaginary line between himself and Tarzan.

"Beyond this line you cannot pass, for my medicine is strong medicine," he cried. "Stop, or you will fall dead as your foot touches this spot. My mother was a voodoo, my father was a snake; I live upon lions' hearts and the entrails of the panther; I eat young babies for breakfast and the demons of the jungle are my slaves. I am the most powerful witch-doctor in the world; I fear nothing, for I cannot die. I —" But he got no further; instead he turned and fled as Tarzan of the Apes crossed the magical dead line and still lived.

As the witch-doctor ran, Tarzan almost lost his temper. This was no way for God to act, at least not in accordance with the conception Tarzan had come to have of God.

"Come back!" he cried. "Come back, God, I will not harm you." But the witch-doctor was in full retreat by this time, stepping high as he leaped over cooking pots and the smoldering embers of small fires that had burned before the huts of villagers. Straight for his own hut ran the witch-doctor, terror-spurred to unwonted speed; but futile was his effort — the ape-man bore down upon him with the speed of Bara, the deer.

Just at the entrance to his hut the witch-doctor was over-hauled. A heavy hand fell upon his shoulder to drag him back. It seized upon a portion of the buffalo hide, dragging the disguise from him. It was a naked black man that Tarzan saw dodge into the darkness of the hut's interior.

So this was what he had thought was God! Tarzan's lip curled in an angry snarl as he leaped into the hut after the terror-stricken witch-doctor. In the blackness within he found the man huddled at the far side and dragged him forth into the comparative lightness of the moonlit night.

The witch-doctor bit and scratched in an attempt to escape; but a few cuffs across the head brought him to a better realization of the futility of resistance. Beneath the moon Tarzan held the cringing figure upon its shaking feet.

"So you are God!" he cried. "If you be God, then Tarzan is greater than God," and so the ape-man thought. "I am Tarzan," he shouted into the ear of the black. "In all the jungle, or above it, or upon the running waters, or the sleeping waters, or upon the big water, or the little water, there is none so great as Tarzan. Tarzan is greater than the Mangani; he is greater than the Gomangani. With his own hands he has slain Numa, the lion, and Sheeta, the panther; there is none so great as Tarzan. Tarzan is greater than God. See!" and with a sudden wrench he twisted the black's neck until the fellow shrieked in pain and then slumped to the earth in a swoon.

Placing his foot upon the neck of the fallen witch-doctor, the ape-man raised his face to the moon and uttered the long, shrill scream of the victorious bull ape. Then he stooped and snatched the zebra's tail from the nerveless fingers of the unconscious man and without a backward glance retraced his footsteps across the village.

From several hut doorways frightened eyes watched him. Mbonga, the chief, was one of those who had seen what passed before the hut of the witch-doctor. Mbonga was greatly concerned. Wise old patriarch that he was, he never had more than half believed in witch-doctors, at least not since greater wisdom had come with age; but as a chief he was well convinced of the power of the witch-doctor as an arm of government, and often it was that Mbonga used the superstitious fears of his people to his own ends through the medium of the medicine-man.

Mbonga and the witch-doctor had worked together and divided the spoils, and now the "face" of the witch-doctor would be lost forever if any saw what Mbonga had seen; nor would this generation again have as much faith in any future witch-doctor.

Mbonga must do something to counteract the evil influence of the forest demon's victory over the witch-doctor. He raised his heavy spear and crept silently from his hut in the wake of the retreating ape-man. Down the village street walked Tarzan, as unconcerned and as deliberate as though only the friendly apes of Kerchak surrounded him instead of a village full of armed enemies.

Seeming only was the indifference of Tarzan, for

alert and watchful was every well-trained sense.
Mbonga, wily stalker of keen-eared jungle creatures,
moved now in utter silence. Not even Bara, the deer,
with his great ears could have guessed from any sound
that Mbonga was near; but the black was not stalking
Bara; he was stalking man, and so he sought only to
avoid noise.

Closer and closer to the slowly moving ape-man he
came. Now he raised his war spear, throwing his spear-
hand far back above his right shoulder. Once and for
all would Mbonga, the chief, rid himself and his people
of the menace of this terrifying enemy. He would make
no poor cast; he would take pains, and he would hurl
his weapon with such great force as would finish the
demon forever.

But Mbonga, sure as he thought himself, erred in
his calculations. He might believe that he was stalking
a man — he did not know, however, that it was a man
with the delicate sense perception of the lower orders.
Tarzan, when he had turned his back upon his enemies,
had noted what Mbonga never would have thought of
considering in the hunting of man — the wind. It was
blowing in the same direction that Tarzan was proceeding, carrying to his delicate nostrils the odors which
arose behind him. Thus it was that Tarzan knew that
he was being followed, for even among the many
stenches of an African village, the ape-man's uncanny
faculty was equal to the task of differentiating one
stench from another and locating with remarkable
precision the source from whence it came.

He knew that a man was following him and coming
closer, and his judgment warned him of the purpose
of the stalker. When Mbonga, therefore, came within
spear range of the ape-man, the latter suddenly wheeled
upon him, so suddenly that the poised spear was shot
a fraction of a second before Mbonga had intended. It
went a trifle high and Tarzan stooped to let it pass over

his head; then he sprang toward the chief. But Mbonga did not wait to receive him. Instead, he turned and fled for the dark doorway of the nearest hut, calling as he went for his warriors to fall upon the stranger and slay him.

Well indeed might Mbonga scream for help, for Tarzan, young and fleet-footed, covered the distance between them in great leaps, at the speed of a charging lion. He was growling, too, not at all unlike Numa himself. Mbonga heard and his blood ran cold. He could feel the wool stiffen upon his pate and a prickly chill run up his spine, as though Death had come and run his cold finger along Mbonga's back.

Others heard, too, and saw, from the darkness of their huts — bold warriors, hideously painted, grasping heavy war spears in nerveless fingers. Against Numa, the lion, they would have charged fearlessly. Against many times their own number of black warriors would they have raced to the protection of their chief; but this weird jungle demon filled them with terror. There was nothing human in the bestial growls that rumbled up from his deep chest; there was nothing human in the bared fangs, or the catlike leaps. Mbonga's warriors were terrified — too terrified to leave the seeming security of their huts while they watched the beast-man spring full upon the back of their old chieftain.

Mbonga went down with a scream of terror. He was too frightened even to attempt to defend himself. He just lay beneath his antagonist in a paralysis of fear, screaming at the top of his lungs. Tarzan half rose and kneeled above the black. He turned Mbonga over and looked him in the face, exposing the man's throat, then he drew his long, keen knife, the knife that John Clayton, Lord Greystoke, had brought from England many years before. He raised it close above Mbonga's neck. The old black whimpered with terror. He pleaded for his life in a tongue which Tarzan could not understand.

For the first time the ape-man had a close view of the chief. He saw an old man, a very old man with scrawny neck and wrinkled face — a dried, parchment-like face which resembled some of the little monkeys Tarzan knew so well. He saw the terror in the man's eyes — never before had Tarzan seen such terror in the eyes of any animal, or such a piteous appeal for mercy upon the face of any creature.

Something stayed the ape-man's hand for an instant. He wondered why it was that he hesitated to make the kill; never before had he thus delayed. The old man seemed to wither and shrink to a bag of puny bones beneath his eyes. So weak and helpless and terror-stricken he appeared that the ape-man was filled with a great contempt; but another sensation also claimed him — something new to Tarzan of the Apes in relation to an enemy. It was pity — pity for a poor, frightened, old man.

Tarzan rose and turned away, leaving Mbonga, the chief, unharmed. With head held high the ape-man walked through the village, swung himself into the branches of the tree which overhung the palisade and disappeared from the sight of the villagers.

All the way back to the stamping ground of the apes, Tarzan sought for an explanation of the strange power which had stayed his hand and prevented him from slaying Mbonga. It was as though someone greater than he had commanded him to spare the life of the old man. Tarzan could not understand, for he could conceive of nothing, or no one, with the authority to dictate to him what he should do, or what he should refrain from doing.

It was late when Tarzan sought a swaying couch among the trees beneath which slept the apes of Kerchak, and he was still absorbed in the solution of his strange problem when he fell asleep.

The sun was well up in the heavens when he awoke. The apes were astir in search of food. Tarzan watched them lazily from above as they scratched in the rotting loam for bugs and beetles and grub worms, or sought among the branches of the trees for eggs and young birds, or luscious caterpillars.

An orchid, dangling close beside his head, opened slowly, unfolding its delicate petals to the warmth and light of the sun which but recently had penetrated to its shady retreat. A thousand times had Tarzan of the Apes witnessed the beauteous miracle; but now it aroused a keener interest, for the ape-man was just commencing to ask himself questions about all the myriad wonders which heretofore he had but taken for granted.

What made the flower open? What made it grow from a tiny bud to a full-blown bloom? Why was it at all? Why was he? Where did Numa, the lion, come from? Who planted the first tree? How did Goro get way up into the darkness of the night sky to cast his welcome light upon the fearsome nocturnal jungle? And the sun! Did the sun merely happen there?

Why were all the peoples of the jungle not trees? Why were the trees not something else? Why was Tarzan different from Taug, and Taug different from Bara, the deer, and Bara different from Sheeta, the panther, and why was not Sheeta like Buto, the rhinoceros? Where and how, anyway, did they all come from — the trees, the flowers, the insects, the countless creatures of the jungle?

Quite unexpectedly an idea popped into Tarzan's head. In following out the many ramifications of the dictionary definition of *God* he had come upon the word *create* — "to cause to come into existence; to form out of nothing."

Tarzan almost had arrived at something tangible when a distant wail startled him from his preoccupation into sensibility of the present and the real. The wail came from the jungle at some little distance from Tarzan's swaying couch. It was the wail of a tiny balu. Tarzan recognized it at once as the voice of Gazan, Teeka's baby. They had called it Gazan because its soft, baby hair had been unusually red, and *Gazan* in the language of the great apes, means red skin.

The wail was immediately followed by a real scream of terror from the small lungs. Tarzan was electrified into instant action. Like an arrow from a bow he shot through the trees in the direction of the sound. Ahead of him he heard the savage snarling of an adult she-ape. It was Teeka to the rescue. The danger must be very real. Tarzan could tell that by the note of rage mingled with fear in the voice of the she.

Running along bending limbs, swinging from one tree to another, the ape-man raced through the middle terraces toward the sounds which now had risen in volume to deafening proportions. From all directions the apes of Kerchak were hurrying in response to the appeal in the tones of the balu and its mother, and as they came, their roars reverberated through the forest.

But Tarzan, swifter than his heavy fellows, distanced them all. It was he who was first upon the scene. What he saw sent a cold chill through his giant frame, for the enemy was the most hated and loathed of all the jungle creatures.

Twined in a great tree was Histah, the snake — huge, ponderous, slimy — and in the folds of its deadly embrace was Teeka's little balu, Gazan. Nothing in the jungle inspired within the breast of Tarzan so near a semblance to fear as did the hideous Histah. The apes, too, loathed the terrifying reptile and feared him even more than they did Sheeta, the panther, or Numa, the lion. Of all their enemies there was none they gave a wider berth than they gave Histah, the snake.

Tarzan knew that Teeka was peculiarly fearful of this

silent, repulsive foe, and as the scene broke upon his vision, it was the action of Teeka which filled him with the greatest wonder, for at the moment that he saw her, the she-ape leaped upon the glistening body of the snake, and as the mighty folds encircled her as well as her offspring, she made no effort to escape, but instead grasped the writhing body in a futile effort to tear it from her screaming balu.

Tarzan knew all too well how deep-rooted was Teeka's terror of Histah. He scarce could believe the testimony of his own eyes then, when they told him that she had voluntarily rushed into that deadly embrace. Nor was Teeka's innate dread of the monster much greater than Tarzan's own. Never, willingly, had he touched a snake. Why, he could not say, for he would admit fear of nothing; nor was it fear, but rather an inherent repulsion bequeathed to him by many generations of civilized ancestors, and back of them, perhaps, by countless myriads of such as Teeka, in the breasts of each of which had lurked the same nameless terror of the slimy reptile.

Yet Tarzan did not hesitate more than had Teeka, but leaped upon Histah with all the speed and impetuosity that he would have shown had he been springing upon Bara, the deer, to make a kill for food. Thus beset the snake writhed and twisted horribly; but not for an instant did it loose its hold upon any of its intended victims, for it had included the ape-man in its cold embrace the minute that he had fallen upon it.

Still clinging to the tree, the mighty reptile held the three as though they had been without weight, the while it sought to crush the life from them. Tarzan had drawn his knife and this he now plunged rapidly into the body of the enemy; but the encircling folds promised to sap his life before he had inflicted a death wound upon the snake. Yet on he fought, nor once did he seek to escape the horrid death that confronted him

— his sole aim was to slay Histah and thus free Teeka and her balu.

The great, wide-gaping jaws of the snake turned and hovered above him. The elastic maw, which could accommodate a rabbit or a horned buck with equal facility, yawned for him; but Histah, in turning his attention upon the ape-man, brought his head within reach of Tarzan's blade. Instantly a brown hand leaped forth and seized the mottled neck, and another drove the heavy hunting knife to the hilt into the little brain.

Convulsively Histah shuddered and relaxed, tensed and relaxed again, whipping and striking with his great body; but no longer sentient or sensible. Histah was dead, but in his death throes he might easily dispatch a dozen apes or men.

Quickly Tarzan seized Teeka and dragged her from the loosened embrace, dropping her to the ground beneath, then he extricated the balu and tossed it to its mother. Still Histah whipped about, clinging to the ape-man; but after a dozen efforts Tarzan succeeded in wriggling free and leaping to the ground out of range of the mighty battering of the dying snake.

A circle of apes surrounded the scene of the battle; but the moment that Tarzan broke safely from the enemy they turned silently away to resume their interrupted feeding, and Teeka turned with them, apparently forgetful of all but her balu and the fact that when the interruption had occurred she just had discovered an ingeniously hidden nest containing three perfectly good eggs.

Tarzan, equally indifferent to a battle that was over, merely cast a parting glance at the still writhing body of Histah and wandered off toward the little pool which served to water the tribe at this point. Strangely, he did not give the victory cry over the vanquished Histah. Why, he could not have told you, other than that to him Histah was not an animal. He differed in some peculiar way from the other denizens of the jungle. Tarzan only knew that he hated him.

At the pool Tarzan drank his fill and lay stretched upon the soft grass beneath the shade of a tree. His mind reverted to the battle with Histah, the snake. It seemed strange to him that Teeka should have placed herself within the folds of the horrid monster. Why had she done it? Why, indeed, had he? Teeka did not belong to him, nor did Teeka's balu. They were both Taug's. Why then had he done this thing? Histah was not food for him when he was dead. There seemed to Tarzan, now that he gave the matter thought, no reason in the world why he should have done the thing he did, and presently it occurred to him that he had acted almost involuntarily, just as he had acted when he had released the old Gomangani the previous evening.

What made him do such things? Somebody more powerful than he must force him to act at times. "All-powerful," thought Tarzan. "The little bugs say that God is all-powerful. It must be that God made me do these things, for I never did them by myself. It was God who made Teeka rush upon Histah. Teeka would never go near Histah of her own volition. It was God who held my knife from the throat of the old Gomangani. God accomplishes strange things for he is 'all-powerful.' I cannot see Him; but I know that it must be God who does these things. No Mangani, no Gomangani, no Tarmangani could do them."

And the flowers — who made them grow? Ah, now it was all explained — the flowers, the trees, the moon, the sun, him-self, every living creature in the jungle — they were all made by God out of nothing.

And what was God? What did God look like? Of that he had no conception; but he was sure that everything that was good came from God. His good act in refraining from slaying the poor, defenseless old Gomangani; Teeka's love that had hurled her into the embrace of death; his own loyalty to Teeka which had jeopardized his life that she might live. The flowers and the trees were good and beautiful. God had made them. He made the other creatures, too, that each might have food upon which to live. He had made Sheeta, the panther, with his beautiful coat; and Numa, the lion, with his noble head and his shaggy mane. He had made Bara, the deer, lovely and graceful.

Yes, Tarzan had found God, and he spent the whole day in attributing to Him all of the good and beautiful things of nature; but there was one thing which troubled him. He could not quite reconcile it to his conception of his newfound God.

Who made Histah, the snake?

Tarzan and the Black Boy

*T*ARZAN OF THE Apes sat at the foot of a great tree braiding a new grass rope. Beside him lay the frayed remnants of the old one, torn and severed by the fangs and talons of Sheeta, the panther. Only half the original rope was there, the balance having been carried off by the angry cat as he bounded away through the jungle with the noose still about his savage neck and the loose end dragging among the underbrush.

Tarzan smiled as he recalled Sheeta's great rage, his frantic efforts to free himself from the entangling strands, his uncanny screams that were part hate, part anger, part terror. He smiled in retrospection at the discomfiture of his enemy, and in anticipation of another day as he added an extra strand to his new rope.

This would be the strongest, the heaviest rope that Tarzan of the Apes ever had fashioned. Visions of Numa, the lion, straining futilely in its embrace thrilled the ape-man. He was quite content, for his hands and his brain were busy. Content, too, were his fellows of the tribe of Kerchak, searching for food in the clearing and the surrounding trees about him.

No perplexing thoughts of the future burdened their minds, and only occasionally, dimly arose recollections of the near past. They were stimulated to a species of brutal content by the delectable business of filling their bellies. Afterward they would sleep — it was their life, and they enjoyed it as we enjoy ours, you and I — as Tarzan enjoyed his. Possibly they enjoyed theirs more than we enjoy ours, for who shall say that the beasts of the jungle do not better fulfill the purposes for which they are created than does man with his many excursions into strange fields and his contraventions of the laws of nature? And what gives greater content and greater happiness than the fulfilling of a destiny?

As Tarzan worked, Gazan, Teeka's little balu, played about him while Teeka sought food upon the opposite side of the clearing. No more did Teeka, the mother, or Taug, the sullen sire, harbor suspicions of Tarzan's intentions toward their first-born. Had he not courted death to save their Gazan from the fangs and talons of Sheeta? Did he not fondle and cuddle the little one with even as great a show of affection as Teeka herself displayed? Their fears were allayed and Tarzan now found himself often in the role of nursemaid to a tiny anthropoid — an avocation which he found by no means irksome, since Gazan was a never-failing fount of surprises and entertainment.

Just now the apeling was developing those arboreal tendencies which were to stand him in such good stead during the years of his youth, when rapid flight into the upper terraces was of far more importance and value than his undeveloped muscles and untried fighting fangs. Backing off fifteen or twenty feet from the bole of the tree beneath the branches of which Tarzan worked upon his rope, Gazan scampered quickly forward, scrambling nimbly upward to the lower limbs. Here he would squat for a moment or two, quite proud of his achievement, then clamber to the ground again and repeat. Sometimes, quite often in fact, for he was an ape, his attention was distracted by other things, a beetle, a caterpillar, a tiny field mouse, and off he would go in pursuit; the caterpillars he always caught, and sometimes the beetles; but the field mice, never.

Now he discovered the tail of the rope upon which Tarzan was working. Grasping it in one small hand he bounced away, for all the world like an animated rubber ball, snatching it from the ape-man's hand and running off across the clearing. Tarzan leaped to his feet and was in pursuit in an instant, no trace of anger on his face or in his voice as he called to the roguish little balu to drop his rope.

Straight toward his mother raced Gazan, and after him came Tarzan. Teeka looked up from her feeding, and in the first instant that she realized that Gazan was fleeing and that another was in pursuit, she bared her fangs and bristled; but when she saw that the pursuer was Tarzan she turned back to the business that had been occupying her attention. At her very feet the ape-man overhauled the balu and, though the youngster squealed and fought when Tarzan seized him, Teeka only glanced casually in their direction. No longer did she fear harm to her first-born at the hands of the ape-man. Had he not saved Gazan on two occasions?

Rescuing his rope, Tarzan returned to his tree and resumed his labor; but thereafter it was necessary to watch carefully the playful balu, who was now possessed to steal it whenever he thought his great, smooth-skinned cousin was momentarily off his guard.

But even under this handicap Tarzan finally completed the rope, a long, pliant weapon, stronger than any he ever had made before. The discarded piece of his former one he gave to Gazan for a plaything, for

Tarzan had it in his mind to instruct Teeka's balu after ideas of his own when the youngster should be old and strong enough to profit by his precepts. At present the little ape's innate aptitude for mimicry would be sufficient to familiarize him with Tarzan's ways and weapons, and so the ape-man swung off into the jungle, his new rope coiled over one shoulder, while little Gazan hopped about the clearing dragging the old one after him in childish glee.

As Tarzan traveled, dividing his quest for food with one for a sufficiently noble quarry whereupon to test his new weapon, his mind often was upon Gazan. The ape-man had realized a deep affection for Teeka's balu almost from the first, partly because the child belonged to Teeka, his first love, and partly for the little ape's own sake, and Tarzan's human longing for some sentient creature upon which to expend those natural affections of the soul which are inherent to all normal members of the *genus homo.* Tarzan envied Teeka. It was true that Gazan evidenced a considerable reciprocation of Tarzan's fondness for him, even preferring him to his own surly sire; but to Teeka the little one turned when in pain or terror, when tired or hungry. Then it was that Tarzan felt quite alone in the world and longed desperately for one who should turn first to him for succor and protection.

Taug had Teeka; Teeka had Gazan; and nearly every other bull and cow of the tribe of Kerchak had one or more to love and by whom to be loved. Of course Tarzan could scarcely formulate the thought in precisely this way — he only knew that he craved something which was denied him; something which seemed to be represented by those relations which existed between Teeka and her balu, and so he envied Teeka and longed for a balu of his own.

He saw Sheeta and his mate with their little family of three; and deeper inland toward the rocky hills, where one might lie up during the heat of the day, in the dense shade of a tangled thicket close under the cool face of an overhanging rock, Tarzan had found the lair of Numa, the lion, and of Sabor, the lioness. Here he had watched them with their little balus — playful creatures, spotted leopard-like. And he had seen the young fawn with Bara, the deer, and with Buto, the rhinoceros, its ungainly little one. Each of the creatures of the jungle had its own — except Tarzan. It made the ape-man sad to think upon this thing, sad and lonely; but presently the scent of game cleared his young mind of all other considerations, as catlike he crawled far out upon a bending limb above the game trail which led down to the ancient watering place of the wild things of this wild world.

How many thousands of times had this great, old limb bent to the savage form of some blood-thirsty hunter in the long years that it had spread its leafy branches above the deep-worn jungle path! Tarzan, the ape-man, Sheeta, the panther, and Histah, the snake, it knew well. They had worn smooth the bark upon its upper surface.

Today it was Horta, the boar, which came down toward the watcher in the old tree — Horta, the boar, whose formidable tusks and diabolical temper preserved him from all but the most ferocious or most famished of the largest carnivora.

But to Tarzan, meat was meat; naught that was edible or tasty might pass a hungry Tarzan unchallenged and unattacked. In hunger, as in battle, the ape-man out-savaged the dreariest denizens of the jungle. He knew neither fear nor mercy, except upon rare occasions when some strange, inexplicable force stayed his hand — a force inexplicable to him, perhaps, because of his ignorance of his own origin and of all the forces of humanitarianism and civilization that were his rightful heritage because of that origin.

So today, instead of staying his hand until a less formidable feast found its way toward him, Tarzan dropped his new noose about the neck of Horta, the boar. It was an excellent test for the untried strands. The angered boar bolted this way and that; but each time the new rope held him where Tarzan had made it fast about the stem of the tree above the branch from which he had cast it.

As Horta grunted and charged, slashing the sturdy jungle patriarch with his mighty tusks until the bark flew in every direction, Tarzan dropped to the ground behind him. In the ape-man's hand was the long, keen blade that had been his constant companion since that distant day upon which chance had directed its point into the body of Bolgani, the gorilla, and saved the torn and bleeding man-child from what else had been certain death.

Tarzan walked in toward Horta, who swung now to face his enemy. Mighty and muscled as was the young giant, it yet would have appeared but the maddest folly for him to face so formidable a creature as Horta, the boar, armed only with a slender hunting knife. So it would have seemed to one who knew Horta even slightly and Tarzan not at all.

For a moment Horta stood motionless facing the ape-man. His wicked, deep-set eyes flashed angrily. He shook his lowered head.

"Mud-eater!" jeered the ape-man. "Wallower in filth. Even your meat stinks, but it is juicy and makes Tarzan strong. Today I shall eat your heart, O Lord of the Great Tusks, that it shall keep savage that which pounds against my own ribs."

Horta, understanding nothing of what Tarzan said, was none the less enraged because of that. He saw only a naked man-thing, hairless and futile, pitting his puny fangs and soft muscles against his own indomitable savagery, and he charged.

Tarzan of the Apes waited until the upcut of a wicked tusk would have laid open his thigh, then he moved — just the least bit to one side; but so quickly that lightning was a sluggard by comparison, and as he moved, he stooped low and with all the great power of his right arm drove the long blade of his father's hunting knife straight into the heart of Horta, the boar. A quick leap carried him from the zone of the creature's death throes, and a moment later the hot and dripping heart of Horta was in his grasp.

His hunger satisfied, Tarzan did not seek a lying-up place for sleep, as was sometimes his way, but continued on through the jungle more in search of adventure than of food, for today he was restless. And so it came that he turned his footsteps toward the village of Mbonga, the black chief, whose people Tarzan had baited remorselessly since that day upon which Kulonga, the chief's son, had slain Kala.

A river winds close beside the village of the black men. Tarzan reached its side a little below the clearing where squat the thatched huts of the Negroes. The river life was ever fascinating to the ape-man. He found pleasure in watching the ungainly antics of Duro, the hippopotamus, and keen sport in tormenting the sluggish crocodile, Gimla, as he basked in the sun. Then, too, there were the shes and the balus of the black men of the Gomangani to frighten as they squatted by the river, the shes with their meager washing, the balus with their primitive toys.

This day he came upon a woman and her child farther down stream than usual. The former was searching for a species of shellfish which was to be found in the mud close to the river bank. She was a young black woman of about thirty. Her teeth were filed to sharp points, for her people ate the flesh of man. Her under lip was slit that it might support a rude pendant of copper which she had worn for so many years that the lip had been dragged downward to prodigious lengths, exposing the teeth and gums of her lower jaw. Her nose, too, was slit, and through the slit was a wooden skewer. Metal ornaments dangled from her ears, and upon her forehead and cheeks; upon her chin and the bridge of her nose were tattooings in colors that were mellowed now by age. She was naked except for a girdle of grasses about her waist. Altogether she was very beautiful in her own estimation and even in the estimation of the men of Mbonga's tribe, though she was of another people — a trophy of war seized in her maidenhood by one of Mbonga's fighting men.

Her child was a boy of ten, lithe, straight and, for a black, handsome. Tarzan looked upon the two from the concealing foliage of a near-by bush. He was about to leap forth before them with a terrifying scream, that he might enjoy the spectacle of their terror and their incontinent flight; but of a sudden a new whim seized him. Here was a balu fashioned as he himself was fashioned. Of course this one's skin was black; but what of it? Tarzan had never seen a white man. In so far as he knew, he was the sole representative of that strange form of life upon the earth. The black boy should make an excellent balu for Tarzan, since he had none of his own. He would tend him carefully, feed him well, protect him as only Tarzan of the Apes could protect his own, and teach him out of his half human, half bestial lore the secrets of the jungle from its rotting surface vegetation to the high tossed pinnacles of the forest's upper terraces.

*T*arzan uncoiled his rope, and shook out the noose. The two before him, all ignorant of the near presence of that terrifying form, continued preoccupied in the search for shellfish, poking about in the mud with short sticks.

Tarzan stepped from the jungle behind them; his noose lay open upon the ground beside him. There was a quick movement of the right arm and the noose rose gracefully into the air, hovered an instant above the head of the unsuspecting youth, then settled. As it encompassed his body below the shoulders, Tarzan gave a quick jerk that tightened it about the boy's arms, pinioning them to his sides. A scream of terror broke from the lad's lips, and as his mother turned, affrighted at his cry, she saw him being dragged quickly toward a great white giant who stood just beneath the shade of a near-by tree, scarcely a dozen long paces from her.

With a savage cry of terror and rage, the woman leaped fearlessly toward the ape-man. In her mien Tarzan saw determination and courage which would shrink not even from death itself. She was very hideous and frightful even when her face was in repose; but convulsed by passion, her expression became terrifyingly fiendish. Even the ape-man drew back, but more in revulsion than fear — fear he knew not.

Biting and kicking was the black she's balu as Tarzan tucked him beneath his arm and vanished into the branches hanging low above him, just as the infuriated mother dashed forward to seize and do battle with him. And as he melted away into the depth of the jungle with his still struggling prize, he meditated upon the possibilities which might lie in the prowess of the Gomangani were the hes as formidable as the shes.

Once at a safe distance from the despoiled mother and out of earshot of her screams and menaces, Tarzan paused to inspect his prize, now so thoroughly terrorized that he had ceased his struggles and his outcries.

The frightened child rolled his eyes fearfully toward his captor, until the whites showed gleaming all about the irises.

"I am Tarzan," said the ape-man, in the vernacular of the anthropoids. "I will not harm you. You are to be Tarzan's balu. Tarzan will protect you. He will feed you. The best in the jungle shall be for Tarzan's balu, for Tarzan is a mighty hunter. None need you fear, not even Numa, the lion, for Tarzan is a mighty fighter. None so great as Tarzan, son of Kala. Do not fear."

But the child only whimpered and trembled, for he did not understand the tongue of the great apes, and the voice of Tarzan sounded to him like the barking and growling of a beast. Then, too, he had heard stories of this bad, white forest god. It was he who had slain Kulonga and others of the warriors of Mbonga, the chief. It was he who entered the village stealthily, by magic, in the darkness of the night, to steal arrows and poison, and frighten the women and the children and even the great warriors. Doubtless this wicked god fed upon little boys. Had his mother not said as much when he was naughty and she threatened to give him to the white god of the jungle if he were not good? Little black Tibo shook as with ague.

"Are you cold, Go-bu-balu?" asked Tarzan, using the simian equivalent of black he-baby in lieu of a better name. "The sun is hot; why do you shiver?"

Tibo could not understand; but he cried for his mamma and begged the great, white god to let him go, promising always to be a good boy thereafter if his plea were granted. Tarzan shook his head. Not a word could he understand. This would never do! He must teach Go-bu-balu a language which sounded like talk. It was quite certain to Tarzan that Go-bu-balu's speech was not talk at all. It sounded quite as senseless as the chattering of the silly birds. It would be best, thought the ape-man, quickly to get him among the tribe of Kerchak where he would hear the Mangani talking among themselves. Thus he would soon learn an intelligible form of speech.

Tarzan rose to his feet upon the swaying branch where he had halted far above the ground, and motioned to the child to follow him; but Tibo only clung tightly to the bole of the tree and wept. Being a boy, and a native African, he had, of course, climbed into trees many times before this; but the idea of racing off through the forest, leaping from one branch to another, as his captor, to his horror, had done when he had carried Tibo away from his mother, filled his childish heart with terror.

Tarzan sighed. His newly acquired balu had much indeed to learn. It was pitiful that a balu of his size and strength should be so backward. He tried to coax Tibo to follow him; but the child dared not, so Tarzan picked him up and carried him upon his back. Tibo no longer scratched or bit. Escape seemed impossible. Even now, were he set upon the ground, the chance was remote, he knew, that he could find his way back to the village of Mbonga, the chief. Even if he could, there were the lions and the leopards and the hyenas, any one of which, as Tibo was well aware, was particularly fond of the meat of little black boys.

So far the terrible white god of the jungle had offered him no harm. He could not expect even this much consideration from the frightful, green-eyed man-eaters. It would be the lesser of two evils, then, to let the white god carry him away without scratching and biting, as he had done at first.

As Tarzan swung rapidly through the trees, little Tibo closed his eyes in terror rather than look longer down into the frightful abysses beneath. Never before in all his life had Tibo been so frightened, yet as the white giant sped on with him through the forest there stole over the child an inexplicable sensation of security as he saw how true were the leaps of the ape-man, how unerring his grasp upon the swaying limbs which gave him hand-hold, and then, too, there was safety in the middle terraces of the forest, far above the reach of the dreaded lions.

And so Tarzan came to the clearing where the tribe fed, dropping among them with his new balu clinging tightly to his shoulders. He was fairly in the midst of them before Tibo spied a single one of the great hairy forms, or before the apes realized that Tarzan was not alone. When they saw the little Gomangani perched upon his back some of them came forward in curiosity with upcurled lips and snarling mien.

An hour before little Tibo would have said that he knew the uttermost depths of fear; but now, as he saw these fearsome beasts surrounding him, he realized that all that had gone before was as nothing by comparison. Why did the great white giant stand there so unconcernedly? Why did he not flee before these horrid, hairy, tree men fell upon them both and tore them to pieces? And then there came to Tibo a numbing recollection. It was none other than the story he had heard passed from mouth to mouth, fearfully, by the people of Mbonga, the chief, that this great white demon of the jungle was naught other than a hairless ape, for had not he been seen in company with these?

Tibo could only stare in wide-eyed horror at the approaching apes. He saw their beetling brows, their great fangs, their wicked eyes. He noted their mighty muscles rolling beneath their shaggy hides. Their every attitude and expression was a menace. Tarzan saw this, too. He drew Tibo around in front of him.

"This is Tarzan's Go-bu-balu," he said. "Do not harm him, or Tarzan will kill you," and he bared his own fangs in the teeth of the nearest ape.

"It is a Gomangani," replied the ape. "Let me kill it. It is a Gomangani. The Gomangani are our enemies. Let me kill it."

"Go away," snarled Tarzan. "I tell you, Gunto, it is Tarzan's balu. Go away or Tarzan will kill you," and the ape-man took a step toward the advancing ape.

The latter sidled off, quite stiff and haughty, after the manner of a dog which meets another and is too proud to fight and too fearful to turn his back and run.

Next came Teeka, prompted by curiosity. At her side skipped little Gazan. They were filled with wonder like the others; but Teeka did not bare her fangs. Tarzan saw this and motioned that she approach.

"Tarzan has a balu now," he said. "He and Teeka's balu can play together."

"It is a Gomangani," replied Teeka. "It will kill my balu. Take it away, Tarzan."

Tarzan laughed. "It could not harm Pamba, the rat," he said. "It is but a little balu and very frightened. Let Gazan play with it."

Teeka still was fearful, for with all their mighty ferocity the great anthropoids are timid; but at last, assured by her great confidence in Tarzan, she pushed Gazan forward toward the little black boy. The small ape, guided by instinct, drew back toward its mother, baring its small fangs and screaming in mingled fear and rage.

Tibo, too, showed no signs of desiring a closer acquaintance with Gazan, so Tarzan gave up his efforts for the time.

During the week which followed, Tarzan found his time much occupied. His balu was a greater responsibility than he had counted upon. Not for a moment did he dare leave it, since of all the tribe, Teeka alone could have been depended upon to refrain from slaying the hapless black had it not been for Tarzan's constant watchfulness. When the ape-man hunted, he must carry Go-bu-balu about with him. It was irksome, and then the little black seemed so stupid and fearful to Tarzan. It was quite helpless against even the lesser of the jungle creatures. Tarzan wondered how it had

survived at all. He tried to teach it, and found a ray of
hope in the fact that Go-bu-balu had mastered a few
words of the language of the anthropoids, and that he
could now cling to a high-tossed branch without
screaming in fear; but there was something about the
child which worried Tarzan. He often had watched the
blacks within their village. He had seen the children
playing, and always there had been much laughter; but
little Go-bu-balu never laughed. It was true that Tarzan
himself never laughed. Upon occasion he smiled,
grimly, but to laughter he was a stranger. The black,
however, should have laughed, reasoned the ape-man.
It was the way of the Gomangani.

Also, he saw that the little fellow often refused food
and was growing thinner day by day. At times he
surprised the boy sobbing softly to himself. Tarzan
tried to comfort him, even as fierce Kala had com-
forted Tarzan when the ape-man was a balu, but all to
no avail. Go-bu-balu merely no longer feared Tarzan —
that was all. He feared every other living thing within
the jungle. He feared the jungle days with their long
excursions through the dizzy tree tops. He feared the
jungle nights with their swaying, perilous couches far
above the ground, and the grunting and coughing of
the great carnivora prowling beneath him.

Tarzan did not know what to do. His heritage of
English blood rendered it a difficult thing even to
consider a surrender of his project, though he was
forced to admit to himself that his balu was not all
that he had hoped. Though he was faithful to his
self-imposed task, and even found that he had grown
to like Go-bu-balu, he could not deceive himself into
believing that he felt for it that fierce heat of passionate
affection which Teeka revealed for Gazan, and which
the black mother had shown for Go-bu-balu.

The little black boy from cringing terror at the sight
of Tarzan passed by degrees into trustfulness and ad-

miration. Only kindness had he ever received at the hands of the great white devil-god, yet he had seen with what ferocity his kindly captor could deal with others. He had seen him leap upon a certain he-ape which persisted in attempting to seize and slay Go-bu-balu. He had seen the strong, white teeth of the ape-man fastened in the neck of his adversary, and the mighty muscles tensed in battle. He had heard the savage, bestial snarls and roars of combat, and he had realized with a shudder that he could not differentiate between those of his guardian and those of the hairy ape.

He had seen Tarzan bring down a buck, just as Numa, the lion, might have done, leaping upon its back and fastening his fangs in the creature's neck. Tibo had shuddered at the sight, but he had thrilled, too, and for the first time there entered his dull, Negroid mind a vague desire to emulate his savage foster parent. But Tibo, the little black boy, lacked the divine spark which had permitted Tarzan, the white boy, to benefit by his training in the ways of the fierce jungle. In imagination he was wanting, and imagination is but another name for super-intelligence.

Imagination it is which builds bridges, and cities, and empires. The beasts know it not, the blacks only a little, while to one in a hundred thousand of earth's dominant race it is given as a gift from heaven that man may not perish from the earth.

While Tarzan pondered his problem concerning the future of his balu, Fate was arranging to take the matter out of his hands. Momaya, Tibo's mother, grief-stricken at the loss of her boy, had consulted the tribal witch-doctor, but to no avail. The medicine he made was not good medicine, for though Momaya paid him two goats for it, it did not bring back Tibo, nor even indicate where she might search for him with reasonable assurance of finding him. Momaya, being of a short temper and of another people, had little respect for the witch-doctor of her husband's tribe, and so, when he suggested that a further payment of two more fat goats would doubtless enable him to make stronger medicine, she promptly loosed her shrewish tongue upon him, and with such good effect that he was glad to take himself off with his zebra's tail and his pot of magic.

When he had gone and Momaya had succeeded in partially subduing her anger, she gave herself over to thought, as she so often had done since the abduction of her Tibo, in the hope that she finally might discover some feasible means of locating him, or at least assuring herself as to whether he were alive or dead.

It was known to the blacks that Tarzan did not eat the flesh of man, for he had slain more than one of their number, yet never tasted the flesh of any. Too, the bodies always had been found, sometimes dropping as though from the clouds to alight in the center of the village. As Tibo's body had not been found, Momaya argued that he still lived, but where?

Then it was that there came to her mind a recollection of Bukawai, the unclean, who dwelt in a cave in the hill-side to the north, and who it was well known entertained devils in his evil lair. Few, if any, had the temerity to visit old Bukawai, firstly because of fear of his black magic and the two hyenas who dwelt with him and were commonly known to be devils masquerading, and secondly because of the loathsome disease which had caused Bukawai to be an outcast — a disease which was slowly eating away his face.

Now it was that Momaya reasoned shrewdly that if any might know the whereabouts of her Tibo, it would be Bukawai, who was in friendly intercourse with gods and demons, since a demon or a god it was who had stolen her baby; but even her great mother love was sorely taxed to find the courage to send her forth into the black jungle toward the distant hills and the uncanny abode of Bukawai, the unclean, and his devils.

Mother love, however, is one of the human passions which closely approximates to the dignity of an irresistible force. It drives the frail flesh of weak women to deeds of heroic measure. Momaya was neither frail nor weak, physically, but she was a woman, an ignorant, superstitious, African savage. She believed in devils, in black magic, and in witchcraft. To Momaya, the jungle was inhabited by far more terrifying things than lions and leopards — horrifying, nameless things which possessed the power of wreaking frightful harm under various innocent guises.

From one of the warriors of the village, whom she knew to have once stumbled upon the lair of Bukawai, the mother of Tibo learned how she might find it — near a spring of water which rose in a small rocky canon between two hills, the easternmost of which was easily recognizable because of a huge granite boulder which rested upon its summit. The westerly hill was lower than its companion, and was quite bare of vegetation except for a single mimosa tree which grew just a little below its summit.

These two hills, the man assured her, could be seen for some distance before she reached them, and together formed an excellent guide to her destination. He warned her, however, to abandon so foolish and dangerous an adventure, emphasizing what she already quite well knew, that if she escaped harm at the hands of Bukawai and his demons, the chances were that she would not be so fortunate with the great carnivora of the jungle through which she must pass going and returning.

The warrior even went to Momaya's husband, who, in turn, having little authority over the vixenish lady of his choice, went to Mbonga, the chief. The latter summoned Momaya, threatening her with the direst punishment should she venture forth upon so unholy an excursion. The old chief's interest in the matter was due solely to that age-old alliance which exists between church and state. The local witch-doctor, knowing his own medicine better than any other knew it, was jealous of all other pretenders to accomplishments in the black art. He long had heard of the power of Bukawai, and feared lest, should he succeed in recovering Momaya's lost child, much of the tribal patronage and consequent fees would be diverted to the unclean one. As Mbonga received, as chief, a certain proportion of the witch-doctor's fees and could expect nothing from Bukawai, his heart and soul were, quite naturally, wrapped up in the orthodox church.

But if Momaya could view with intrepid heart an excursion into the jungle and a visit to the fear-haunted abode of Bukawai, she was not likely to be deterred by threats of future punishment at the hands of old Mbonga, whom she secretly despised. Yet she appeared to accede to his injunctions, returning to her hut in silence.

She would have preferred starting upon her quest by day-light, but this was now out of the question, since she must carry food and a weapon of some sort — things which she never could pass out of the village with by day without being subjected to curious questioning that surely would come immediately to the ears of Mbonga.

So Momaya bided her time until night, and just before the gates of the village were closed, she slipped through into the darkness and the jungle. She was much frightened, but she set her face resolutely toward the north, and though she paused often to listen, breathlessly, for the huge cats which, here, were her greatest terror, she nevertheless continued her way staunchly for several hours, until a low moan a little to her right and behind her brought her to a sudden stop.

With palpitating heart the woman stood, scarce daring to breathe, and then, very faintly but unmistakable to her keen ears, came the stealthy crunching of twigs and grasses beneath padded feet.

All about Momaya grew the giant trees of the tropical jungle, festooned with hanging vines and mosses. She seized upon the nearest and started to clamber, apelike, to the branches above. As she did so, there was a sudden rush of a great body behind her, a menacing roar that caused the earth to tremble, and something crashed into the very creepers to which she was clinging — but below her.

Momaya drew herself to safety among the leafy branches and thanked the foresight which had prompted her to bring along the dried human ear which hung from a cord about her neck. She always had known that that ear was good medicine. It had been given her, when a girl, by the witch-doctor of her town tribe, and was nothing like the poor, weak medicine of Mbonga's witch-doctor.

All night Momaya clung to her perch, for although the lion sought other prey after a short time, she dared not descend into the darkness again, for fear she might encounter him or another of his kind; but at daylight she clambered down and resumed her way.

Tarzan of the Apes, finding that his balu never ceased to give evidence of terror in the presence of the apes of the tribe, and also that most of the adult apes were a constant menace to Go-bu-balu's life, so that Tarzan dared not leave him alone with them, took to hunting with the little black boy farther and farther from the stamping grounds of the anthropoids.

Little by little his absences from the tribe grew in length as he wandered farther away from them, until finally he found himself a greater distance to the north than he ever before had hunted, and with water and ample game and fruit, he felt not at all inclined to return to the tribe.

Little Go-bu-balu gave evidences of a greater interest in life, an interest which varied in direct proportion to the distance he was from the apes of Kerchak. He now trotted along behind Tarzan when the ape-man went upon the ground, and in the trees he even did his best to follow his mighty foster parent. The boy was still sad and lonely. His thin, little body had grown steadily thinner since he had come among the apes, for while, as a young cannibal, he was not overnice in the matter of diet, he found it not always to his taste to stomach the weird things which tickled the palates of epicures among the apes.

His large eyes were very large indeed now, his cheeks sunken, and every rib of his emaciated body plainly discernible to whomsoever should care to count them. Constant terror, perhaps, had had as much to do with his physical condition as had improper food. Tarzan noticed the change and was worried. He had hoped to see his balu wax sturdy and strong. His disappointment was great. In only one respect did Go-bu-balu seem to progress — he readily was mastering the language of the apes. Even now he and Tarzan could converse in a fairly satisfactory manner by supplementing the meager ape speech with signs; but for the most part, Go-bu-balu was silent other than to answer questions put to him. His great sorrow was yet too new and too poignant to be laid aside even momentarily. Always he pined for Momaya — shrewish, hideous, repulsive, perhaps, she would have been to you or me, but to Tibo she was mamma, the personification of that one great love which knows no selfishness and which does not consume itself in its own fires.

As the two hunted, or rather as Tarzan hunted and Go-bu-balu tagged along in his wake, the ape-man noticed many things and thought much. Once they came upon Sabor moaning in the tall grasses. About her romped and played two little balls of fur, but her eyes were for one which lay between her great forepaws and did not romp, one who never would romp again.

Tarzan read aright the anguish and the suffering of the huge mother cat. He had been minded to bait her. It was to do this that he had sneaked silently through the trees until he had come almost above her, but something held the ape-man as he saw the lioness grieving over her dead cub. With the acquisition of Go-bu-balu, Tarzan had come to realize the responsibilities and sorrows of parentage, without its joys. His heart went out to Sabor as it might not have done a few weeks before. As he watched her, there rose quite unbidden before him a vision of Momaya, the skewer through the septum of her nose, her pendulous under lip sagging beneath the weight which dragged it down. Tarzan saw not her unloveliness; he saw only the same anguish that was Sabor's, and he winced. That strange functioning of the mind which sometimes is called association of ideas snapped Teeka and Gazan before the ape-man's mental vision. What if one should come and take Gazan from Teeka. Tarzan uttered a low and ominous growl as though Gazan were his own. Go-bu-balu glanced here and there apprehensively, thinking that Tarzan had espied an enemy. Sabor sprang suddenly to her feet, her yellow-green eyes blazing, her tail lashing as she cocked her ears, and raising her muzzle, sniffed the air for possible danger. The two little cubs, which had been playing, scampered quickly to her, and standing beneath her, peered out from between her forelegs, their big ears upstanding, their little heads cocked first upon one side and then upon the other.

With a shake of his black shock, Tarzan turned away and resumed his hunting in another direction; but all day there rose one after another, above the threshold of his objective mind, memory portraits of Sabor, of Momaya, and of Teeka — a lioness, a cannibal, and a she-ape, yet to the ape-man they were identical through motherhood.

It was noon of the third day when Momaya came within sight of the cave of Bukawai, the unclean. The old witch-doctor had rigged a framework of interlaced boughs to close the mouth of the cave from predatory beasts. This was now set to one side, and the black cavern beyond yawned mysterious and repellent. Momaya shivered as from a cold wind of the rainy season. No sign of life appeared about the cave, yet Momaya experienced that uncanny sensation as of unseen eyes regarding her malevolently. Again she shuddered. She tried to force her unwilling feet onward toward the cave, when from its depths issued an uncanny sound that was neither brute nor human, a weird sound that was akin to mirthless laughter.

With a stifled scream, Momaya turned and fled into the jungle. For a hundred yards she ran before she could control her terror, and then she paused, listening. Was all her labor, were all the terrors and dangers through which she had passed to go for naught? She tried to steel herself to return to the cave, but again fright overcame her.

Saddened, disheartened, she turned slowly upon the back trail toward the village of Mbonga. Her young shoulders now were drooped like those of an old woman who bears a great burden of many years with their accumulated pains and sorrows, and she walked with tired feet and a halting step. The spring of youth was gone from Momaya.

For another hundred yards she dragged her weary way, her brain half paralyzed from dumb terror and suffering, and then there came to her the memory of a little babe that suckled at her breast, and of a slim boy who romped, laughing, about her, and they were both Tibo — her Tibo!

Her shoulders straightened. She shook her savage

head, and she turned about and walked boldly back to the mouth of the cave of Bukawai, the unclean — of Bukawai, the witch-doctor.

Again, from the interior of the cave came the hideous laughter that was not laughter. This time Momaya recognized it for what it was, the strange cry of a hyena. No more did she shudder, but she held her spear ready and called aloud to Bukawai to come out.

Instead of Bukawai came the repulsive head of a hyena. Momaya poked at it with her spear, and the ugly, sullen brute drew back with an angry growl. Again Momaya called Bukawai by name, and this time there came an answer in mumbling tones that were scarce more human than those of the beast.

"Who comes to Bukawai?" queried the voice.

"It is Momaya," replied the woman; "Momaya from the village of Mbonga, the chief.

"What do you want?"

"I want good medicine, better medicine than Mbonga's witch-doctor can make," replied Momaya. "The great, white, jungle god has stolen my Tibo, and I want medicine to bring him back, or to find where he is hidden that I may go and get him."

"Who is Tibo?" asked Bukawai.

Momaya told him.

"Bukawai's medicine is very strong," said the voice. "Five goats and a new sleeping mat are scarce enough in exchange for Bukawai's medicine."

"Two goats are enough," said Momaya, for the spirit of barter is strong in the breasts of the blacks.

The pleasure of haggling over the price was a sufficiently potent lure to draw Bukawai to the mouth of the cave. Momaya was sorry when she saw him that he had not remained within. There are some things too horrible, too hideous, too repulsive for description — Bukawai's face was of these. When Momaya saw him she understood why it was that he was almost inarticulate.

Beside him were two hyenas, which rumor had said were his only and constant companions. They made an excellent trio — the most repulsive of beasts with the most repulsive of humans.

"Five goats and a new sleeping mat," mumbled Bukawai.

"Two fat goats and a sleeping mat." Momaya raised her bid; but Bukawai was obdurate. He stuck for the five goats and the sleeping mat for a matter of half an hour, while the hyenas sniffed and growled and laughed hideously. Momaya was determined to give all that Bukawai asked if she could do no better, but haggling is second nature to black barterers, and in the end it partly repaid her, for a compromise finally was reached which included three fat goats, a new sleeping mat, and a piece of copper wire.

"Come back tonight," said Bukawai, "when the moon is two hours in the sky. Then will I make the strong medicine which shall bring Tibo back to you. Bring with you the three fat goats, the new sleeping mat, and the piece of copper wire the length of a large man's forearm."

"I cannot bring them," said Momaya. "You will have to come after them. When you have restored Tibo to me, you shall have them all at the village of Mbonga.

Bukawai shook his head.

"I will make no medicine," he said, "until I have the goats and the mat and the copper wire."

Momaya pleaded and threatened, but all to no avail. Finally, she turned away and started off through the jungle toward the village of Mbonga. How she could get three goats and a sleeping mat out of the village and through the jungle to the cave of Bukawai, she did not know, but that she would do it somehow she was quite positive — she would do it or die. Tibo must be restored to her.

Tarzan coming lazily through the jungle with little Go-bu-balu, caught the scent of Bara, the deer. Tarzan hungered for the flesh of Bara. Naught tickled his palate so greatly; but to stalk Bara with Go-bu-balu at his heels, was out of the question, so he hid the child in the crotch of a tree where the thick foliage screened him from view, and set off swiftly and silently upon the spoor of Bara.

Tibo alone was more terrified than Tibo even among the apes. Real and apparent dangers are less disconcerting than those which we imagine, and only the gods of his people knew how much Tibo imagined.

He had been but a short time in his hiding place when he heard something approaching through the jungle. He crouched closer to the limb upon which he lay and prayed that Tarzan would return quickly. His wide eyes searched the jungle in the direction of the moving creature.

What if it was a leopard that had caught his scent! It would be upon him in a minute. Hot tears flowed from the large eyes of little Tibo. The curtain of jungle foliage rustled close at hand. The thing was but a few paces from his tree! His eyes fairly popped from his black face as he watched for the appearance of the dread creature which presently would thrust a snarling countenance from between the vines and creepers.

And then the curtain parted and a woman stepped into full view. With a gasping cry, Tibo tumbled from his perch and raced toward her. Momaya suddenly started back and raised her spear, but a second later she cast it aside and caught the thin body in her strong arms.

Crushing it to her, she cried and laughed all at one and the same time, and hot tears of joy, mingled with the tears of Tibo, trickled down the crease between her naked breasts.

Disturbed by the noise so close at hand, there arose

from his sleep in a near-by thicket Numa, the lion. He looked through the tangled underbrush and saw the black woman and her young. He licked his chops and measured the distance between them and himself. A short charge and a long leap would carry him upon them. He flicked the end of his tail and sighed.

A vagrant breeze, swirling suddenly in the wrong direction, carried the scent of Tarzan to the sensitive nostrils of Bara, the deer. There was a startled tensing of muscles and cocking of ears, a sudden dash, and Tarzan's meat was gone. The ape-man angrily shook his head and turned back toward the spot where he had left Go-bu-balu. He came softly, as was his way. Before he reached the spot he heard strange sounds — the sound of a woman laughing and of a woman weeping, and the two which seemed to come from one throat were mingled with the convulsive sobbing of a child. Tarzan hastened, and when Tarzan hastened, only the birds and the wind went faster.

And as Tarzan approached the sounds, he heard another, a deep sigh. Momaya did not hear it, nor did Tibo; but the ears of Tarzan were as the ears of Bara, the deer. He heard the sigh, and he knew, so he unloosed the heavy spear which dangled at his back. Even as he sped through the branches of the trees, with the same ease that you or I might take out a pocket handkerchief as we strolled nonchalantly down a lazy country lane, Tarzan of the Apes took the spear from its thong that it might be ready against any emergency.

Numa, the lion, did not rush madly to attack. He reasoned again, and reason told him that already the prey was his, so he pushed his great bulk through the foliage and stood eyeing his meat with baleful, glaring eyes.

Momaya saw him and shrieked, drawing Tibo closer to her breast. To have found her child and to lose him, all in a moment! She raised her spear, throwing her hand far back of her shoulder. Numa roared and stepped slowly forward. Momaya cast her weapon. It grazed the tawny shoulder, inflicting a flesh wound which aroused all the terrific bestiality of the carnivore, and the lion charged.

Momaya tried to close her eyes, but could not. She saw the flashing swiftness of the huge, oncoming death, and then she saw something else. She saw a mighty, naked white man drop as from the heavens into the path of the charging lion. She saw the muscles of a great arm flash in the light of the equatorial sun as it filtered, dappling, through the foliage above. She saw a heavy hunting spear hurtle through the air to meet the lion in midleap.

Numa brought up upon his haunches, roaring terribly and striking at the spear which protruded from his breast. His great blows bent and twisted the weapon. Tarzan, crouching and with hunting knife in hand, circled warily about the frenzied cat. Momaya, wide-eyed, stood rooted to the spot, watching, fascinated.

In sudden fury Numa hurled himself toward the ape-man, but the wiry creature eluded the blundering charge, side-stepping quickly only to rush in upon his foe. Twice the hunting blade flashed in the air. Twice it fell upon the back of Numa, already weakening from the spear point so near his heart. The second stroke of the blade pierced far into the beast's spine, and with a last convulsive sweep of the fore-paws, in a vain attempt to reach his tormentor, Numa sprawled upon the ground, paralyzed and dying.

Bukawai, fearful lest he should lose any recompense, followed Momaya with the intention of persuading her to part with her ornaments of copper and iron against her return with the price of the medicine — to pay, as it were, for an option on his services as one pays a retaining fee to an attorney, for, like an attorney, Bukawai knew the value of his medicine and that it was well to collect as much as possible in advance.

The witch-doctor came upon the scene as Tarzan leaped to meet the lion's charge. He saw it all and marveled, guessing immediately that this must be the strange white demon concerning whom he had heard vague rumors before Momaya came to him.

Momaya, now that the lion was past harming her or hers, gazed with new terror upon Tarzan. It was he who had stolen her Tibo. Doubtless he would attempt to steal him again. Momaya hugged the boy close to her. She was determined to die this time rather than suffer Tibo to be taken from her again.

Tarzan eyed them in silence. The sight of the boy clinging, sobbing, to his mother aroused within his savage breast a melancholy loneliness. There was none thus to cling to Tarzan, who yearned so for the love of someone, of something.

At last Tibo looked up, because of the quiet that had fallen upon the jungle, and saw Tarzan. He did not shrink.

"Tarzan," he said, in the speech of the great apes of the tribe of Kerchak, "do not take me from Momaya, my mother. Do not take me again to the lair of the hairy, tree men, for I fear Taug and Gunto and the others. Let me stay with Momaya, O Tarzan, God of the Jungle! Let me stay with Momaya, my mother, and to the end of our days we will bless you and put food before the gates of the village of Mbonga that you may never hunger."

Tarzan sighed.

"Go," he said, "back to the village of Mbonga, and Tarzan will follow to see that no harm befalls you."

Tibo translated the words to his mother, and the two turned their backs upon the ape-man and started off toward home. In the heart of Momaya was a great fear and a great exultation, for never before had she walked with God, and never had she been so happy. She strained little Tibo to her, stroking his thin cheek. Tarzan saw and sighed again.

"For Teeka there is Teeka's balu," he soliloquized; "for Sabor there are balus, and for the she-Gomangani, and for Bara, and for Manu, and even for Pamba, the rat; but for Tarzan there can be none — neither a she nor a balu. Tarzan of the Apes is a man, and it must be that man walks alone."

Bukawai saw them go, and he mumbled through his rotting face, swearing a great oath that he would yet have the three fat goats, the new sleeping mat, and the bit of copper wire.

The Witch~Doctor
Seeks Vengeance

LORD GREYSTOKE was hunting, or, to be more accurate, he was shooting pheasants at Chamston-Hedding. Lord Greystoke was immaculately and appropriately garbed — to the minutest detail he was vogue. To be sure, he was among the forward guns, not being considered a sporting shot, but what he lacked in skill he more than made up in appearance. At the end of the day he would, doubtless, have many birds to his credit, since he had two guns and a smart loader — many more birds than he could eat in a year, even had he been hungry, which he was not, having but just arisen from the breakfast table.

The beaters — there were twenty-three of them, in white smocks — had but just driven the birds into a patch of gorse, and were now circling to the opposite side that they might drive down toward the guns. Lord Greystoke was quite as excited as he ever permitted himself to become. There was an exhilaration in the sport that would not be denied. He felt his blood tingling through his veins as the beaters approached closer and closer to the birds. In a vague and stupid sort of way Lord Greystoke felt, as he always felt upon such occasions, that he was experiencing a sensation somewhat akin to a reversion to a prehistoric type — that the blood of an ancient forbear was coursing hot through him, a hairy, half-naked forbear who had lived by the hunt.

And far away in a matted equatorial jungle another Lord Greystoke, the real Lord Greystoke, hunted. By the standards which he knew, he, too, was vogue — utterly vogue, as was the primal ancestor before the first eviction. The day being sultry, the leopard skin had been left behind. The real Lord Greystoke had not two guns, to be sure, nor even one, neither did he have a smart loader; but he possessed something infinitely more efficacious than guns, or loaders, or even twenty-three beaters in white smocks — he possessed an appetite, an uncanny woodcraft, and muscles that were as steel springs.

Later that day, in England, a Lord Greystoke ate bountifully of things he had not killed, and he drank other things which were uncorked to the accompaniment of much noise. He patted his lips with snowy linen to remove the faint traces of his repast, quite ignorant of the fact that he was an impostor and that the rightful owner of his noble title was even then finishing his own dinner in far-off Africa. He was not using snowy linen, though. Instead he drew the back of a brown forearm and hand across his mouth and wiped his bloody fingers upon his thighs. Then he moved slowly through the jungle to the drinking place, where, upon all fours, he drank as drank his fellows, the other beasts of the jungle.

As he quenched his thirst, another denizen of the gloomy forest approached the stream along the path behind him. It was Numa, the lion, tawny of body and black of mane, scowling and sinister, rumbling out low, coughing roars. Tarzan of the Apes heard him long before he came within sight, but the ape-man went on with his drinking until he had had his fill; then he arose, slowly, with the easy grace of a creature of the wilds and all the quiet dignity that was his birthright.

Numa halted as he saw the man standing at the very spot where the king would drink. His jaws were parted, and his cruel eyes gleamed. He growled and advanced slowly. The man growled, too, backing slowly to one side, and watching, not the lion's face, but its tail. Should that commence to move from side to side in quick, nervous jerks, it would be well to be upon the alert, and should it rise suddenly erect, straight and stiff, then one might prepare to fight or flee; but it did neither, so Tarzan merely backed away and the lion came down and drank scarce fifty feet from where the man stood.

Tomorrow they might be at one another's throats, but today there existed one of those strange and inexplicable truces which so often are seen among the savage ones of the jungle. Before Numa had finished drinking, Tarzan had returned into the forest, and was swinging away in the direction of the village of Mbonga, the black chief.

It had been at least a moon since the ape-man had called upon the Gomangani. Not since he had restored little Tibo to his grief-stricken mother had the whim seized him to do so. The incident of the adopted balu was a closed one to Tarzan. He had sought to find something upon which to lavish such an affection as Teeka lavished upon her balu, but a short experience of the little black boy had made it quite plain to the ape-man that no such sentiment could exist between them.

The fact that he had for a time treated the little black as he might have treated a real balu of his own had in

no way altered the vengeful sentiments with which he
considered the murderers of Kala. The Gomangani
were his deadly enemies, nor could they ever be aught
else. Today he looked forward to some slight relief from
the monotony of his existence in such excitement as
he might derive from baiting the blacks.

It was not yet dark when he reached the village and
took his place in the great tree overhanging the palisade. From beneath came a great wailing out of the
depths of a near-by hut. The noise fell disagreeably
upon Tarzan's ears — it jarred and grated. He did not
like it, so he decided to go away for a while in the hopes
that it might cease; but though he was gone for a couple
of hours the wailing still continued when he returned.

With the intention of putting a violent termination
to the annoying sound, Tarzan slipped silently from
the tree into the shadows beneath. Creeping stealthily
and keeping well in the cover of other huts, he approached that from which rose the sounds of lamentation. A fire burned brightly before the doorway as it
did before other doorways in the village. A few females
squatted about, occasionally adding their own mourn-
ful howlings to those of the master artist within.

The ape-man smiled a slow smile as he thought of
the consternation which would follow the quick leap
that would carry him among the females and into the
full light of the fire. Then he would dart into the hut
during the excitement, throttle the chief screamer, and
be gone into the jungle before the blacks could gather
their scattered nerves for an assault.

Many times had Tarzan behaved similarly in the
village of Mbonga, the chief. His mysterious and un-
expected appearances always filled the breasts of the
poor, superstitious blacks with the panic of terror;
never, it seemed, could they accustom themselves to
the sight of him. It was this terror which lent to the
adventures the spice of interest and amusement which

the human mind of the ape-man craved. Merely to kill was not in itself sufficient. Accustomed to the sight of death, Tarzan found no great pleasure in it. Long since had he avenged the death of Kala, but in the accomplishment of it, he had learned the excitement and the pleasure to be derived from the baiting of the blacks. Of this he never tired.

It was just as he was about to spring forward with a savage roar that a figure appeared in the doorway of the hut. It was the figure of the wailer whom he had come to still, the figure of a young woman with a wooden skewer through the split septum of her nose, with a heavy metal ornament depending from her lower lip, which it had dragged down to hideous and repulsive deformity, with strange tattooing upon forehead, cheeks, and breasts, and a wonderful coiffure built up with mud and wire.

A sudden flare of the fire threw the grotesque figure into high relief, and Tarzan recognized her as Momaya, the mother of Tibo. The fire also threw out a fitful flame which carried to the shadows where Tarzan lurked, picking out his light brown body from the surrounding darkness. Momaya saw him and knew him. With a cry, she leaped forward and Tarzan came to meet her. The other women, turning, saw him, too; but they did not come toward him. Instead they rose as one, shrieked as one, fled as one.

Momaya threw herself at Tarzan's feet, raising supplicating hands toward him and pouring forth from her mutilated lips a perfect cataract of words, not one of which the ape-man comprehended. For a moment he looked down upon the upturned, frightful face of the woman. He had come to slay, but that overwhelming torrent of speech filled him with consternation and with awe. He glanced about him apprehensively, then back at the woman. A revulsion of feeling seized him. He could not kill little Tibo's mother, nor could he stand and face this verbal geyser. With a quick gesture of impatience at the spoiling of his evening's entertainment, he wheeled and leaped away into the darkness. A moment later he was swinging through the black jungle night, the cries and lamentations of Momaya growing fainter in the distance.

It was with a sigh of relief that he finally reached a point from which he could no longer hear them, and finding a comfortable crotch high among the trees, composed himself for a night of dreamless slumber, while a prowling lion moaned and coughed beneath him, and in far-off England the other Lord Greystoke, with the assistance of a valet, disrobed and crawled between spotless sheets, swearing irritably as a cat meowed beneath his window.

As Tarzan followed the fresh spoor of Horta, the boar, the following morning, he came upon the tracks of two Gomangani, a large one and a small one. The ape-man, accustomed as he was to questioning closely all that fell to his perceptions, paused to read the story written in the soft mud of the game trail. You or I would have seen little of interest there, even if, by chance, we could have seen aught. Perhaps had one been there to point them out to us, we might have noted indentations in the mud, but there were countless indentations, one overlapping another into a confusion that would have been entirely meaningless to us. To Tarzan each told its own story. Tantor, the elephant, had passed that way as recently as three suns since. Numa had hunted here the night just gone, and Horta, the boar, had walked slowly along the trail within an hour; but what held Tarzan's attention was the spoor tale of the Gomangani. It told him that the day before an old man had gone toward the north in company with a little boy, and that with them had been two hyenas.

Tarzan scratched his head in puzzled incredulity. He

could see by the overlapping of the footprints that the beasts had not been following the two, for sometimes one was ahead of them and one behind, and again both were in advance, or both were in the rear. It was very strange and quite inexplicable, especially where the spoor showed where the hyenas in the wider portions of the path had walked one on either side of the human pair, quite close to them. Then Tarzan read in the spoor of the smaller Gomangani a shrinking terror of the beast that brushed his side, but in that of the old man was no sign of fear.

At first Tarzan had been solely occupied by the remarkable juxtaposition of the spoor of Dango and Gomangani, but now his keen eyes caught something in the spoor of the little Gomangani which brought him to a sudden stop. It was as though, finding a letter in the road, you suddenly had discovered in it the familiar handwriting of a friend.

"Go-bu-balu!" exclaimed the ape-man, and at once memory flashed upon the screen of recollection the supplicating attitude of Momaya as she had hurled herself before him in the village of Mbonga the night before. Instantly all was explained — the wailing and lamentation, the pleading of the black mother, the sympathetic howling of the shes about the fire. Little Go-bu-balu had been stolen again, and this time by another than Tarzan. Doubtless the mother had thought that he was again in the power of Tarzan of the Apes, and she had been beseeching him to return her balu to her.

Yes, it was all quite plain now; but who could have stolen Go-bu-balu this time? Tarzan wondered, and he wondered, too, about the presence of Dango. He would investigate. The spoor was a day old and it ran toward the north. Tarzan set out to follow it. In places it was totally obliterated by the passage of many beasts, and where the way was rocky, even Tarzan of the Apes was almost baffled; but there was still the faint effluvium which clung to the human spoor, appreciable only to such highly trained perceptive powers as were Tarzan's.

It had all happened to little Tibo very suddenly and unexpectedly within the brief span of two suns. First had come Bukawai, the witch-doctor — Bukawai, the unclean — with the ragged bit of flesh which still clung to his rotting face. He had come alone and by day to the place at the river where Momaya went daily to wash her body and that of Tibo, her little boy. He had stepped out from behind a great bush quite close to Momaya, frightening little Tibo so that he ran screaming to his mother's protecting arms.

But Momaya, though startled, had wheeled to face the fearsome thing with all the savage ferocity of a she-tiger at bay. When she saw who it was, she breathed a sigh of partial relief, though she still clung tightly to Tibo.

"I have come," said Bukawai without preliminary, "for the three fat goats, the new sleeping mat, and the bit of copper wire as long as a tall man's arm."

"I have no goats for you," snapped Momaya, "nor a sleeping mat, nor any wire. Your medicine was never made. The white jungle god gave me back my Tibo. You had nothing to do with it."

"But I did," mumbled Bukawai through his fleshless jaws. "It was I who commanded the white jungle god to give back your Tibo."

Momaya laughed in his face. "Speaker of lies," she cried, "go back to your foul den and your hyenas. Go back and hide your stinking face in the belly of the mountain, lest the sun, seeing it, cover his face with a black cloud."

"I have come," reiterated Bukawai, "for the three fat goats, the new sleeping mat, and the bit of copper wire the length of a tall man's arm, which you were to pay me for the return of your Tibo."

"It was to be the length of a man's forearm," corrected Momaya, "but you shall have nothing, old thief. You would not make medicine until I had brought the payment in advance, and when I was returning to my village the great, white jungle god gave me back my Tibo — gave him to me out of the jaws of Numa. His medicine is true medicine — yours is the weak medicine of an old man with a hole in his face."

"I have come," repeated Bukawai patiently, "for the three fat —" But Momaya had not waited to hear more of what she already knew by heart. Clasping Tibo close to her side, she was hurrying away toward the palisaded village of Mbonga, the chief.

And the next day, when Momaya was working in the plantain field with others of the women of the tribe, and little Tibo had been playing at the edge of the jungle, casting a small spear in anticipation of the distant day when he should be a full-fledged warrior, Bukawai had come again.

Tibo had seen a squirrel scampering up the bole of a great tree. His childish mind had transformed it into the menacing figure of a hostile warrior. Little Tibo had raised his tiny spear, his heart filled with the savage blood lust of his race, as he pictured the night's orgy when he should dance about the corpse of his human kill as the women of his tribe prepared the meat for the feast to follow.

But when he cast the spear, he missed both squirrel and tree, losing his missile far among the tangled undergrowth of the jungle. However, it could be but a few steps within the forbidden labyrinth. The women were all about in the field. There were warriors on guard within easy hail, and so little Tibo boldly ventured into the dark place.

Just behind the screen of creepers and matted foliage lurked three horrid figures — an old, old man, black as the pit, with a face half eaten away by leprosy, his sharp-filed teeth, the teeth of a cannibal, showing yellow and repulsive through the great gaping hole where his mouth and nose had been. And beside him, equally hideous, stood two powerful hyenas — carrion-eaters consorting with carrion.

Tibo did not see them until, head down, he had forced his way through the thickly growing vines in search of his little spear, and then it was too late. As he looked up into the face of Bukawai, the old witch-doctor seized him, muffling his screams with a palm across his mouth. Tibo struggled futilely.

A moment later he was being hustled away through the dark and terrible jungle, the frightful old man still muffling his screams, and the two hideous hyenas pacing now on either side, now before, now behind, always prowling, always growling, snapping, snarling, or, worst of all, laughing hideously.

To little Tibo, who within his brief existence had passed through such experiences as are given to few to pass through in a lifetime, the northward journey was a nightmare of terror. He thought now of the time that he had been with the great, white jungle god, and he prayed with all his little soul that he might be back again with the white-skinned giant who consorted with the hairy tree men. Terror-stricken he had been then, but his surroundings had been nothing by comparison with those which he now endured.

The old man seldom addressed Tibo, though he kept up an almost continuous mumbling throughout the long day. Tibo caught repeated references to fat goats, sleeping mats, and pieces of copper wire. "Ten fat goats, ten fat goats," the old Negro would croon over and over again. By this little Tibo guessed that the price of his ransom had risen. Ten fat goats? Where would his mother get ten fat goats, or thin ones, either, for that matter, to buy back just a poor little boy? Mbonga would never let her have them, and Tibo knew that his father never had owned more than three goats at the same time in all his life. Ten fat goats! Tibo sniffled. The putrid old man would kill him and eat him, for the goats would never be forthcoming. Bukawai would throw his bones to the hyenas. The little black boy shuddered and became so weak that he almost fell in his tracks. Bukawai cuffed him on an ear and jerked him along.

After what seemed an eternity to Tibo, they arrived at the mouth of a cave between two rocky hills. The opening was low and narrow. A few saplings bound together with strips of rawhide closed it against stray beasts. Bukawai removed the primitive door and pushed Tibo within. The hyenas, snarling, rushed past him and were lost to view in the blackness of the interior. Bukawai replaced the saplings and seizing Tibo roughly by the arm, dragged him along a narrow, rocky passage. The floor was comparatively smooth, for the dirt which lay thick upon it had been trodden and tramped by many feet until few inequalities remained.

The passage was tortuous, and as it was very dark and the walls rough and rocky, Tibo was scratched and bruised from the many bumps he received. Bukawai walked as rapidly through the winding gallery as one would traverse a familiar lane by daylight. He knew every twist and turn as a mother knows the face of her child, and he seemed to be in a hurry. He jerked poor little Tibo possibly a trifle more ruthlessly than necessary even at the pace Bukawai set; but the old witch-doctor, an outcast from the society of man, diseased, shunned, hated, feared, was far from possessing an angelic temper. Nature had given him few of the kindlier characteristics of man, and these few Fate had eradicated entirely. Shrewd, cunning, cruel, vindictive, was Bukawai, the witch-doctor.

Frightful tales were whispered of the cruel tortures

he inflicted upon his victims. Children were frightened into obedience by the threat of his name. Often had Tibo been thus frightened, and now he was reaping a grisly harvest of terror from the seeds his mother had innocently sown. The darkness, the presence of the dreaded witch-doctor, the pain of the contusions, with a haunting premonition of the future, and the fear of the hyenas combined to almost paralyze the child. He stumbled and reeled until Bukawai was dragging rather than leading him.

Presently Tibo saw a faint lightness ahead of them, and a moment later they emerged into a roughly circular chamber to which a little daylight filtered through a rift in the rocky ceiling. The hyenas were there ahead of them, waiting. As Bukawai entered with Tibo, the beasts slunk toward them, baring yellow fangs. They were hungry. Toward Tibo they came, and one snapped at his naked legs. Bukawai seized a stick from the floor of the chamber and struck a vicious blow at the beast, at the same time mumbling forth a volley of execrations. The hyena dodged and ran to the side of the chamber, where he stood growling. Bukawai took a step toward the creature, which bristled with rage at his approach. Fear and hatred shot from its evil eyes, but, fortunately for Bukawai, fear predominated.

Seeing that he was unnoticed, the second beast made a short, quick rush for Tibo. The child screamed and darted after the witch-doctor, who now turned his attention to the second hyena. This one he reached with his heavy stick, striking it repeatedly and driving it to the wall. There the two carrion-eaters commenced to circle the chamber while the human carrion, their master, now in a perfect frenzy of demoniacal rage, ran to and fro in an effort to intercept them, striking out with his cudgel and lashing them with his tongue, calling down upon them the curses of whatever gods and demons he could summon to memory, and de-

scribing in lurid figures the ignominy of their ancestors.

Several times one or the other of the beasts would
turn to make a stand against the witch-doctor, and then
Tibo would hold his breath in agonized terror, for
never in his brief life had he seen such frightful hatred
depicted upon the countenance of man or beast; but
always fear overcame the rage of the savage creatures,
so that they resumed their flight, snarling and bare-
fanged, just at the moment that Tibo was certain they
would spring at Bukawai's throat.

At last the witch-doctor tired of the futile chase. With
a snarl quite as bestial as those of the beast, he turned
toward Tibo. "I go to collect the ten fat goats, the new
sleeping mat, and the two pieces of copper wire that
your mother will pay for the medicine I shall make to
bring you back to her," he said. "You will stay here.
There," and he pointed toward the passage which they
had followed to the chamber, "I will leave the hyenas.
If you try to escape, they will eat you."

He cast aside the stick and called to the beasts. They
came, snarling and slinking, their tails between their
legs. Bukawai led them to the passage and drove them
into it. Then he dragged a rude lattice into place before
the opening after he, himself, had left the chamber.
"This will keep them from you," he said. "If I do not
get the ten fat goats and the other things, they shall at
least have a few bones after I am through." And he left
the boy to think over the meaning of his all-too-sug-
gestive words.

When he was gone, Tibo threw himself upon the
earth floor and broke into childish sobs of terror and
loneliness. He knew that his mother had no ten fat
goats to give and that when Bukawai returned, little
Tibo would be killed and eaten. How long he lay there
he did not know, but presently he was aroused by the
growling of the hyenas. They had returned through the

passage and were glaring at him from beyond the lattice. He could see their yellow eyes blazing through the darkness. They reared up and clawed at the barrier. Tibo shivered and withdrew to the opposite side of the chamber. He saw the lattice sag and sway to the attacks of the beasts. Momentarily he expected that it would fall inward, letting the creatures upon him.

Wearily the horror-ridden hours dragged their slow way. Night came, and for a time Tibo slept, but it seemed that the hungry beasts never slept. Always they stood just beyond the lattice growling their hideous growls or laughing their hideous laughs. Through the narrow rift in the rocky roof above him, Tibo could see a few stars, and once the moon crossed. At last daylight came again. Tibo was very hungry and thirsty, for he had not eaten since the morning before, and only once upon the long march had he been permitted to drink, but even hunger and thirst were almost forgotten in the terror of his position.

It was after daylight that the child discovered a second opening in the walls of the subterranean chamber, almost opposite that at which the hyenas still stood glaring hungrily at him. It was only a narrow slit in the rocky wall. It might lead in but a few feet, or it might lead to freedom! Tibo approached it and looked within. He could see nothing. He extended his arm into the blackness, but he dared not venture farther. Bukawai never would have left open a way of escape, Tibo reasoned, so this passage must lead either nowhere or to some still more hideous danger.

To the boy's fear of the actual dangers which menaced him — Bukawai and the two hyenas — his superstition added countless others quite too horrible even to name, for in the lives of the blacks, through the shadows of the jungle day and the black horrors of the jungle night, flit strange, fantastic shapes peopling the already hideously peopled forests with menacing figures, as though the lion and the leopard, the snake and the hyena, and the countless poisonous insects were not quite sufficient to strike terror to the hearts of the poor, simple creatures whose lot is cast in earth's most fearsome spot.

And so it was that little Tibo cringed not only from real menaces but from imaginary ones. He was afraid even to venture upon a road that might lead to escape, lest Bukawai had set to watch it some frightful demon of the jungle.

But the real menaces suddenly drove the imaginary ones from the boy's mind, for with the coming of daylight the half-famished hyenas renewed their efforts to break down the frail barrier which kept them from their prey. Rearing upon their hind feet they clawed and struck at the lattice. With wide eyes Tibo saw it sag and rock. Not for long, he knew, could it withstand the assaults of these two powerful and determined brutes. Already one corner had been forced past the rocky protuberance of the entrance way which had held it in place. A shaggy forearm protruded into the chamber. Tibo trembled as with ague, for he knew that the end was near.

Backing against the farther wall he stood flattened out as far from the beasts as he could get. He saw the lattice give still more. He saw a savage, snarling head forced past it, and grinning jaws snapping and gaping toward him. In another instant the pitiful fabric would fall inward, and the two would be upon him, rending his flesh from his bones, gnawing the bones themselves, fighting for possession of his entrails.

*B*ukawai came upon Momaya outside the palisade of Mbonga, the chief. At sight of him the woman drew back in revulsion, then she flew at him, tooth and nail; but Bukawai threatening her with a spear held her at a safe distance.

"Where is my baby?" she cried. "Where is my little Tibo?"

Bukawai opened his eyes in well-simulated amazement. "Your baby!" he exclaimed. "What should I know of him, other than that I rescued him from the white god of the jungle and have not yet received my pay. I come for the goats and the sleeping mat and the piece of copper wire the length of a tall man's arm from the shoulder to the tips of his fingers."

"Offal of a hyena!" shrieked Momaya. "My child has been stolen, and you, rotting fragment of a man, have taken him. Return him to me or I shall tear your eyes from your head and feed your heart to the wild hogs."

Bukawai shrugged his shoulders. "What do I know about your child?" he asked. "I have not taken him. If he is stolen again, what should Bukawai know of the matter? Did Bukawai steal him before? No, the white jungle god stole him, and if he stole him once he would steal him again. It is nothing to me. I returned him to you before and I have come for my pay. If he is gone and you would have him returned, Bukawai will return him — for ten fat goats, a new sleeping mat and two pieces of copper wire the length of a tall man's arm from the shoulder to the tips of his fingers, and Bukawai will say nothing more about the goats and the sleeping mat and the copper wire which you were to pay for the first medicine."

"Ten fat goats!" screamed Momaya. "I could not pay you ten fat goats in as many years. Ten fat goats, indeed!"

"Ten fat goats," repeated Bukawai. "Ten fat goats, the new sleeping mat and two pieces of copper wire the length of —"

Momaya stopped him with an impatient gesture.

"Wait! she cried."I have no goats. You waste your breath. Stay here while I go to my man. He has but three goats, yet something may be done. Wait!"

Bukawai sat down beneath a tree. He felt quite content, for he knew that he should have either payment or revenge. He did not fear harm at the hands of these people of another tribe, although he well knew that they must fear and hate him. His leprosy alone would prevent their laying hands upon him, while his reputation as a witch-doctor rendered him doubly immune from attack. He was planning upon compelling them to drive the ten goats to the mouth of his cave when Momaya returned. With her were three warriors — Mbonga, the chief, Rabba Kega, the village witch-doctor, and Ibeto, Tibo's father. They were not pretty men even under ordinary circumstances, and now, with their faces marked by anger, they well might have inspired terror in the heart of anyone; but if Bukawai felt any fear, he did not betray it. Instead he greeted them with an insolent stare, intended to awe them, as they came and squatted in a semi-circle before him.

"Where is Ibeto's son?" asked Mbonga.

"How should I know?" returned Bukawai. "Doubtless the white devil-god has him. If I am paid I will make strong medicine and then we shall know where is Ibeto's son, and shall get him back again. It was my medicine which got him back the last time, for which I got no pay."

"I have my own witch-doctor to make medicine," replied Mbonga with dignity.

Bukawai sneered and rose to his feet. "Very well," he said, "let him make his medicine and see if he can bring Ibeto's son back." He took a few steps away from them, and then he turned angrily back. "His medicine will not bring the child back — that I know, and I also know that when you find him it will be too late for any medicine to bring him back, for he will be dead. This have I just found out, the ghost of my father's sister but now came to me and told me."

Now Mbonga and Rabba Kega might not take much stock in their own magic, and they might even be skeptical as to the magic of another; but there was always a chance of *some- thing* being in it, especially if it were not their own. Was it not well known that old Bukawai had speech with the demons themselves and that two even lived with him in the forms of hyenas! Still they must not accede too hastily. There was the price to be considered, and Mbonga had no intention of parting lightly with ten goats to obtain the return of a single little boy who might die of smallpox long before he reached a warrior's estate.

"Wait," said Mbonga. "Let us see some of your magic, that we may know if it be good magic. Then we can talk about payment. Rabba Kega will make some magic, too. We will see who makes the best magic. Sit down, Bukawai."

"The payment will be ten goats — fat goats — a new sleeping mat and two pieces of copper wire the length of a tall man's arm from the shoulder to the ends of his fingers, and it will be made in advance, the goats being driven to my cave. Then will I make the medicine, and on the second day the boy will be returned to his mother. It cannot be done more quickly than that because it takes time to make such strong medicine."

"Make us some medicine now," said Mbonga. "Let us see what sort of medicine you make."

"Bring me fire," replied Bukawai, "and I will make you a little magic."

Momaya was dispatched for the fire, and while she was away Mbonga dickered with Bukawai about the price. Ten goats, he said, was a high price for an able-bodied warrior. He also called Bukawai's attention to the fact that he, Mbonga, was very poor, that his people were very poor, and that ten goats were at least eight too many, to say nothing of a new sleeping mat and the copper wire; but Bukawai was adamant. His medicine was very expensive and he would have to give at least five goats to the gods who helped him make it. They were still arguing when Momaya returned with the fire.

Bukawai placed a little on the ground before him, took a pinch of powder from a pouch at his side and sprinkled it on the embers. A cloud of smoke rose with a puff. Bukawai closed his eyes and rocked back and forth. Then he made a few passes in the air and pretended to swoon. Mbonga and the others were much impressed. Rabba Kega grew nervous. He saw his reputation waning. There was some fire left in the vessel which Momaya had brought. He seized the vessel, dropped a handful of dry leaves into it while no one was watching and then uttered a frightful scream which drew the attention of Bukawai's audience to him. It also brought Bukawai quite miraculously out of his swoon, but when the old witch-doctor saw the reason for the disturbance he quickly relapsed into unconsciousness before anyone discovered his *faux pas.*

Rabba Kega, seeing that he had the attention of Mbonga, Ibeto, and Momaya, blew suddenly into the vessel, with the result that the leaves commenced to smolder, and smoke issued from the mouth of the receptacle. Rabba Kega was careful to hold it so that none might see the dry leaves. Their eyes opened wide at this remarkable demonstration of the village witch-doctor's powers. The latter, greatly elated, let himself out. He shouted, jumped up and down, and made frightful grimaces; then he put his face close over the mouth of the vessel and appeared to be communing with the spirits within.

It was while he was thus engaged that Bukawai came out of his trance, his curiosity finally having gotten the better of him. No one was paying him the slightest attention. He blinked his one eye angrily, then he, too, let out a loud roar, and when he was sure that Mbonga had turned toward him, he stiffened rigidly and made spasmodic movements with his arms and legs.

"I see him!" he cried. "He is far away. The white devil-god did not get him. He is alone and in great danger; but," he added, "if the ten fat goats and the other things are paid to me quickly there is yet time to save him."

Rabba Kega had paused to listen. Mbonga looked toward him. The chief was in a quandary. He did not know which medicine was the better. "What does your magic tell you?" he asked of Rabba Kega.

"I, too, see him," screamed Rabba Kega; "but he is not where Bukawai says he is. He is dead at the bottom of the river."

At this Momaya commenced to howl loudly.

Tarzan had followed the spoor of the old man, the two hyenas, and the little black boy to the mouth of the cave in the rocky canon between the two hills. Here he paused a moment before the sapling barrier which Bukawai had set up, listening to the snarls and growls which came faintly from the far recesses of the cavern.

Presently, mingled with the beastly cries, there came faintly to the keen ears of the ape-man, the agonized moan of a child. No longer did Tarzan hesitate. Hurling the door aside, he sprang into the dark opening. Narrow and black was the corridor; but long use of his eyes in the Stygian blackness of the jungle nights had given to the ape-man something of the nocturnal visionary powers of the wild things with which he had consorted since babyhood.

He moved rapidly and yet with caution, for the place was dark, unfamiliar and winding. As he advanced, he heard more and more loudly the savage snarls of the two hyenas, mingled with the scraping and scratching of their paws upon wood. The moans of a child grew in volume, and Tarzan recognized in them the voice of the little black boy he once had sought to adopt as his balu.

There was no hysteria in the ape-man's advance. Too accustomed was he to the passing of life in the jungle to be greatly wrought even by the death of one whom he knew; but the lust for battle spurred him on. He was only a wild beast at heart and his wild beast's heart beat high in anticipation of conflict.

In the rocky chamber of the hill's center, little Tibo crouched low against the wall as far from the hunger-crazed beasts as he could drag himself. He saw the lattice giving to the frantic clawing of the hyenas. He knew that in a few minutes his little life would flicker out horribly beneath the rending, yellow fangs of these loathsome creatures.

Beneath the buffetings of the powerful bodies, the lattice sagged inward, until, with a crash it gave way, letting the carnivora in upon the boy. Tibo cast one affrighted glance toward them, then closed his eyes and buried his face in his arms, sobbing piteously.

For a moment the hyenas paused, caution and cowardice holding them from their prey. They stood thus glaring at the lad, then slowly, stealthily, crouching, they crept toward him. It was thus that Tarzan came upon them, bursting into the chamber swiftly and silently; but not so silently that the keen-eared beasts did not note his coming. With angry growls they turned from Tibo upon the ape-man, as, with a smile upon his lips, he ran toward them. For an instant one of the animals stood its ground; but the ape-man did not deign even to draw his hunting knife against despised Dango. Rushing in upon the brute he grasped it by the scruff of the neck, just as it attempted to dodge past him, and hurled it across the cavern after its fellow which already was slinking into the corridor, bent upon escape.

Then Tarzan picked Tibo from the floor, and when the child felt human hands upon him instead of the paws and fangs of the hyenas, he rolled his eyes upward in surprise and incredulity, and as they fell upon Tarzan, sobs of relief broke from the childish lips and his hands clutched at his deliverer as though the white devil-god was not the most feared of jungle creatures.

When Tarzan came to the cave mouth the hyenas were nowhere in sight, and after permitting Tibo to quench his thirst in the spring which rose near by, he lifted the boy to his shoulders and set off toward the jungle at a rapid trot, determined to still the annoying howlings of Momaya as quickly as possible, for he shrewdly had guessed that the absence of her balu was the cause of her lamentation.

"He is not dead at the bottom of the river," cried Bukawai. "What does this fellow know about making magic? Who is he, anyway, that he dare say Bukawai's magic is not good magic? Bukawai sees Momaya's son. He is far away and alone and in great danger. Hasten then with the ten fat goats, the —"

But he got no further. There was a sudden interruption from above, from the branches of the very tree beneath which they squatted, and as the five blacks looked up they almost swooned in fright as they saw the great, white devil-god looking down upon them; but before they could flee they saw another face, that of the lost little Tibo, and his face was laughing and very happy.

And then Tarzan dropped fearlessly among them, the boy still upon his back, and deposited him before his mother. Momaya, Ibeto, Rabba Kega, and Mbonga were all crowding around the lad trying to question him at the same time. Suddenly Momaya turned ferociously to fall upon Bukawai, for the boy had told her all that he had suffered at the hands of the cruel old man; but Bukawai was no longer there — he had required no recourse to black art to assure him that the vicinity of Momaya would be no healthful place for him after Tibo had told his story, and now he was running through the jungle as fast as his old legs would carry him toward the distant lair where he knew no black would dare pursue him.

Tarzan, too, had vanished, as he had a way of doing, to the mystification of the blacks. Then Momaya's eyes lighted upon Rabba Kega. The village witch-doctor saw something in those eyes of hers which boded no good to him, and backed away.

"So my Tibo is dead at the bottom of the river, is he?" the woman shrieked. "And he's far away and alone and in great danger, is he? Magic!" The scorn which Momaya crowded into that single word would have done credit to a Thespian of the first magnitude. "Magic, indeed!" she screamed. "Momaya will show you some magic of her own," and with that she seized upon a broken limb and struck Rabba Kega across the head. With a howl of pain, the man turned and fled, Momaya pursuing him and beating him across the shoulders, through the gateway and up the length of the village street, to the intense amusement of the warriors, the women, and the children who were so fortunate as to witness the spectacle, for one and all feared Rabba Kega, and to fear is to hate.

Thus it was that to his host of passive enemies, Tarzan of the Apes added that day two active foes, both of whom remained awake long into the night planning means of revenge upon the white devil-god who had brought them into ridicule and disrepute, but with their most malevolent schemings was mingled a vein of real fear and awe that would not down.

Young Lord Greystoke did not know that they planned against him, nor, knowing, would have cared. He slept as well that night as he did on any other night, and though there was no roof above him, and no doors to lock against intruders, he slept much better than his noble relative in England, who had eaten altogether too much lobster and drank too much wine at dinner that night.

The End of Bukawai

*W*HEN TARZAN OF the Apes was still but a boy he had learned, among other things, to fashion pliant ropes of fibrous jungle grass. Strong and tough were the ropes of Tarzan, the little Tarmangani. Tublat, his foster father, would have told you this much and more. Had you tempted him with a handful of fat caterpillars he even might have sufficiently unbended to narrate to you a few stories of the many indignities which Tarzan had heaped upon him by means of his hated rope; but then Tublat always worked himself into such a frightful rage when he devoted any considerable thought either to the rope or to Tarzan, that it might not have proved comfortable for you to have remained close enough to him to hear what he had to say.

So often had that snakelike noose settled unexpectedly over Tublat's head, so often had he been jerked ridiculously and painfully from his feet when he was least looking for such an occurrence, that there is little wonder he found scant space in his savage heart for love of his white-skinned foster child, or the inventions thereof. There had been other times, too, when Tublat had swung helplessly in midair, the noose tightening about his neck, death staring him in the face, and little Tarzan dancing upon a near-by limb, taunting him and making unseemly grimaces.

Then there had been another occasion in which the rope had figured prominently — an occasion, and the only one connected with the rope, which Tublat recalled with pleasure. Tarzan, as active in brain as he was in body, was always inventing new ways in which to play. It was through the medium of play that he learned much during his childhood. This day he learned something, and that he did not lose his life in the learning of it, was a matter of great surprise to Tarzan, and the fly in the ointment, to Tublat.

The man-child had, in throwing his noose at a play-mate in a tree above him, caught a projecting branch instead. When he tried to shake it loose it but drew the tighter. Then Tarzan started to climb the rope to remove it from the branch. When he was part way up a frolicsome playmate seized that part of the rope which lay upon the ground and ran off with it as far as he could go. When Tarzan screamed at him to desist, the young ape released the rope a little and then drew it tight again. The result was to impart a swinging motion to Tarzan's body which the ape-boy suddenly realized was a new and pleasurable form of play. He urged the ape to continue until Tarzan was swinging to and fro as far as the short length of rope would permit, but the distance was not great enough, and, too, he was not far enough above the ground to give the necessary thrills which add so greatly to the pastimes of the young.

So he clambered to the branch where the noose was caught and after removing it carried the rope far aloft and out upon a long and powerful branch. Here he again made it fast, and taking the loose end in his hand, clambered quickly down among the branches as far as the rope would permit him to go; then he swung out upon the end of it, his lithe, young body turning and twisting — a human bob upon a pendulum of grass — thirty feet above the ground.

Ah, how delectable! This was indeed a new play of the first magnitude. Tarzan was entranced. Soon he discovered that by wriggling his body in just the right way at the proper time he could diminish or accelerate his oscillation, and, being a boy, he chose, naturally, to accelerate. Presently he was swinging far and wide, while below him, the apes of the tribe of Kerchak looked on in mild amaze.

Had it been you or I swinging there at the end of that grass rope, the thing which presently happened would not have happened, for we could not have hung on so long as to have made it possible; but Tarzan was quite as much at home swinging by his hands as he was standing upon his feet, or, at least, almost. At any rate he felt no fatigue long after the time that an ordinary mortal would have been numb with the strain of the physical exertion. And this was his undoing.

Tublat was watching him as were others of the tribe. Of all the creatures of the wild, there was none Tublat so cordially hated as he did this hideous, hairless, white-skinned, caricature of an ape. But for Tarzan's nimbleness, and the zealous watchfulness of savage Kala's mother love, Tublat would long since have rid himself of this stain upon his family escutcheon. So long had it been since Tarzan became a member of the tribe, that Tublat had forgotten the circumstances surrounding the entrance of the jungle waif into his family, with the result that he now imagined that Tarzan was his own offspring, adding greatly to his chagrin.

Wide and far swung Tarzan of the Apes, until at last, as he reached the highest point of the arc the rope, which rapidly had frayed on the rough bark of the tree limb, parted suddenly. The watching apes saw the smooth, brown body shoot outward, and down, plummet-like. Tublat leaped high in the air, emitting what in a human being would have been an exclamation of delight. This would be the end of Tarzan and most of Tublat's troubles. From now on he could lead his life in peace and security.

Tarzan fell quite forty feet, alighting on his back in a thick bush. Kala was the first to reach his side — ferocious, hideous, loving Kala. She had seen the life crushed from her own balu in just such a fall years before. Was she to lose this one too in the same way? Tarzan was lying quite still when she found him, embedded deeply in the bush. It took Kala several minutes to disentangle him and drag him forth; but he was not killed. He was not even badly injured. The bush had broken the force of the fall. A cut upon the back of his head showed where he had struck the tough stem of the shrub and explained his unconsciousness.

In a few minutes he was as active as ever. Tublat was furious. In his rage he snapped at a fellow-ape without first discovering the identity of his victim, and was badly mauled for his ill temper, having chosen to vent his spite upon a husky and belligerent young bull in the full prime of his vigor.

But Tarzan had learned something new. He had learned that continued friction would wear through the strands of his rope, though it was many years before this knowledge did more for him than merely to keep him from swinging too long at a time, or too far above the ground at the end of his rope.

The day came, however, when the very thing that had once all but killed him proved the means of saving his life.

He was no longer a child, but a mighty jungle male. There was none now to watch over him, solicitously, nor did he need such. Kala was dead. Dead, too, was Tublat, and though with Kala passed the one creature that ever really had loved him, there were still many who hated him after Tublat departed unto the arms of his fathers. It was not that he was more cruel or more savage than they that they hated him, for though he was both cruel and savage as were the beasts, his fellows, yet too was he often tender, which they never were. No, the thing which brought Tarzan most into disrepute with those who did not like him, was the possession and practice of a characteristic which they had not and could not understand — the human sense of humor. In Tarzan it was a trifle broad, perhaps, manifesting itself in rough and painful practical jokes upon his friends and cruel baiting of his enemies.

But to neither of these did he owe the enmity of Bukawai, the witch-doctor, who dwelt in the cave between the two hills far to the north of the village of Mbonga, the chief. Bukawai was jealous of Tarzan, and Bukawai it was who came near proving the undoing of the ape-man. For months Bukawai had nursed his hatred while revenge seemed remote indeed, since Tarzan of the Apes frequented another part of the jungle, miles away from the lair of Bukawai. Only once had the black witch-doctor seen the devil-god, as he was most often called among the blacks, and upon that occasion Tarzan had robbed him of a fat fee, at the same time putting the lie in the mouth of Bukawai, and making his medicine seem poor medicine. All this Bukawai never could forgive, though it seemed unlikely that the opportunity would come to be revenged.

Yet it did come, and quite unexpectedly. Tarzan was hunting far to the north. He had wandered away from the tribe, as he did more and more often as he approached maturity, to hunt alone for a few days. As a child he had enjoyed romping and playing with the young apes, his companions; but now these play-fellows of his had grown to surly, lowering bulls, or to touchy, suspicious mothers, jealously guarding helpless balus. So Tarzan found in his own man-mind a greater and a truer companionship than any or all of the apes of Kerchak could afford him.

This day, as Tarzan hunted, the sky slowly became over-cast. Torn clouds, whipped to ragged streamers, fled low above the tree tops. They reminded Tarzan of frightened antelope fleeing the charge of a hungry lion. But though the light clouds raced so swiftly, the jungle was motionless. Not a leaf quivered and the silence was a great, dead weight — insupportable. Even the insects seemed stilled by apprehension of some frightful thing impending, and the larger things were soundless. Such a forest, such a jungle might have stood there in the beginning of that unthinkably far-gone age before God peopled the world with life, when there were no sounds because there were no ears to hear.

And over all lay a sickly, pallid ocher light through which the scourged clouds raced. Tarzan had seen all these conditions many times before, yet he never could escape a strange feeling at each recurrence of them. He knew no fear, but in the face of Nature's manifestations of her cruel, immeasurable powers, he felt very small — very small and very lonely.

Now he heard a low moaning, far away. "The lions seek their prey," he murmured to himself, looking up once again at the swift-flying clouds. The moaning rose to a great volume of sound. "They come!" said Tarzan of the Apes, and sought the shelter of a thickly foliaged tree. Quite suddenly the trees bent their tops simulta-neously as though God had stretched a hand from the heavens and pressed His flat palm down upon the world. "They pass!" whispered Tarzan. "The lions pass." Then came a vivid flash of lightning, followed by deafening thunder. "The lions have sprung," cried Tarzan, "and now they roar above the bodies of their kills."

The trees were waving wildly in all directions now, a perfectly demoniacal wind threshed the jungle pitilessly. In the midst of it the rain came — not as it comes upon us of the northlands, but in a sudden, choking, blinding deluge. "The blood of the kill," thought Tarzan, huddling himself closer to the bole of the great tree beneath which he stood.

He was close to the edge of the jungle, and at a little distance he had seen two hills before the storm broke; but now he could see nothing. It amused him to look out into the beating rain, searching for the two hills and imagining that the torrents from above had washed them away, yet he knew that presently the rain would cease, the sun come out again and all be as it was before, except where a few branches had fallen and here and there some old and rotted patriarch had crashed back to enrich the soil upon which he had fatted for, maybe, centuries. All about him branches and leaves filled the air or fell to earth, torn away by the strength of the tornado and the weight of the water upon them. A gaunt corpse toppled and fell a few yards away; but Tarzan was protected from all these dangers by the wide-spreading branches of the sturdy young giant beneath which his jungle craft had guided him. Here there was but a single danger, and that a remote one. Yet it came. Without warning the tree above him was riven by lightning, and when the rain ceased and the sun came out Tarzan lay stretched as he had fallen, upon his face amidst the wreckage of the jungle giant that should have shielded him.

Bukawai came to the entrance of his cave after the rain and the storm had passed and looked out upon the scene. From his one eye Bukawai could see; but had he had a dozen eyes he could have found no beauty in the fresh sweetness of the revivified jungle, for to such things, in the chemistry of temperament, his brain failed to react; nor, even had he had a nose, which he had not for years, could he have found enjoyment or sweetness in the clean-washed air.

At either side of the leper stood his sole and constant companions, the two hyenas, sniffing the air. Presently one of them uttered a low growl and with flattened head started, sneaking and wary, toward the jungle. The other followed. Bukawai, his curiosity aroused, trailed after them, in his hand a heavy knob-stick.

The hyenas halted a few yards from the prostrate Tarzan, sniffing and growling. Then came Bukawai, and at first he could not believe the witness of his own eyes; but when he did and saw that it was indeed the devil-god his rage knew no bounds, for he thought him dead and himself cheated of the revenge he had so long dreamed upon.

The hyenas approached the ape-man with bared fangs. Bukawai, with an inarticulate scream, rushed upon them, striking cruel and heavy blows with his knob-stick, for there might still be life in the apparently lifeless form. The beasts, snapping and snarling, half turned upon their master and their tormentor, but long fear still held them from his putrid throat. They slunk away a few yards and squatted upon their haunches, hatred and baffled hunger gleaming from their savage eyes.

Bukawai stooped and placed his ear above the ape-man's heart. It still beat. As well as his sloughed features could register pleasure they did so; but it was not a pretty sight. At the ape-man's side lay his long, grass rope. Quickly Bukawai bound the limp arms behind his prisoner's back, then he raised him to one of his shoulders, for, though Bukawai was old and diseased, he was still a strong man. The hyenas fell in behind as the witch-doctor set off toward the cave, and through the long black corridors they followed as Bukawai bore his victim into the bowels of the hills. Through subterranean chambers, connected by winding passageways, Bukawai staggered with his load. At a sudden turning of the corridor, daylight flooded them and

Bukawai stepped out into a small, circular basin in the hill, apparently the crater of an ancient volcano, one of those which never reached the dignity of a mountain and are little more than lava-rimmed pits closed to the earth's surface.

Steep walls rimmed the cavity. The only exit was through the passageway by which Bukawai had entered. A few stunted trees grew upon the rocky floor. A hundred feet above could be seen the ragged lips of this cold, dead mouth of hell.

Bukawai propped Tarzan against a tree and bound him there with his own grass rope, leaving his hands free but securing the knots in such a way that the ape-man could not reach them. The hyenas slunk to and fro, growling. Bukawai hated them and they hated him. He knew that they but waited for the time when he should be helpless, or when their hatred should rise to such a height as to submerge their cringing fear of him.

In his own heart was not a little fear of these repulsive creatures, and because of that fear, Bukawai always kept the beasts well fed, often hunting for them when their own forages for food failed, but ever was he cruel to them with the cruelty of a little brain, diseased, bestial, primitive.

He had had them since they were puppies. They had known no other life than that with him, and though they went abroad to hunt, always they returned. Of late Bukawai had come to believe that they returned not so much from habit as from a fiendish patience which would submit to every indignity and pain rather than forego the final vengeance, and Bukawai needed but little imagination to picture what that vengeance would be. Today he would see for himself what his end would be; but another should impersonate Bukawai.

When he had trussed Tarzan securely, Bukawai went back into the corridor, driving the hyenas ahead of him, and pulling across the opening a lattice of laced branches, which shut the pit from the cave during the night that Bukawai might sleep in security, for then the hyenas were penned in the crater that they might not sneak upon a sleeping Bukawai in the darkness.

Bukawai returned to the outer cave mouth, filled a vessel with water at the spring which rose in the little canon close at hand and returned toward the pit. The hyenas stood before the lattice looking hungrily toward Tarzan. They had been fed in this manner before.

With his water, the witch-doctor approached Tarzan and threw a portion of the contents of the vessel in the ape-man's face. There was fluttering of the eyelids, and at the second application Tarzan opened his eyes and looked about.

"Devil-god," cried Bukawai, "I am the great witch-doctor. My medicine is strong. Yours is weak. If it is not, why do you stay tied here like a goat that is bait for lions?"

Tarzan understood nothing the witch-doctor said, therefore he did not reply, but only stared straight at Bukawai with cold and level gaze. The hyenas crept up behind him. He heard them growl; but he did not even turn his head. He was a beast with a man's brain. The beast in him refused to show fear in the face of a death which the man-mind already admitted to be inevitable.

Bukawai, not yet ready to give his victim to the beasts, rushed upon the hyenas with his knob-stick. There was a short scrimmage in which the brutes came off second best, as they always did. Tarzan watched it. He saw and realized the hatred which existed between the two animals and the hideous semblance of a man.

With the hyenas subdued, Bukawai returned to the baiting of Tarzan; but finding that the ape-man understood nothing he said, the witch-doctor finally desisted. Then he withdrew into the corridor and pulled the latticework barrier across the opening. He went back into the cave and got a sleeping mat, which he brought to the opening, that he might lie down and watch the spectacle of his revenge in comfort.

The hyenas were sneaking furtively around the ape-man. Tarzan strained at his bonds for a moment, but soon realized that the rope he had braided to hold Numa, the lion, would hold him quite as successfully. He did not wish to die; but he could look death in the face now as he had many times before without a quaver.

As he pulled upon the rope he felt it rub against the small tree about which it was passed. Like a flash of the cinematograph upon the screen, a picture was flashed before his mind's eye from the storehouse of his memory. He saw a lithe, boyish figure swinging high above the ground at the end of a rope. He saw many apes watching from below, and then he saw the rope part and the boy hurtle downward toward the ground. Tarzan smiled. Immediately he commenced to draw the rope rapidly back and forth across the tree trunk.

The hyenas, gaining courage, came closer. They sniffed at his legs; but when he struck at them with his free arms they slunk off. He knew that with the growth of hunger they would attack. Coolly, methodically, without haste, Tarzan drew the rope back and forth against the rough trunk of the small tree.

In the entrance to the cavern Bukawai fell asleep. He thought it would be some time before the beasts gained sufficient courage or hunger to attack the captive. Their growls and the cries of the victim would awaken him. In the mean-time he might as well rest, and he did.

Thus the day wore on, for the hyenas were not famished, and the rope with which Tarzan was bound was a stronger one than that of his boyhood, which had parted so quickly to the chafing of the rough tree bark. Yet, all the while hunger was growing upon the beasts and the strands of the grass rope were wearing thinner and thinner. Bukawai slept.

It was late afternoon before one of the beasts, irritated by the gnawing of appetite, made a quick, growling dash at the ape-man. The noise awoke Bukawai. He sat up quickly and watched what went on within the crater. He saw the hungry hyena charge the man, leaping for the unprotected throat. He saw Tarzan reach out and seize the growling animal, and then he saw the second beast spring for the devil-god's shoulder. There was a mighty heave of the great, smooth-skinned body. Rounded muscles shot into great, tensed piles beneath the brown hide — the ape-man surged forward with all his weight and all his great strength — the bonds parted, and the three were rolling upon the floor of the crater snarling, snapping, and rending.

Bukawai leaped to his feet. Could it be that the devil-god was to prevail against his servants? Impossible! The creature was unarmed, and he was down with two hyenas on top of him; but Bukawai did not know Tarzan.

The ape-man fastened his fingers upon the throat of one of the hyenas and rose to one knee, though the other beast tore at him frantically in an effort to pull him down. With a single hand Tarzan held the one, and with the other hand he reached forth and pulled toward him the second beast.

And then Bukawai, seeing the battle going against his forces, rushed forward from the cavern brandishing his knob-stick. Tarzan saw him coming, and rising now to both feet, a hyena in each hand, he hurled one of the foaming beasts straight at the witch-doctor's head. Down went the two in a snarling, biting heap. Tarzan tossed the second hyena across the crater, while the first gnawed at the rotting face of its master; but this did not suit the ape-man. With a kick he sent the beast howling after its companion, and springing to the side of the prostrate witch-doctor, dragged him to his feet.

Bukawai, still conscious, saw death, immediate and terrible, in the cold eyes of his captor, so he turned upon Tarzan with teeth and nails. The ape-man shuddered at the proximity of that raw face to his. The hyenas had had enough and disappeared through the small aperture leading into the cave. Tarzan had little difficulty in overpowering and binding Bukawai. Then he led him to the very tree to which he had been bound; but in binding Bukawai, Tarzan saw to it that escape after the same fashion that he had escaped would be out of the question; then he left him.

As he passed through the winding corridors and the subterranean apartments, Tarzan saw nothing of the hyenas.

"They will return," he said to himself.

In the crater between the towering walls Bukawai, cold with terror, trembled, trembled as with ague.

"They will return!" he cried, his voice rising to a fright-filled shriek.

And they did.

The Lion

NUMA, THE LION, crouched behind a thorn bush close beside the drinking pool where the river eddied just below the bend. There was a ford there and on either bank a well-worn trail, broadened far out at the river's brim, where, for countless centuries, the wild things of the jungle and of the plains beyond had come down to drink, the carnivora with bold and fearless majesty, the herbivora timorous, hesitating, fearful.

Numa, the lion, was hungry, he was very hungry, and so he was quite silent now. On his way to the drinking place he had moaned often and roared not a little; but as he neared the spot where he would lie in wait for Bara, the deer, or Horta, the boar, or some other of the many luscious-fleshed creatures who came hither to drink, he was silent. It was a grim, a terrible silence, shot through with yellow-green light of ferocious eyes, punctuated with undulating tremors of sinuous tail.

It was Pacco, the zebra, who came first, and Numa, the lion, could scarce restrain a roar of anger, for of all the plains people, none are more wary than Pacco, the zebra. Behind the black-striped stallion came a herd of thirty or forty of the plump and vicious little horselike beasts. As he neared the river, the leader paused often, cocking his ears and raising his muzzle to sniff the gentle breeze for the tell-tale scent spoor of the dread flesh-eaters.

Numa shifted uneasily, drawing his hind quarters far beneath his tawny body, gathering himself for the sudden charge and the savage assault. His eyes shot hungry fire. His great muscles quivered to the excitement of the moment.

Pacco came a little nearer, halted, snorted, and wheeled. There was a pattering of scurrying hoofs and the herd was gone; but Numa, the lion, moved not. He was familiar with the ways of Pacco, the zebra. He knew that he would return, though many times he might wheel and fly before he summoned the courage to lead his harem and his offspring to the water. There was the chance that Pacco might be frightened off entirely. Numa had seen this happen before, and so he became almost rigid lest he be the one to send them galloping, waterless, back to the plain.

Again and again came Pacco and his family, and again and again did they turn and flee; but each time they came closer to the river, until at last the plump stallion dipped his velvet muzzle daintily into the water. The others, stepping warily, approached their leader. Numa selected a sleek, fat filly and his flaming eyes burned greedily as they feasted upon her, for Numa, the lion, loves scarce anything better than the meat of Pacco, perhaps because Pacco is, of all the grass-eaters, the most difficult to catch.

Slowly the lion rose, and as he rose, a twig snapped beneath one of his great, padded paws. Like a shot from a rifle he charged upon the filly; but the snapped twig had been enough to startle the timorous quarry, so that they were in instant flight simultaneously with Numa's charge.

The stallion was last, and with a prodigious leap, the lion catapulted through the air to seize him; but the snapping twig had robbed Numa of his dinner, though his mighty talons raked the zebra's glossy rump, leaving four crimson bars across the beautiful coat.

It was an angry Numa that quitted the river and prowled, fierce, dangerous, and hungry, into the jungle. Far from particular now was his appetite. Even Dango, the hyena, would have seemed a tidbit to that ravenous maw. And in this temper it was that the lion came upon the tribe of Kerchak, the great ape.

One does not look for Numa, the lion, this late in the morning. He should be lying up asleep beside his last night's kill by now; but Numa had made no kill last night. He was still hunting, hungrier than ever.

The anthropoids were idling about the clearing, the first keen desire of the morning's hunger having been satisfied. Numa scented them long before he saw them. Ordinarily he would have turned away in search of other game, for even Numa respected the mighty muscles and the sharp fangs of the great bulls of the tribe of Kerchak, but today he kept on steadily toward them, his bristled snout wrinkled into a savage snarl.

Without an instant's hesitation, Numa charged the moment he reached a point from where the apes were visible to him. There were a dozen or more of the hairy, manlike creatures upon the ground in a little glade. In a tree at one side sat a brown-skinned youth. He saw Numa's swift charge; he saw the apes turn and flee, huge bulls trampling upon little balus; only a single she held her ground to meet the charge, a young she inspired by new motherhood to the great sacrifice that her balu might escape.

Tarzan leaped from his perch, screaming at the flying bulls beneath and at those who squatted in the safety of surrounding trees. Had the bulls stood their ground, Numa would not have carried through that charge

unless goaded by great rage or the gnawing pangs of
starvation. Even then he would not have come off
unscathed.

If the bulls heard, they were too slow in responding,
for Numa had seized the mother ape and dragged her
into the jungle before the males had sufficiently col-
lected their wits and their courage to rally in defense
of their fellow. Tarzan's angry voice aroused similar
anger in the breasts of the apes. Snarling and barking
they followed Numa into the dense labyrinth of foliage
wherein he sought to hide himself from them. The
ape-man was in the lead, moving rapidly and yet with
caution, depending even more upon his ears and nose
than upon his eyes for information of the lion's whereabouts.

The spoor was easy to follow, for the dragged body
of the victim left a plain trail, blood-spattered and
scentful. Even such dull creatures as you or I might
easily have followed it. To Tarzan and the apes of
Kerchak it was as obvious as a cement sidewalk.

Tarzan knew that they were nearing the great cat even
before he heard an angry growl of warning just ahead.
Calling to the apes to follow his example, he swung
into a tree and a moment later Numa was surrounded
by a ring of growling beasts, well out of reach of his
fangs and talons but within plain sight of him. The
carnivore crouched with his fore-quarters upon the
she-ape. Tarzan could see that the latter was already
dead; but something within him made it seem quite
necessary to rescue the useless body from the clutches
of the enemy and to punish him.

He shrieked taunts and insults at Numa, and tearing
dead branches from the tree in which he danced,
hurled them at the lion. The apes followed his example.
Numa roared out in rage and vexation. He was hungry,
but under such conditions he could not feed.

The apes, if they had been left to themselves, would

doubtless soon have left the lion to peaceful enjoyment of his feast, for was not the she dead? They could not restore her to life by throwing sticks at Numa, and they might even now be feeding in quiet themselves; but Tarzan was of a different mind. Numa must be punished and driven away. He must be taught that even though he killed a Mangani, he would not be permitted to feed upon his kill. The man-mind looked into the future, while the apes perceived only the immediate present. They would be content to escape today the menace of Numa, while Tarzan saw the necessity, and the means as well, of safeguarding the days to come.

So he urged the great anthropoids on until Numa was showered with missiles that kept his head dodging and his voice pealing forth its savage protest; but still he clung desperately to his kill.

The twigs and branches hurled at Numa, Tarzan soon realized, did not hurt him greatly even when they struck him, and did not injure him at all, so the ape-man looked about for more effective missiles, nor did he have to look long. An out-cropping of decomposed granite not far from Numa suggested ammunition of a much more painful nature. Calling to the apes to watch him, Tarzan slipped to the ground and gathered a handful of small fragments. He knew that when once they had seen him carry out his idea they would be much quicker to follow his lead than to obey his instructions, were he to command them to procure pieces of rock and hurl them at Numa, for Tarzan was not then king of the apes of the tribe of Kerchak. That came in later years. Now he was but a youth, though one who already had wrested for himself a place in the councils of the savage beasts among whom a strange fate had cast him. The sullen bulls of the older generation still hated him as beasts hate those of whom they are suspicious, whose scent characteristic is the scent characteristic of an alien order and, therefore, of an enemy order. The younger bulls, those who had grown up through childhood as his playmates, were as accustomed to Tarzan's scent as to that of any other member of the tribe. They felt no greater suspicion of him than of any other bull of their acquaintance; yet they did not love him, for they loved none outside the mating season, and the animosities aroused by other bulls during that season lasted well over until the next. They were a morose and peevish band at best, though here and there were those among them in whom germinated the primal seeds of humanity — reversions to type, these, doubtless; reversions to the ancient progenitor who took the first step out of apehood toward humanness, when he walked more often upon his hind feet and discovered other things for idle hands to do.

So now Tarzan led where he could not yet command. He had long since discovered the apish propensity for mimicry and learned to make use of it. Having filled his arms with fragments of rotted granite, he clambered again into a tree, and it pleased him to see that the apes had followed his example.

During the brief respite while they were gathering their ammunition, Numa had settled himself to feed; but scarce had he arranged himself and his kill when a sharp piece of rock hurled by the practiced hand of the ape-man struck him upon the cheek. His sudden roar of pain and rage was smothered by a volley from the apes, who had seen Tarzan's act. Numa shook his massive head and glared upward at his tormentors. For a half hour they pursued him with rocks and broken branches, and though he dragged his kill into densest thickets, yet they always found a way to reach him with their missiles, giving him no opportunity to feed, and driving him on and on.

The hairless ape-thing with the man scent was worst of all, for he had even the temerity to advance upon the ground to within a few yards of the Lord of the

Jungle, that he might with greater accuracy and force hurl the sharp bits of granite and the heavy sticks at him. Time and again did Numa charge — sudden, vicious charges — but the lithe, active tormentor always managed to elude him and with such insolent ease that the lion forgot even his great hunger in the consuming passion of his rage, leaving his meat for considerable spaces of time in vain efforts to catch his enemy.

The apes and Tarzan pursued the great beast to a natural clearing, where Numa evidently determined to make a last stand, taking up his position in the center of the open space, which was far enough from any tree to render him practically immune from the rather erratic throwing of the apes, though Tarzan still found him with most persistent and aggravating frequency.

This, however, did not suit the ape-man, since Numa now suffered an occasional missile with no more than a snarl, while he settled himself to partake of his delayed feast. Tarzan scratched his head, pondering some more effective method of offense, for he had determined to prevent Numa from profiting in any way through his attack upon the tribe. The man-mind reasoned against the future, while the shaggy apes thought only of their present hatred of this ancestral enemy. Tarzan guessed that should Numa find it an easy thing to snatch a meal from the tribe of Kerchak, it would be but a short time before their existence would be one living nightmare of hideous watchfulness and dread. Numa must be taught that the killing of an ape brought immediate punishment and no rewards. It would take but a few lessons to insure the former safety of the tribe. This must be some old lion whose failing strength and agility had forced him to any prey that he could catch; but even a single lion, undisputed, could exterminate the tribe, or at least make its existence so precarious and so terrifying that life would no longer be a pleasant condition.

"Let him hunt among the Gomangani," thought Tarzan. "He will find them easier prey. I will teach ferocious Numa that he may not hunt the Mangani."

But how to wrest the body of his victim from the feeding lion was the first question to be solved. At last Tarzan hit upon a plan. To anyone but Tarzan of the Apes it might have seemed rather a risky plan, and perhaps it did even to him; but Tarzan rather liked things that contained a considerable element of danger. At any rate, I rather doubt that you or I would have chosen a similar plan for foiling an angry and a hungry lion.

Tarzan required assistance in the scheme he had hit upon and his assistant must be equally as brave and almost as active as he. The ape-man's eyes fell upon Taug, the play-mate of his childhood, the rival in his first love and now, of all the bulls of the tribe, the only one that might be thought to hold in his savage brain any such feeling toward Tarzan as we describe among ourselves as friendship. At least, Tarzan knew, Taug was courageous, and he was young and agile and wonderfully muscled.

"Taug!" cried the ape-man. The great ape looked up from a dead limb he was attempting to tear from a lightning-blasted tree. "Go close to Numa and worry him," said Tarzan. "Worry him until he charges. Lead him away from the body of Mamka. Keep him away as long as you can."

Taug nodded. He was across the clearing from Tarzan. Wresting the limb at last from the tree he dropped to the ground and advanced toward Numa, growling and barking out his insults. The worried lion looked up and rose to his feet. His tail went stiffly erect and Taug turned in flight, for he knew that warming signal of the charge.

From behind the lion, Tarzan ran quickly toward the center of the clearing and the body of Mamka. Numa, all his eyes for Taug, did not see the ape-man. Instead he shot forward after the fleeing bull, who had turned in flight not an instant too soon, since he reached the nearest tree but a yard or two ahead of the pursuing demon. Like a cat the heavy anthropoid scampered up the bole of his sanctuary. Numa's talons missed him by little more than inches.

For a moment the lion paused beneath the tree, glaring up at the ape and roaring until the earth trembled, then he turned back again toward his kill, and as he did so, his tail shot once more to rigid erectness and he charged back even more ferociously than he had come, for what he saw was the naked man-thing running toward the farther trees with the bloody carcass of his prey across a giant shoulder.

The apes, watching the grim race from the safety of the trees, screamed taunts at Numa and warnings to Tarzan. The high sun, hot and brilliant, fell like a spotlight upon the actors in the little clearing, portraying them in glaring relief to the audience in the leafy shadows of the surrounding trees. The light-brown body of the naked youth, all but hidden by the shaggy carcass of the killed ape, the red blood streaking his smooth hide, his muscles rolling, velvety, beneath. Behind him the black-maned lion, head flattened, tail extended, racing, a jungle thoroughbred, across the sunlit clearing.

Ah, but this was life! With death at his heels, Tarzan thrilled with the joy of such living as this; but would he reach the trees ahead of the rampant death so close behind?

Gunto swung from a limb in a tree before him. Gunto was screaming warnings and advice.

"Catch me!" cried Tarzan, and with his heavy burden leaped straight for the big bull hanging there by his hind feet and one forepaw. And Gunto caught them — the big ape-man and the dead weight of the slain she-ape — caught them with one great, hairy paw and whirled them upward until Tarzan's fingers closed upon a near-by branch.

Beneath, Numa leaped; but Gunto, heavy and awkward as he may have appeared, was as quick as Manu, the monkey, so that the lion's talons but barely grazed him, scratching a bloody streak beneath one hairy arm.

Tarzan carried Mamka's corpse to a high crotch, where even Sheeta, the panther, could not get it. Numa paced angrily back and forth beneath the tree, roaring frightfully. He had been robbed of his kill and his revenge also. He was very savage indeed; but his despoilers were well out of his reach, and after hurling a few taunts and missiles at him they swung away through the trees, fiercely reviling him.

Tarzan thought much upon the little adventure of that day. He foresaw what might happen should the great carnivora of the jungle turn their serious attention upon the tribe of Kerchak, the great ape, but equally he thought upon the wild scramble of the apes for safety when Numa first charged among them. There is little humor in the jungle that is not grim and awful. The beasts have little or no conception of humor; but the young Englishman saw humor in many things which presented no humorous angle to his associates.

Since earliest childhood he had been a searcher after fun, much to the sorrow of his fellow-apes, and now he saw the humor of the frightened panic of the apes and the baffled rage of Numa even in this grim jungle adventure which had robbed Mamka of life, and jeopardized that of many members of the tribe.

It was but a few weeks later that Sheeta, the panther, made a sudden rush among the tribe and snatched a little balu from a tree where it had been hidden while its mother sought food. Sheeta got away with his small prize unmolested. Tarzan was very wroth. He spoke to the bulls of the ease with which Numa and Sheeta, in a single moon, had slain two members of the tribe.

"They will take us all for food," he cried. "We hunt as we will through the jungle, paying no heed to approaching enemies. Even Manu, the monkey, does not so. He keeps two or three always watching for enemies. Pacco, the zebra, and Wappi, the antelope, have those about the herd who keep watch while the others feed, while we, the great Mangani, let Numa, and Sabor, and Sheeta come when they will and carry us off to feed their balus.

"Gr-r-rmph," said Numgo.

"What are we to do?" asked Taug.

"We, too, should have two or three always watching for the approach of Numa, and Sabor, and Sheeta," replied Tarzan. "No others need we fear, except Histah, the snake, and if we watch for the others we will see Histah if he comes, though gliding ever so silently."

And so it was that the great apes of the tribe of Kerchak posted sentries thereafter, who watched upon three sides while the tribe hunted, scattered less than had been their wont.

But Tarzan went abroad alone, for Tarzan was a man-thing and sought amusement and adventure and such humor as the grim and terrible jungle offers to those who know it and do not fear it — a weird humor shot with blazing eyes and dappled with the crimson of lifeblood. While others sought only food and love, Tarzan of the Apes sought food and joy.

One day he hovered above the palisaded village of Mbonga, the chief, the jet cannibal of the jungle primeval. He saw, as he had seen many times before, the witch-doctor, Rabba Kega, decked out in the head and hide of Gorgo, the buffalo. It amused Tarzan to see a Gomangani parading as Gorgo; but it suggested nothing in particular to him until he chanced to see stretched against the side of Mbonga's hut the skin of a lion with the head still on. Then a broad grin widened the handsome face of the savage beast-youth.

Back into the jungle he went until chance, agility, strength, and cunning backed by his marvelous powers of perception, gave him an easy meal. If Tarzan felt that the world owed him a living he also realized that it was for him to collect it, nor was there ever a better collector than this son of an English lord, who knew even less of the ways of his forbears than he did of the forbears themselves, which was nothing.

It was quite dark when Tarzan returned to the village of Mbonga and took his now polished perch in the tree which overhangs the palisade upon one side of the walled enclosure. As there was nothing in particular to feast upon in the village there was little life in the single street, for only an orgy of flesh and native beer could draw out the people of Mbonga. Tonight they sat gossiping about their cooking fires, the older members of the tribe; or, if they were young, paired off in the shadows cast by the palm-thatched huts.

Tarzan dropped lightly into the village, and sneaking stealthily in the concealment of the denser shadows, approached the hut of the chief, Mbonga. Here he found that which he sought. There were warriors all about him; but they did not know that the feared devil-god slunk noiselessly so near them, nor did they see him possess himself of that which he coveted and depart from their village as noiselessly as he had come.

Later that night, as Tarzan curled himself for sleep, he lay for a long time looking up at the burning planets and the twinkling stars and at Goro the moon, and he smiled. He recalled how ludicrous the great bulls had appeared in their mad scramble for safety that day when Numa had charged among them and seized Mamka, and yet he knew them to be fierce and coura- geous. It was the sudden shock of surprise that always sent them into a panic; but of this Tarzan was not as yet fully aware. That was something he was to learn in the near future.

He fell asleep with a broad grin upon his face.

Manu, the monkey, awoke him in the morning by dropping discarded bean pods upon his upturned face from a branch a short distance above him. Tarzan looked up and smiled. He had been awakened thus before many times. He and Manu were fairly good friends, their friendship operating upon a reciprocal basis. Sometimes Manu would come running early in the morning to awaken Tarzan and tell him that Bara, the deer, was feeding close at hand, or that Horta, the boar, was asleep in a mudhole hard by, and in return Tarzan broke open the shells of the harder nuts and fruits for Manu, or frightened away Histah, the snake, and Sheeta, the panther.

The sun had been up for some time, and the tribe had already wandered off in search of food. Manu indicated the direction they had taken with a wave of his hand and a few piping notes of his squeaky little voice.

"Come, Manu," said Tarzan, "and you will see that which shall make you dance for joy and squeal your wrinkled little head off. Come, follow Tarzan of the Apes."

With that he set off in the direction Manu had indicated and above him, chattering, scolding and squealing, skipped Manu, the monkey. Across Tarzan's shoulders was the thing he had stolen from the village of Mbonga, the chief, the evening before.

The tribe was feeding in the forest beside the clearing where Gunto, and Taug, and Tarzan had so harassed Numa and finally taken away from him the fruit of his kill. Some of them were in the clearing itself. In peace and content they fed, for were there not three sentries, each watching upon a different side of the herd? Tarzan had taught them this, and though he had been away for several days hunting alone, as he often did, or visiting at the cabin by the sea, they had not as yet forgotten his admonitions, and if they continued for a short time longer to post sentries, it would become a habit of their tribal life and thus be perpetuated indefinitely.

But Tarzan, who knew them better than they knew themselves, was confident that they had ceased to place the watchers about them the moment that he had left them, and now he planned not only to have a little fun at their expense but to teach them a lesson in preparedness, which, by the way, is even a more vital issue in the jungle than in civilized places. That you and I exist today must be due to the preparedness of some shaggy anthropoid of the Oligocene. Of course the apes of Kerchak were always prepared, after their own way — Tarzan had merely suggested a new and additional safeguard.

Gunto was posted today to the north of the clearing. He squatted in the fork of a tree from where he might view the jungle for quite a distance about him. It was he who first discovered the enemy. A rustling in the undergrowth attracted his attention, and a moment later he had a partial view of a shaggy mane and tawny yellow back. Just a glimpse it was through the matted foliage beneath him; but it brought from Gunto's leathern lungs a shrill "Kreeg-ah!" which is the ape for beware, or danger.

Instantly the tribe took up the cry until "Kreeg-ahs!" rang through the jungle about the clearing as apes swung quickly to places of safety among the lower branches of the trees and the great bulls hastened in the direction of Gunto.

And then into the clearing strode Numa, the lion — majestic and mighty, and from a deep chest issued the moan and the cough and the rumbling roar that set stiff hairs to bristling from shaggy craniums down the length of mighty spines.

Inside the clearing, Numa paused and on the instant there fell upon him from the trees near by a shower of broken rock and dead limbs torn from age-old trees. A dozen times he was hit, and then the apes ran down and gathered other rocks, pelting him unmercifully.

Numa turned to flee, but his way was barred by a fusillade of sharp-cornered missiles, and then, upon the edge of the clearing, great Taug met him with a huge fragment of rock as large as a man's head, and down went the Lord of the Jungle beneath the stunning blow.

With shrieks and roars and loud barkings the great apes of the tribe of Kerchak rushed upon the fallen lion. Sticks and stones and yellow fangs menaced the still form. In another moment, before he could regain consciousness, Numa would be battered and torn until only a bloody mass of broken bones and matted hair remained of what had once been the most dreaded of jungle creatures.

But even as the sticks and stones were raised above him and the great fangs bared to tear him, there descended like a plummet from the trees above a diminutive figure with long, white whiskers and a wrinkled face. Square upon the body of Numa it alighted and there it danced and screamed and shrieked out its challenge against the bulls of Kerchak.

For an instant they paused, paralyzed by the wonder of the thing. It was Manu, the monkey, Manu, the little coward, and here he was daring the ferocity of the great Mangani, hopping about upon the carcass of Numa, the lion, and crying out that they must not strike it again.

And when the bulls paused, Manu reached down and seized a tawny ear. With all his little might he tugged upon the heavy head until slowly it turned back, revealing the tousled, black head and clean-cut profile of Tarzan of the Apes.

Some of the older apes were for finishing what they had commenced; but Taug, sullen, mighty Taug, sprang quickly to the ape-man's side and straddling the unconscious form warned back those who would have struck his childhood playmate. And Teeka, his mate, came too, taking her place with bared fangs at Taug's side. others followed their example, until at last Tarzan was surrounded by a ring of hairy champions who would permit no enemy to approach him.

It was a surprised and chastened Tarzan who opened his eyes to consciousness a few minutes later. He looked about him at the surrounding apes and slowly there returned to him a realization of what had occurred.

Gradually a broad grin illuminated his features. His bruises were many and they hurt; but the good that had come from his adventure was worth all that it had cost. He had learned, for instance, that the apes of Kerchak had heeded his teaching, and he had learned that he had good friends among the sullen beasts whom he had thought without sentiment. He had discovered that Manu, the monkey — even little, cowardly Manu — had risked his life in his defense.

It made Tarzan very glad to know these things; but at the other lesson he had been taught he reddened. He had always been a joker, the only joker in the grim and terrible company; but now as he lay there half dead from his hurts, he almost swore a solemn oath forever to forego practical joking — almost; but not quite.

The Nightmare

THE BLACKS OF the village of Mbonga, the chief, were feasting, while above them in a large tree sat Tarzan of the Apes — grim, terrible, empty, and envious. Hunting had proved poor that day, for there are lean days as well as fat ones for even the greatest of the jungle hunters. Oftentimes Tarzan went empty for more than a full sun, and he had passed through entire moons during which he had been but barely able to stave off starvation; but such times were infrequent.

There once had been a period of sickness among the grass-eaters which had left the plains almost bare of game for several years, and again the great cats had increased so rapidly and so overrun the country that their prey, which was also Tarzan's, had been frightened off for a considerable time.

But for the most part Tarzan had fed well always. Today, though, he had gone empty, one misfortune following another as rapidly as he raised new quarry, so that now, as he sat perched in the tree above the feasting blacks, he experienced all the pangs of famine and his hatred for his lifelong enemies waxed strong in his breast. It was tantalizing, indeed, to sit there hungry while these Gomangani filled themselves so full of food that their stomachs seemed almost upon the point of bursting, and with elephant steaks at that!

It was true that Tarzan and Tantor were the best of friends, and that Tarzan never yet had tasted of the flesh of the elephant; but the Gomangani evidently had slain one, and as they were eating of the flesh of their kill, Tarzan was assailed by no doubts as to the ethics of his doing likewise, should he have the opportunity. Had he known that the elephant had died of sickness several days before the blacks discovered the carcass, he might not have been so keen to partake of the feast, for Tarzan of the Apes was no carrion-eater. Hunger, however, may blunt the most epicurean taste, and Tarzan was not exactly an epicure.

What he was at this moment was a very hungry wild beast whom caution was holding in leash, for the great cooking pot in the center of the village was surrounded by black warriors, through whom not even Tarzan of the Apes might hope to pass unharmed. It would be necessary, therefore, for the watcher to remain there hungry until the blacks had gorged themselves to stupor, and then, if they had left any scraps, to make the best meal he could from such; but to the impatient Tarzan it seemed that the greedy Gomangani would rather burst than leave the feast before the last morsel had been devoured. For a time they broke the monotony of eating by executing portions of a hunting dance, a maneuver which sufficiently stimulated digestion to permit them to fall to once more with renewed vigor; but with the consumption of appalling quantities of elephant meat and native beer they presently became too logy for physical exertion of any sort, some reaching a stage where they no longer could rise from the ground, but lay conveniently close to the great cooking pot, stuffing themselves into unconsciousness.

It was well past midnight before Tarzan even could begin to see the end of the orgy. The blacks were now falling asleep rapidly; but a few still persisted. From before their condition Tarzan had no doubt but that he easily could enter the village and snatch a handful of meat from before their noses; but a handful was not what he wanted. Nothing less than a stomachful would allay the gnawing craving of that great emptiness. He must therefore have ample time to forage in peace.

At last but a single warrior remained true to his ideals — an old fellow whose once wrinkled belly was now as smooth and as tight as the head of a drum. With evidences of great discomfort, and even pain, he would crawl toward the pot and drag himself slowly to his knees, from which position he could reach into the receptacle and seize a piece of meat. Then he would roll over on his back with a loud groan and lie there while he slowly forced the food between his teeth and down into his gorged stomach.

It was evident to Tarzan that the old fellow would eat until he died, or until there was no more meat. The ape-man shook his head in disgust. What foul creatures were these Gomangani? Yet of all the jungle folk they alone resembled Tarzan closely in form. Tarzan was a man, and they, too, must be some manner of men, just as the little monkeys, and the great apes, and Bolgani, the gorilla, were quite evidently of one great family, though differing in size and appearance and customs. Tarzan was ashamed, for of all the beasts of the jungle, then, man was the most disgusting — man and Dango, the hyena. Only man and Dango ate until they swelled up like a dead rat. Tarzan had seen Dango eat his way into the carcass of a dead elephant and then continue to eat so much that he had been unable to get out of the hole through which he had entered. Now he could readily believe that man, given the opportunity, would do the same. Man, too, was the most unlovely of creatures — with his skinny legs and his big stomach, his filed teeth, and his thick, red lips. Man was disgusting. Tarzan's gaze was riveted upon the hideous old warrior wallowing in filth beneath him.

There! the thing was struggling to its knees to reach for another morsel of flesh. It groaned aloud in pain and yet it persisted in eating, eating, ever eating. Tarzan could endure it no longer — neither his hunger nor his disgust. Silently he slipped to the ground with the bole of the great tree between himself and the feaster.

The man was still kneeling, bent almost double in agony, before the cooking pot. His back was toward the ape-man. Swiftly and noiselessly Tarzan approached him. There was no sound as steel fingers closed about the black throat. The struggle was short, for the man was old and already half stupefied from the effects of the gorging and the beer.

Tarzan dropped the inert mass and scooped several large pieces of meat from the cooking pot — enough to satisfy even his great hunger — then he raised the body of the feaster and shoved it into the vessel. When the other blacks awoke they would have something to think about! Tarzan grinned. As he turned toward the tree with his meat, he picked up a vessel containing beer and raised it to his lips, but at the first taste he spat the stuff from his mouth and tossed the primitive tankard aside. He was quite sure that even Dango would draw the line at such filthy tasting drink as that, and his contempt for man increased with the conviction.

Tarzan swung off into the jungle some half mile or so before he paused to partake of his stolen food. He noticed that it gave forth a strange and unpleasant odor, but assumed that this was due to the fact that it had stood in a vessel of water above a fire. Tarzan was, of course, unaccustomed to cooked food. He did not like it; but he was very hungry and had eaten a considerable portion of his haul before it was really borne in upon him that the stuff was nauseating. It required far less than he had imagined it would to satisfy his appetite.

Throwing the balance to the ground he curled up in a convenient crotch and sought slumber; but slumber seemed difficult to woo. Ordinarily Tarzan of the Apes was asleep as quickly as a dog after it curls itself upon a hearthrug before a roaring blaze; but tonight he squirmed and twisted, for at the pit of his stomach was a peculiar feeling that resembled nothing more closely than an attempt upon the part of the fragments of elephant meat reposing there to come out into the night and search for their elephant; but Tarzan was adamant. He gritted his teeth and held them back. He was not to be robbed of his meal after waiting so long to obtain it.

He had succeeded in dozing when the roaring of a lion awoke him. He sat up to discover that it was broad daylight. Tarzan rubbed his eyes. Could it be that he had really slept? He did not feel particularly refreshed as he should have after a good sleep. A noise attracted his attention, and he looked down to see a lion standing at the foot of the tree gazing hungrily at him. Tarzan made a face at the king of beasts, whereat Numa, greatly to the ape-man's surprise, started to climb up into the branches toward him. Now, never before had Tarzan seen a lion climb a tree, yet, for some unaccountable reason, he was not greatly surprised that this particular lion should do so.

As the lion climbed slowly toward him, Tarzan sought higher branches; but to his chagrin, he discovered that it was with the utmost difficulty that he could climb at all. Again and again he slipped back, losing all that he had gained, while the lion kept steadily at his climbing, coming ever closer and closer to the ape-man. Tarzan could see the hungry light in the

yellow-green eyes. He could see the slaver on the drooping jowls, and the great fangs agape to seize and destroy
him. Clawing desperately, the ape-man at last succeeded in gaining a little upon his pursuer. He reached
the more slender branches far aloft where he well knew
no lion could follow; yet on and on came devil-faced
Numa. It was incredible; but it was true. Yet what most
amazed Tarzan was that though he realized the incredi-
bility of it all, he at the same time accepted it as a matter
of course, first that a lion should climb at all and
second that he should enter the upper terraces where
even Sheeta, the panther, dared not venture.

To the very top of a tall tree the ape-man clawed his
awkward way and after him came Numa, the lion,
moaning dismally. At last Tarzan stood balanced upon
the very utmost pinnacle of a swaying branch, high
above the forest. He could go no farther. Below him
the lion came steadily upward, and Tarzan of the Apes
realized that at last the end had come. He could not
do battle upon a tiny branch with Numa, the lion,
especially with such a Numa, to which swaying
branches two hundred feet above the ground provided
as substantial footing as the ground itself.

Nearer and nearer came the lion. Another moment
and he could reach up with one great paw and drag the
ape-man downward to those awful jaws. A whirring
noise above his head caused Tarzan to glance apprehensively upward. A great bird was circling close above
him. He never had seen so large a bird in all his life,
yet he recognized it immediately, for had he not seen
it hundreds of times in one of the books in the little
cabin by the land-locked bay — the moss-grown cabin
that with its contents was the sole heritage left by his
dead and unknown father to the young Lord Greystoke?

In the picture-book the great bird was shown flying
far above the ground with a small child in its talons

while, beneath, a distracted mother stood with uplifted hands. The lion was already reaching forth a taloned paw to seize him when the bird swooped and buried no less formidable talons in Tarzan's back. The pain was numbing; but it was with a sense of relief that the ape-man felt himself snatched from the clutches of Numa.

With a great whirring of wings the bird rose rapidly until the forest lay far below. It made Tarzan sick and dizzy to look down upon it from so great a height, so he closed his eyes tight and held his breath. Higher and higher climbed the huge bird. Tarzan opened his eyes. The jungle was so far away that he could see only a dim, green blur below him, but just above and quite close was the sun. Tarzan reached out his hands and warmed them, for they were very cold. Then a sudden madness seized him. Where was the bird taking him? Was he to submit thus passively to a feathered creature however enormous? Was he, Tarzan of the Apes, mighty fighter, to die without striking a blow in his own defense? Never!

He snatched the hunting blade from his gee-string and thrusting upward drove it once, twice, thrice into the breast above him. The mighty wings fluttered a few more times, spasmodically, the talons relaxed their hold, and Tarzan of the Apes fell hurtling downward toward the distant jungle.

It seemed to the ape-man that he fell for many minutes before he crashed through the leafy verdure of the tree tops. The smaller branches broke his fall, so that he came to rest for an instant upon the very branch upon which he had sought slumber the previous night. For an instant he toppled there in a frantic attempt to regain his equilibrium; but at last he rolled off, yet, clutching wildly, he succeeded in grasping the branch and hanging on.

Once more he opened his eyes, which he had closed

during the fall. Again it was night. With all his old
agility he clambered back to the crotch from which he
had toppled. Below him a lion roared, and, looking
downward, Tarzan could see the yellow-green eyes shining in the moonlight as they bored hungrily upward
through the darkness of the jungle night toward him.

The ape-man gasped for breath. Cold sweat stood
out from every pore, there was a great sickness at the
pit of Tarzan's stomach. Tarzan of the Apes had
dreamed his first dream.

For a long time he sat watching for Numa to climb
into the tree after him, and listening for the sound of
the great wings from above, for to Tarzan of the Apes
his dream was a reality.

He could not believe what he had seen and yet,
having seen even these incredible things, he could not
disbelieve the evidence of his own perceptions. Never
in all his life had Tarzan's senses deceived him badly,
and so, naturally, he had great faith in them. Each
perception which ever had been transmitted to Tarzan's brain had been, with varying accuracy, a true
perception. He could not conceive of the possibility
of apparently having passed through such a weird
adventure in which there was no grain of truth. That
a stomach, disordered by decayed elephant flesh, a lion
roaring in the jungle, a picture-book, and sleep could
have so truly portrayed all the clear-cut details of what
he had seemingly experienced was quite beyond his
knowledge; yet he knew that Numa could not climb a
tree, he knew that there existed in the jungle no such
bird as he had seen, and he knew, too, that he could
not have fallen a tiny fraction of the distance he had
hurtled downward, and lived.

To say the least, he was a very puzzled Tarzan as he
tried to compose himself once more for slumber — a
very puzzled and a very nauseated Tarzan.

As he thought deeply upon the strange occurrences

of the night, he witnessed another remarkable happening. It was indeed quite preposterous, yet he saw it all with his own eyes — it was nothing less than Histah, the snake, wreathing his sinuous and slimy way up the bole of the tree below him — Histah, with the head of the old man Tarzan had shoved into the cooking pot — the head and the round, tight, black, distended stomach. As the old man's frightful face, with upturned eyes, set and glassy, came close to Tarzan, the jaws opened to seize him. The ape-man struck furiously at the hideous face, and as he struck the apparition disappeared.

Tarzan sat straight up upon his branch trembling in every limb, wide-eyed and panting. He looked all around him with his keen, jungle-trained eyes, but he saw naught of the old man with the body of Histah, the snake, but on his naked thigh the ape-man saw a caterpillar, dropped from a branch above him. With a grimace he flicked it off into the darkness beneath.

And so the night wore on, dream following dream, nightmare following nightmare, until the distracted ape-man started like a frightened deer at the rustling of the wind in the trees about him, or leaped to his feet as the uncanny laugh of a hyena burst suddenly upon a momentary jungle silence. But at last the tardy morning broke and a sick and feverish Tarzan wound sluggishly through the dank and gloomy mazes of the forest in search of water. His whole body seemed on fire, a great sickness surged upward to his throat. He saw a tangle of almost impenetrable thicket, and, like the wild beast he was, he crawled into it to die alone and unseen, safe from the attacks of predatory carnivora.

But he did not die. For a long time he wanted to; but presently nature and an outraged stomach relieved themselves in their own therapeutic manner, the ape-man broke into a violent perspiration and then fell into a normal and untroubled sleep which persisted well into the afternoon. When he awoke he found himself weak but no longer sick.

Once more he sought water, and after drinking deeply, took his way slowly toward the cabin by the sea. In times of loneliness and trouble it had long been his custom to seek there the quiet and restfulness which he could find nowhere else.

As he approached the cabin and raised the crude latch which his father had fashioned so many years before, two small, blood-shot eyes watched him from the concealing foliage of the jungle close by. From beneath shaggy, beetling brows they glared maliciously upon him, maliciously and with a keen curiosity; then Tarzan entered the cabin and closed the door after him. Here, with all the world shut out from him, he could dream without fear of interruption. He could curl up and look at the pictures in the strange things which were books, he could puzzle out the printed word he had learned to read without knowledge of the spoken language it represented, he could live in a wonderful world of which he had no knowledge beyond the covers of his beloved books. Numa and Sabor might prowl about close to him, the elements might rage in all their fury; but here at least, Tarzan might be entirely off his guard in a delightful relaxation which gave him all his faculties for the uninterrupted pursuit of this greatest of all his pleasures.

Today he turned to the picture of the huge bird which bore off the little Tarmangani in its talons. Tarzan puckered his brows as he examined the colored print. Yes, this was the very bird that had carried him off the day before, for to Tarzan the dream had been so great a reality that he still thought another day and a night had passed since he had lain down in the tree to sleep.

But the more he thought upon the matter the less

positive he was as to the verity of the seeming adventure through which he had passed, yet where the real had ceased and the unreal commenced he was quite unable to determine. Had he really then been to the village of the blacks at all, had he killed the old Gomangani, had he eaten of the elephant meat, had he been sick? Tarzan scratched his tousled black head and wondered. It was all very strange, yet he knew that he never had seen Numa climb a tree, or Histah with the head and belly of an old black man whom Tarzan already had slain.

Finally, with a sigh he gave up trying to fathom the unfathomable, yet in his heart of hearts he knew that something had come into his life that he never before had experienced, another life which existed when he slept and the consciousness of which was carried over into his waking hours.

Then he commenced to wonder if some of these strange creatures which he met in his sleep might not slay him, for at such times Tarzan of the Apes seemed to be a different Tarzan, sluggish, helpless and timid — wishing to flee his enemies as fled Bara, the deer, most fearful of creatures.

Thus, with a dream, came the first faint tinge of a knowledge of fear, a knowledge which Tarzan, awake, had never experienced, and perhaps he was experiencing what his early forbears passed through and transmitted to posterity in the form of superstition first and religion later; for they, as Tarzan, had seen things at night which they could not explain by the daylight standards of sense perception or of reason, and so had built for themselves a weird explanation which included grotesque shapes, possessed of strange and uncanny powers, to whom they finally came to attribute all those inexplicable phenomena of nature which with each recurrence filled them with awe, with wonder, or with terror.

And as Tarzan concentrated his mind on the little bugs upon the printed page before him, the active recollection of the strange adventures presently merged into the text of that which he was reading — a story of Bolgani, the gorilla, in captivity. There was a more or less lifelike illustration of Bolgani in colors and in a cage, with many remarkable looking Tarmangani standing against a rail and peering curiously at the snarling brute. Tarzan wondered not a little, as he always did, at the odd and seemingly useless array of colored plumage which covered the bodies of the Tarmangani. It always caused him to grin a trifle when he looked at these strange creatures. He wondered if they so covered their bodies from shame of their hairlessness or because they thought the odd things they wore added any to the beauty of their appearance. Particularly was Tarzan amused by the grotesque headdresses of the pictured people. He wondered how some of the shes succeeded in balancing theirs in an upright position, and he came as near to laughing aloud as he ever had, as he contemplated the funny little round things upon the heads of the hes.

Slowly the ape-man picked out the meaning of the various combinations of letters on the printed page, and as he read, the little bugs, for as such he always thought of the letters, commenced to run about in a most confusing manner, blurring his vision and befuddling his thoughts. Twice he brushed the back of a hand smartly across his eyes; but only for a moment could he bring the bugs back to coherent and intelligible form. He had slept ill the night before and now he was exhausted from loss of sleep, from sickness, and from the slight fever he had had, so that it became more and more difficult to fix his attention, or to keep his eyes open.

Tarzan realized that he was falling asleep, and just as the realization was borne in upon him and he had decided to relinquish himself to an inclination which had assumed almost the proportions of a physical pain, he was aroused by the opening of the cabin door. Turning quickly toward the interruption Tarzan was amazed, for a moment, to see bulking large in the doorway the huge and hairy form of Bolgani, the gorilla.

Now there was scarcely a denizen of the great jungle with whom Tarzan would rather not have been cooped up inside the small cabin than Bolgani, the gorilla, yet he felt no fear, even though his quick eye noted that Bolgani was in the throes of that jungle madness which seizes upon so many of the fiercer males. Ordinarily the huge gorillas avoid conflict, hide themselves from the other jungle folk, and are generally the best of neighbors; but when they are attacked, or the madness seizes them, there is no jungle denizen so bold and fierce as to deliberately seek a quarrel with them.

But for Tarzan there was no escape. Bolgani was glowering at him from red-rimmed, wicked eyes. In a moment he would rush in and seize the ape-man. Tarzan reached for the hunting knife where he had lain it on the table beside him; but as his fingers did not immediately locate the weapon, he turned a quick glance in search of it. As he did so his eyes fell upon the book he had been looking at which still lay open at the picture of Bolgani. Tarzan found his knife, but he merely fingered it idly and grinned in the direction of the advancing gorilla.

Not again would he be fooled by empty things which came while he slept! In a moment, no doubt, Bolgani would turn into Pamba, the rat, with the head of Tantor, the elephant. Tarzan had seen enough of such strange happenings recently to have some idea as to what he might expect; but this time Bolgani did not alter his form as he came slowly toward the young ape-man.

Tarzan was a bit puzzled, too, that he felt no desire to rush frantically to some place of safety, as had been the sensation most conspicuous in the other of his new and remarkable adventures. He was just himself now, ready to fight, if necessary; but still sure that no flesh and blood gorilla stood before him.

The thing should be fading away into thin air by now, thought Tarzan, or changing into something else; yet it did not. Instead it loomed clear-cut and real as Bolgani himself, the magnificent dark coat glistening with life and health in a bar of sunlight which shot across the cabin through the high window behind the young Lord Greystoke. This was quite the most realistic of his sleep adventures, thought Tarzan, as he passively awaited the next amusing incident.

And then the gorilla charged. Two mighty, calloused hands seized upon the ape-man, great fangs were bared close to his face, a hideous growl burst from the cavernous throat and hot breath fanned Tarzan's cheek, and still he sat grinning at the apparition. Tarzan might be fooled once or twice, but not for so many times in succession! He knew that this Bolgani was no real Bolgani, for had he been he never could have gained entrance to the cabin, since only Tarzan knew how to operate the latch.

The gorilla seemed puzzled by the strange passivity of the hairless ape. He paused an instant with his jaws snarling close to the other's throat, then he seemed suddenly to come to some decision. Whirling the ape-man across a hairy shoulder, as easily as you or I might lift a babe in arms, Bolgani turned and dashed out into the open, racing toward the great trees.

Now, indeed, was Tarzan sure that this was a sleep adventure, and so grinned largely as the giant gorilla bore him, unresisting, away. Presently, reasoned Tarzan, he would awaken and find himself back in the cabin where he had fallen asleep. He glanced back at the thought and saw the cabin door standing wide open. This would never do! Always had he been careful to close and latch it against wild intruders. Manu, the monkey, would make sad havoc there among Tarzan's treasures should he have access to the interior for even a few minutes. The question which arose in Tarzan's mind was a baffling one. Where did sleep adventures end and reality commence? How was he to be sure that the cabin door was not really open? Everything about him appeared quite normal — there were none of the grotesque exaggerations of his former sleep adventures. It would be better then to be upon the safe side and make sure that the cabin door was closed — it would do no harm even if all that seemed to be happening were not happening at all.

Tarzan essayed to slip from Bolgani's shoulder; but the great beast only growled ominously and gripped him tighter. With a mighty effort the ape-man wrenched himself loose, and as he slid to the ground, the dream gorilla turned ferociously upon him, seized him once more and buried great fangs in a sleek, brown shoulder.

The grin of derision faded from Tarzan's lips as the pain and the hot blood aroused his fighting instincts. Asleep or awake, this thing was no longer a joke! Biting, tearing, and snarling, the two rolled over upon the ground. The gorilla now was frantic with insane rage. Again and again he loosed his hold upon the ape-man's shoulder in an attempt to seize the jugular; but Tarzan of the Apes had fought before with creatures who struck first for the vital vein, and each time he wriggled out of harm's way as he strove to get his fingers upon his adversary's throat. At last he succeeded — his great muscles tensed and knotted beneath his smooth hide as he forced with every ounce of his mighty strength to push the hairy torso from him. And as he choked Bolgani and strained him away, his other hand crept slowly upward between them until the point of the hunting knife rested over the savage heart — there was a quick movement of the steel-thewed wrist and the blade plunged to its goal.

Bolgani, the gorilla, voiced a single frightful shriek, tore himself loose from the grasp of the ape-man, rose to his feet, staggered a few steps and then plunged to earth. There were a few spasmodic movements of the limbs and the brute was still.

Tarzan of the Apes stood looking down upon his kill, and as he stood there he ran his fingers through his thick, black shock of hair. Presently he stooped and touched the dead body. Some of the red life-blood of the gorilla crimsoned his fingers. He raised them to his nose and sniffed. Then he shook his head and turned toward the cabin. The door was still open. He closed it and fastened the latch. Returning toward the body of his kill he again paused and scratched his head.

If this was a sleep adventure, what then was reality? How was he to know the one from the other? How much of all that had happened in his life had been real and how much unreal?

He placed a foot upon the prostrate form and raising his face to the heavens gave voice to the kill cry of the bull ape. Far in the distance a lion answered. It was very real and, yet, he did not know. Puzzled, he turned away into the jungle.

No, he did not know what was real and what was not; but there was one thing that he did know — never again would he eat of the flesh of Tantor, the elephant.

The Battle for Teeka

*T*HE DAY WAS perfect. A cool breeze tempered the heat of the equatorial sun. Peace had reigned within the tribe for weeks and no alien enemy had trespassed upon its preserves from without. To the ape-mind all this was sufficient evidence that the future would be identical with the immediate past — that Utopia would persist.

The sentinels, now from habit become a fixed tribal custom, either relaxed their vigilance or entirely deserted their posts, as the whim seized them. The tribe was far scattered in search of food. Thus may peace and prosperity undermine the safety of the most primitive community even as it does that of the most cultured.

Even the individuals became less watchful and alert, so that one might have thought Numa and Sabor and Sheeta entirely deleted from the scheme of things. The shes and the balus roamed unguarded through the sullen jungle, while the greedy males foraged far afield, and thus it was that Teeka and Gazan, her balu, hunted upon the extreme southern edge of the tribe with no great male near them.

Still farther south there moved through the forest a

sinister figure — a huge bull ape, maddened by solitude and defeat. A week before he had contended for the kingship of a tribe far distant, and now battered, and still sore, he roamed the wilderness an outcast. Later he might return to his own tribe and submit to the will of the hairy brute he had attempted to dethrone; but for the time being he dared not do so, since he had sought not only the crown but the wives, as well, of his lord and master. It would require an entire moon at least to bring forgetfulness to him he had wronged, and so Toog wandered a strange jungle, grim, terrible, hate-filled.

It was in this mental state that Toog came unexpectedly upon a young she feeding alone in the jungle — a stranger she, lithe and strong and beautiful beyond compare. Toog caught his breath and slunk quickly to one side of the trail where the dense foliage of the tropical underbrush concealed him from Teeka while permitting him to feast his eyes upon her loveliness.

But not alone were they concerned with Teeka — they roved the surrounding jungle in search of the bulls and cows and balus of her tribe, though principally for the bulls. When one covets a she of an alien tribe one must take into consideration the great, fierce, hairy guardians who seldom wander far from their wards and who will fight a stranger to the death in protection of the mate or offspring of a fellow, precisely as they would fight for their own.

Toog could see no sign of any ape other than the strange she and a young balu playing near by. His wicked, bloodshot eyes half closed as they rested upon the charms of the former — as for the balu, one snap of those great jaws upon the back of its little neck would prevent it from raising any unnecessary alarm.

Toog was a fine, big male, resembling in many ways Teeka's mate, Taug. Each was in his prime, and each was wonderfully muscled, perfectly fanged and as horrifyingly ferocious as the most exacting and particular she could wish. Had Toog been of her own tribe, Teeka might as readily have yielded to him as to Taug when her mating time arrived; but now she was Taug's and no other male could claim her without first defeating Taug in personal combat. And even then Teeka retained some rights in the matter. If she did not favor a correspondent, she could enter the lists with her rightful mate and do her part toward discouraging his advances, a part, too, which would prove no mean assistance to her lord and master, for Teeka, even though her fangs were smaller than a male's, could use them to excellent effect.

Just now Teeka was occupied in a fascinating search for beetles, to the exclusion of all else. She did not realize how far she and Gazan had become separated from the balance of the tribe, nor were her defensive senses upon the alert as they should have been. Months of immunity from danger under the protecting watchfulness of the sentries, which Tarzan had taught the tribe to post, had lulled them all into a sense of peaceful security based on that fallacy which has wrecked many enlightened communities in the past and will continue to wreck others in the future — that because they have not been attacked they never will be.

Toog, having satisfied himself that only the she and her balu were in the immediate vicinity, crept stealthily forward. Teeka's back was toward him when he finally rushed upon her; but her senses were at last awakened to the presence of danger and she wheeled to face the strange bull just before he reached her. Toog halted a few paces from her. His anger had fled before the seductive feminine charms of the stranger. He made conciliatory noises — a species of clucking sound with his broad, flat lips — that were, too, not greatly dissimilar to that which might be produced in an osculatory solo.

But Teeka only bared her fangs and growled. Little Gazan started to run toward his mother, but she warned him away with a quick "Kreeg-ah!" telling him to run high into a tall tree. Evidently Teeka was not favorably impressed by her new suitor. Toog realized this and altered his methods accordingly. He swelled his giant chest, beat upon it with his calloused knuckles and swaggered to and fro before her.

"I am Toog," he boasted. "Look at my fighting fangs. Look at my great arms and my mighty legs. With one bite I can slay your biggest bull. Alone have I slain Sheeta. I am Toog. Toog wants you." Then he waited for the effect, nor did he have long to wait. Teeka turned with a swiftness which belied her great weight and bolted in the opposite direction. Toog, with an angry growl, leaped in pursuit; but the smaller, lighter female was too fleet for him. He chased her for a few yards and then, foaming and barking, he halted and beat upon the ground with his hard fists.

From the tree above him little Gazan looked down and witnessed the stranger bull's discomfiture. Being young, and thinking himself safe above the reach of the heavy male, Gazan screamed an ill-timed insult at their tormentor. Toog looked up. Teeka had halted at a little distance — she would not go far from her balu; that Toog quickly realized and as quickly determined to take advantage of. He saw that the tree in which the young ape squatted was isolated and that Gazan could not reach another without coming to earth. He would obtain the mother through her love for her young.

He swung himself into the lower branches of the tree. Little Gazan ceased to insult him; his expression of deviltry changed to one of apprehension, which was quickly followed by fear as Toog commenced to ascend toward him. Teeka screamed to Gazan to climb higher, and the little fellow scampered upward among the tiny branches which would not support the weight of the great bull; but nevertheless Toog kept on climbing. Teeka was not fearful. She knew that he could not ascend far enough to reach Gazan, so she sat at a little distance from the tree and applied jungle opprobrium to him. Being a female, she was a past master of the art.

But she did not know the malevolent cunning of Toog's little brain. She took it for granted that the bull would climb as high as he could toward Gazan and then, finding that he could not reach him, resume his pursuit of her, which she knew would prove equally fruitless. So sure was she of the safety of her balu and her own ability to take care of herself that she did not voice the cry for help which would soon have brought the other members of the tribe flocking to her side.

Toog slowly reached the limit to which he dared risk his great weight to the slender branches. Gazan was still fifteen feet above him. The bull braced himself and seized the main branch in his powerful hands, then he commenced shaking it vigorously. Teeka was appalled. Instantly she realized what the bull purposed. Gazan clung far out upon a swaying limb. At the first shake he lost his balance, though he did not quite fall, clinging still with his four hands; but Toog redoubled his efforts; the shaking produced a violent snapping of the limb to which the young ape clung. Teeka saw all too plainly what the outcome must be and forgetting her own danger in the depth of her mother love, rushed forward to ascend the tree and give battle to the fearsome creature that menaced the life of her little one.

But before ever she reached the bole, Toog had succeeded, by violent shaking of the branch, to loosen Gazan's hold. With a cry the little fellow plunged down through the foliage, clutching futilely for a new hold, and alighted with a sickening thud at his mother's feet, where he lay silent and motionless. Moaning, Teeka stooped to lift the still form in her arms; but at the same instant Toog was upon her.

Struggling and biting she fought to free herself; but the giant muscles of the great bull were too much for her lesser strength. Toog struck and choked her repeatedly until finally, half unconscious, she lapsed into quasi submission. Then the bull lifted her to his shoulder and turned back to the trail toward the south from whence he had come.

Upon the ground lay the quiet form of little Gazan. He did not moan. He did not move. The sun rose slowly toward meridian. A mangy thing, lifting its nose to scent the jungle breeze, crept through the underbrush. It was Dango, the hyena. Presently its ugly muzzle broke through some near-by foliage and its cruel eyes fastened upon Gazan.

Early that morning, Tarzan of the Apes had gone to the cabin by the sea, where he passed many an hour at such times as the tribe was ranging in the vicinity. On the floor lay the skeleton of a man — all that remained of the former Lord Greystoke — lay as it had fallen some twenty years before when Kerchak, the great ape, had thrown it, lifeless, there. Long since had the termites and the small rodents picked clean the sturdy English bones. For years Tarzan had seen it lying there, giving it no more attention than he gave the countless thousand bones that strewed his jungle haunts. On the bed another, smaller, skeleton reposed and the youth ignored it as he ignored the other. How could he know that the one had been his father, the other his mother? The little pile of bones in the rude cradle, fashioned with such loving care by the former Lord Greystoke, meant nothing to him — that one day that little skull was to help prove his right to a proud title was as far beyond his ken as the satellites of the suns of Orion. To Tarzan they were bones — just bones. He did not need them, for there was no meat left upon them, and they were not in his way, for he knew no necessity for a bed, and the skeleton upon the floor he easily could step over.

Today he was restless. He turned the pages first of one book and then of another. He glanced at pictures which he knew by heart, and tossed the books aside. He rummaged for the thousandth time in the cupboard. He took out a bag which contained several small, round pieces of metal. He had played with them many times in the years gone by; but always he replaced them carefully in the bag, and the bag in the cupboard, upon the very shelf where first he had discovered it. In strange ways did heredity manifest itself in the ape-man. Come of an orderly race, he himself was orderly without knowing why. The apes dropped things wherever their interest in them waned — in the tall grass or from the high-flung branches of the trees. What they dropped they sometimes found again, by accident; but not so the ways of Tarzan. For his few belongings he had a place and scrupulously he returned each thing to its proper place when he was done with it. The round pieces of metal in the little bag always interested him. Raised pictures were upon either side, the meaning of which he did not quite understand. The pieces were bright and shiny. It amused him to arrange them in various figures upon the table. Hundreds of times had he played thus. Today, while so engaged, he dropped a lovely yellow piece — an English sovereign — which rolled beneath the bed where lay all that was mortal of the once beautiful Lady Alice.

True to form, Tarzan at once dropped to his hands and knees and searched beneath the bed for the lost gold piece. Strange as it might appear, he had never before looked beneath the bed. He found the gold piece, and something else he found, too — a small wooden box with a loose cover. Bringing them both out he returned the sovereign to its bag and the bag to its shelf within the cupboard; then he investigated the box. It contained a quantity of cylindrical bits of metal, cone-shaped at one end and flat at the other, with a projecting rim. They were all quite green and dull, coated with years of verdigris.

Tarzan removed a handful of them from the box and examined them. He rubbed one upon another and discovered that the green came off, leaving a shiny surface for two-thirds of their length and a dull gray over the cone-shaped end. Finding a bit of wood he rubbed one of the cylinders rapidly and was rewarded by a lustrous sheen which pleased him.

At his side hung a pocket pouch taken from the body of one of the numerous black warriors he had slain. Into this pouch he put a handful of the new playthings, thinking to polish them at his leisure; then he replaced the box beneath the bed, and finding nothing more to amuse him, left the cabin and started back in the direction of the tribe.

Shortly before he reached them he heard a great commotion ahead of him — the loud screams of shes and balus, the savage, angry barking and growling of the great bulls. Instantly he increased his speed, for the "Kreeg-ahs" that came to his ears warned him that something was amiss with his fellows.

While Tarzan had been occupied with his own devices in the cabin of his dead sire, Taug, Teeka's mighty mate, had been hunting a mile to the north of the tribe. At last, his belly filled, he had turned lazily back toward the clearing where he had last seen the tribe and presently commenced passing its members scattered alone or in twos or threes. Nowhere did he see Teeka or Gazan, and soon he began inquiring of the other apes where they might be; but none had seen them recently.

Now the lower orders are not highly imaginative. They do not, as you and I, paint vivid mental pictures of things which might have occurred, and so Taug did not now apprehend that any misfortune had overtaken his mate and their off-spring — he merely knew that he wished to find Teeka that he might lie down in the shade and have her scratch his back while his breakfast digested; but though he called to her and searched for her and asked each whom he met, he could find no trace of Teeka, nor of Gazan either.

He was beginning to become peeved and had about made up his mind to chastise Teeka for wandering so far afield when he wanted her. He was moving south along a game trail, his calloused soles and knuckles giving forth no sound, when he came upon Dango at the opposite side of a small clearing. The eater of carrion did not see Taug, for all his eyes were for something which lay in the grass beneath a tree — something upon which he was sneaking with the cautious stealth of his breed.

Taug, always cautious himself, as it behooves one to be who fares up and down the jungle and desires to survive, swung noiselessly into a tree, where he could have a better view of the clearing. He did not fear Dango; but he wanted to see what it was that Dango stalked. In a way, possibly, he was actuated as much by curiosity as by caution.

And when Taug reached a place in the branches from which he could have an unobstructed view of the clearing he saw Dango already sniffing at something directly beneath him — something which Taug instantly recognized as the lifeless form of his little Gazan.

With a cry so frightful, so bestial, that it momentarily paralyzed the startled Dango, the great ape launched his mighty bulk upon the surprised hyena. With a cry and a snarl, Dango, crushed to earth, turned to tear at his assailant; but as effectively might a sparrow turn upon a hawk. Taug's great, gnarled fingers closed upon the hyena's throat and back, his jaws snapped once on the mangy neck, crushing the vertebrae, and then he hurled the dead body contemptuously aside.

Again he raised his voice in the call of the bull ape to its mate, but there was no reply; then he leaned down to sniff at the body of Gazan. In the breast of this savage, hideous beast there beat a heart which was moved, however slightly, by the same emotions of paternal love which affect us. Even had we no actual evidence of this, we must know it still, since only thus might be explained the survival of the human race in which the jealousy and selfishness of the bulls would, in the earliest stages of the race, have wiped out the young as rapidly as they were brought into the world had not God implanted in the savage bosom that paternal love which evidences itself most strongly in the protective instinct of the male.

In Taug the protective instinct was not alone highly developed; but affection for his offspring as well, for Taug was an unusually intelligent specimen of these great, manlike apes which the natives of the Gobi speak of in whispers; but which no white man ever had seen, or, if seeing, lived to tell of until Tarzan of the Apes came among them.

And so Taug felt sorrow as any other father might feel sorrow at the loss of a little child. To you little Gazan might have seemed a hideous and repulsive creature, but to Taug and Teeka he was as beautiful and as cute as is your little Mary or Johnnie or Elizabeth Ann to you, and he was their firstborn, their only balu, and a he — three things which might make a young ape the apple of any fond father's eye.

For a moment Taug sniffed at the quiet little form. With his muzzle and his tongue he smoothed and caressed the rumpled coat. From his savage lips broke a low moan; but quickly upon the heels of sorrow came the overmastering desire for revenge.

Leaping to his feet he screamed out a volley of

"Kreeg-ahs," punctuated from time to time by the blood-freezing cry of an angry, challenging bull — a rage-mad bull with the blood lust strong upon him.

Answering his cries came the cries of the tribe as they swung through the trees toward him. It was these that Tarzan heard on his return from his cabin, and in reply to them he raised his own voice and hurried forward with increased speed until he fairly flew through the middle terraces of the forest.

When at last he came upon the tribe he saw their members gathered about Taug and something which lay quietly upon the ground. Dropping among them, Tarzan approached the center of the group. Taug was stiff roaring out his challenges; but when he saw Tarzan he ceased and stooping picked up Gazan in his arms and held him out for Tarzan to see. Of all the bulls of the tribe, Taug held affection for Tarzan only. Tarzan he trusted and looked up to as one wiser and more cunning. To Tarzan he came now — to the playmate of his balu days, the companion of innumerable battles of his maturity.

When Tarzan saw the still form in Taug's arms, a low growl broke from his lips, for he too loved Teeka's little balu.

"Who did it?" he asked. "Where is Teeka?"

"I do not know," replied Taug. "I found him lying here with Dango about to feed upon him; but it was not Dango that did it — there are no fang marks upon him."

Tarzan came closer and placed an ear against Gazan's breast. "He is not dead," he said. "Maybe he will not die." He pressed through the crowd of apes and circled once about them, examining the ground step by step. Suddenly he stopped and placing his nose close to the earth sniffed. Then he sprang to his feet, giving a peculiar cry. Taug and the others pressed forward, for the sound told them that the hunter had found the spoor of his quarry.

"A stranger bull has been here," said Tarzan. "It was he that hurt Gazan. He has carried off Teeka."

Taug and the other bulls commenced to roar and threaten; but they did nothing. Had the stranger bull been within sight they would have torn him to pieces; but it did not occur to them to follow him.

"If the three bulls had been watching around the tribe this would not have happened," said Tarzan. "Such things will happen as long as you do not keep the three bulls watching for an enemy. The jungle is full of enemies, and yet you let your shes and your balus feed where they will, alone and unprotected. Tarzan goes now — he goes to find Teeka and bring her back to the tribe."

The idea appealed to the other bulls. "We will all go," they cried.

"No," said Tarzan, "you will not all go. We cannot take shes and balus when we go out to hunt and fight. You must remain to guard them or you will lose them all."

They scratched their heads. The wisdom of his advice was dawning upon them, but at first they had been carried away by the new idea — the idea of following up an enemy offender to wrest his prize from him and punish him. The community instinct was ingrained in their characters through ages of custom. They did not know why they had not thought to pursue and punish the offender — they could not know that it was because they had as yet not reached a mental plane which would permit them to work as individuals. In times of stress, the community instinct sent them huddling into a compact herd where the great bulls, by the weight of their combined strength and ferocity, could best protect them from an enemy. The idea of separating to do battle with a foe had not yet occurred to them — it was too foreign to custom, too inimical to community interests; but to Tarzan it was the first and most natural thought. His senses told him that there was but a single bull connected with the attack upon Teeka and Gazan. A single enemy did not require the entire tribe for his punishment. Two swift bulls could quickly overhaul him and rescue Teeka.

In the past no one ever had thought to go forth in search of the shes that were occasionally stolen from the tribe. If Numa, Sabor, Sheeta or a wandering bull ape from another tribe chanced to carry off a maid or a matron while no one was looking, that was the end of it — she was gone, that was all. The bereaved husband, if the victim chanced to have been mated, growled around for a day or two and then, if he were strong enough, took another mate within the tribe, and if not, wandered far into the jungle on the chance of stealing one from another community.

In the past Tarzan of the Apes had condoned this practice for the reason that he had had no interest in those who had been stolen; but Teeka had been his first love and Teeka's balu held a place in his heart such as a balu of his own would have held. Just once before had Tarzan wished to follow and revenge. That had been years before when Kulonga, the son of Mbonga, the chief, had slain Kala. Then, single-handed, Tarzan had pursued and avenged. Now, though to a lesser degree, he was moved by the same passion.

He turned toward Taug. "Leave Gazan with Mumga," he said. "She is old and her fangs are broken and she is no good; but she can take care of Gazan until we return with Teeka, and if Gazan is dead when we come back," he turned to address Mumga, "I will kill you, too."

"Where are we going?" asked Taug.

"We are going to get Teeka," replied the ape-man, "and kill the bull who has stolen her. Come!"

He turned again to the spoor of the stranger bull,

which showed plainly to his trained senses, nor did he glance back to note if Taug followed. The latter laid Gazan in Mumga's arms with a parting: "If he dies Tarzan will kill you," and he followed after the brown-skinned figure that already was moving at a slow trot along the jungle trail.

No other bull of the tribe of Kerchak was so good a trailer as Tarzan, for his trained senses were aided by a high order of intelligence. His judgment told him the natural trail for a quarry to follow, so that he need but note the most apparent marks upon the way, and today the trail of Toog was as plain to him as type upon a printed page to you or me.

Following close behind the lithe figure of the ape-man came the huge and shaggy bull ape. No words passed between them. They moved as silently as two shadows among the myriad shadows of the forest. Alert as his eyes and ears, was Tarzan's patrician nose. The spoor was fresh, and now that they had passed from the range of the strong ape odor of the tribe he had little difficulty in following Toog and Teeka by scent alone. Teeka's familiar scent spoor told both Tarzan and Taug that they were upon her trail, and soon the scent of Toog became as familiar as the other.

They were progressing rapidly when suddenly dense clouds overcast the sun. Tarzan accelerated his pace. Now he fairly flew along the jungle trail, or, where Toog had taken to the trees, followed nimbly as a squirrel along the bending, undulating pathway of the foliage branches, swinging from tree to tree as Toog had swung before them; but more rapidly because they were not handicapped by a burden such as Toog's.

Tarzan felt that they must be almost upon the quarry, for the scent spoor was becoming stronger and stronger, when the jungle was suddenly shot by livid lightning, and a deafening roar of thunder reverberated through the heavens and the forest until the earth trembled and shook. Then came the rain — not as it comes to us of the temperate zones, but as a mighty avalanche of water — a deluge which spills tons instead of drops upon the bending forest giants and the terrified creatures which haunt their shade.

And the rain did what Tarzan knew that it would do — it wiped the spoor of the quarry from the face of the earth. For a half hour the torrents fell — then the sun burst forth, jewelling the forest with a million scintillant gems; but today the ape-man, usually alert to the changing wonders of the jungle, saw them not. Only the fact that the spoor of Teeka and her abductor was obliterated found lodgment in his thoughts.

Even among the branches of the trees there are well-worn trails, just as there are trails upon the surface of the ground; but in the trees they branch and cross more often, since the way is more open than among the dense undergrowth at the surface. Along one of these well-marked trails Tarzan and Taug continued after the rain had ceased, because the ape-man knew that this was the most logical path for the thief to follow; but when they came to a fork, they were at a loss. Here they halted, while Tarzan examined every branch and leaf which might have been touched by the fleeing ape.

He sniffed the bole of the tree, and with his keen eyes he sought to find upon the bark some sign of the way the quarry had taken. It was slow work and all the time, Tarzan knew, the bull of the alien tribe was forging steadily away from them — gaining precious minutes that might carry him to safety before they could catch up with him.

First along one fork he went, and then another, applying every test that his wonderful junglecraft was cognizant of; but again and again he was baffled, for the scent had been washed away by the heavy downpour, in every exposed place. For a half hour Tarzan and Taug searched, until at last, upon the bottom of a broad leaf, Tarzan's keen nose caught the faint trace of the scent spoor of Toog, where the leaf had brushed a hairy shoulder as the great ape passed through the foliage.

Once again the two took up the trail, but it was slow work now and there were many discouraging delays when the spoor seemed lost beyond recovery. To you or me there would have been no spoor, even before the coming of the rain, except, possibly, where Toog had come to earth and followed a game trail. In such places the imprint of a huge handlike foot and the knuckles of one great hand were sometimes plain enough for an ordinary mortal to read. Tarzan knew from these and other indications that the ape was yet carrying Teeka. The depth of the imprint of his feet indicated a much greater weight than that of any of the larger bulls, for they were made under the combined weight of Toog and Teeka, while the fact that the knuckles of but one hand touched the ground at any time showed that the other hand was occupied in some other business — the business of holding the prisoner to a hairy shoulder. Tarzan could follow, in sheltered places, the changing of the burden from one shoulder to another, as indicated by the deepening of the foot imprint upon the side of the load, and the changing of the knuckle imprints from one side of the trail to the other.

There were stretches along the surface paths where the ape had gone for considerable distances entirely erect upon his hind feet — walking as a man walks; but the same might have been true of any of the great anthropoids of the same species, for, unlike the chimpanzee and the gorilla, they walk without the aid of their hands quite as readily as with. It was such things, however, which helped to identify to Tarzan and to Taug the appearance of the abductor, and with his individual scent characteristic already indelibly impressed upon their memories, they were in a far better position to know him when they came upon him, even should he have disposed of Teeka before, than is a modern sleuth with his photographs and Bertillon measurements, equipped to recognize a fugitive from civilized justice.

But with all their high-strung and delicately attuned perceptive faculties the two bulls of the tribe of Kerchak were often sore pressed to follow the trail at all, and at best were so delayed that in the afternoon of the second day, they still had not overhauled the fugitive. The scent was now strong, for it had been made since the rain, and Tarzan knew that it would not be long before they came upon the thief and his loot. Above them, as they crept stealthily forward, chattered Manu, the monkey, and his thousand fellows; squawked and screamed the brazen-throated birds of plumage; buzzed and hummed the countless insects amid the rustling of the forest leaves, and, as they passed, a little graybeard, squeaking and scolding upon a swaying branch, looked down and saw them. Instantly the scolding and squeaking ceased, and off tore the long-tailed mite as though Sheeta, the panther, had been endowed with wings and was in close pursuit of him. To all appearances he was only a very much frightened little monkey, fleeing for his life — there seemed nothing sinister about him.

And what of Teeka during all this time? Was she at last resigned to her fate and accompanying her new mate in the proper humility of a loving and tractable spouse? A single glance at the pair would have answered these questions to the utter satisfaction of the most captious. She was torn and bleeding from many wounds, inflicted by the sullen Toog in his vain efforts to subdue her to his will, and Toog too was disfigured and mutilated; but with stubborn ferocity, he still clung to his now useless prize.

On through the jungle he forced his way in the direction of the stamping ground of his tribe. He hoped that his king would have forgotten his treason; but if not he was still resigned to his fate — any fate would be better than suffering longer the sole companionship of this frightful she, and then, too, he wished to exhibit his captive to his fellows. Maybe he could wish her on the king — it is possible that such a thought urged him on.

At last they came upon two bulls feeding in a parklike grove — a beautiful grove dotted with huge boulders half embedded in the rich loam — mute monuments, possibly, to a forgotten age when mighty glaciers rolled their slow course where now a torrid sun beats down upon a tropic jungle.

The two bulls looked up, baring long fighting fangs, as Toog appeared in the distance. The latter recognized the two as friends. "It is Toog," he growled. "Toog has come back with a new she."

The apes waited his nearer approach. Teeka turned a snarling, fanged face toward them. She was not pretty to look upon, yet through the blood and hatred upon her countenance they realized that she was beautiful, and they envied Toog — alas! they did not know Teeka.

As they squatted looking at one another there raced through the trees toward them a long-tailed little monkey with gray whiskers. He was a very excited little monkey when he came to a halt upon the limb of a tree directly overhead. "Two strange bulls come," he cried. One is a Mangani, the other a hideous ape without hair upon his body. They follow the spoor of Toog. I saw them."

The four apes turned their eyes backward along the trail Toog had just come; then they looked at one another for a minute. "Come," said the larger of Toog's two friends, "we will wait for the strangers in the thick bushes beyond the clearing."

He turned and waddled away across the open place, the others following him. The little monkey danced about, all excitement. His chief diversion in life was to bring about bloody encounters between the larger denizens of the forest, that he might sit in the safety of the trees and witness the spectacles. He was a glutton for gore, was this little, whiskered, gray monkey, so long as it was the gore of others — a typical fight fan was the graybeard.

The apes hid themselves in the shrubbery beside the trail along which the two stranger bulls would pass. Teeka trembled with excitement. She had heard the words of Manu, and she knew that the hairless ape must be Tarzan, while the other was, doubtless, Taug. Never, in her wildest hopes, had she expected succor of this sort. Her one thought had been to escape and find her way back to the tribe of Kerchak; but even this had appeared to her practically impossible, so closely did Toog watch her.

As Taug and Tarzan reached the grove where Toog had come upon his friends, the ape scent became so strong that both knew the quarry was but a short distance ahead. And so they went even more cautiously, for they wished to come upon the thief from behind if they could and charge him before he was aware of their presence. That a little gray-whiskered monkey had forestalled them they did not know, nor that three pairs of savage eyes were already watching their every move and waiting for them to come within reach of itching paws and slavering jowls.

On they came across the grove, and as they entered the path leading into the dense jungle beyond, a sudden "Kreeg-ah!" shrilled out close before them — a "Kreeg-ah" in the familiar voice of Teeka. The small brains of Toog and his companions had not been able to foresee that Teeka might betray them, and now that she had, they went wild with rage. Toog struck the she a mighty blow that felled her, and then the three rushed forth to do battle with Tarzan and Taug. The little monkey danced upon his perch and screamed with delight.

And indeed he might well be delighted, for it was a lovely fight. There were no preliminaries, no formalities, no introductions — the five bulls merely charged and clinched. They rolled in the narrow trail and into the thick verdure beside it. They bit and clawed and scratched and struck, and all the while they kept up the most frightful chorus of growlings and barkings and roarings. In five minutes they were torn and bleeding, and the little graybeard leaped high, shrilling his primitive bravos; but always his attitude was "thumbs down." He wanted to see something killed. He did not care whether it were friend or foe. It was blood he wanted — blood and death.

Taug had been set upon by Toog and another of the apes, while Tarzan had the third — a huge brute with the strength of a buffalo. Never before had Tarzan's assailant beheld so strange a creature as this slippery, hairless bull with which he battled. Sweat and blood covered Tarzan's sleek, brown hide. Again and again he slipped from the clutches of the great bull, and all the while he struggled to free his hunting knife from the scabbard in which it had stuck.

At length he succeeded — a brown hand shot out and clutched a hairy throat, another flew upward clutching the sharp blade. Three swift, powerful strokes and the bull relaxed with a groan, falling limp beneath his antagonist. Instantly Tarzan broke from the clutches of the dying bull and sprang to Taug's assistance. Toog saw him coming and wheeled to meet him. In the impact of the charge, Tarzan's knife was wrenched from his hand and then Toog closed with him. Now was the battle even — two against two — while on the verge, Teeka, now recovered from the blow that had felled her, slunk waiting for an opportunity to aid. She saw Tarzan's knife and picked it up. She never had used it, but knew how Tarzan used it. Always had she been afraid of the thing which dealt death to the mightiest of the jungle people with the ease that Tantor's great tusks deal death to Tantor's enemies.

She saw Tarzan's pocket pouch torn from his side, and with the curiosity of an ape, that even danger and excitement cannot entirely dispel, she picked this up, too.

Now the bulls were standing — the clinches had been broken. Blood streamed down their sides — their faces were crimsoned with it. Little graybeard was so fascinated that at last he had even forgotten to scream and dance; but sat rigid with delight in the enjoyment of the spectacle.

Back across the grove Tarzan and Taug forced their adversaries. Teeka followed slowly. She scarce knew what to do. She was lame and sore and exhausted from the frightful ordeal through which she had passed, and she had the confidence of her sex in the prowess of her mate and the other bull of her tribe — they would not need the help of a she in their battle with these two strangers.

The roars and screams of the fighters reverberated through the jungle, awakening the echoes in the distant hills. From the throat of Tarzan's antagonist had come a score of "Kreeg-ahs!" and now from behind came the reply he had awaited. Into the grove, barking and growling, came a score of huge bull apes — the fighting men of Toog's tribe.

Teeka saw them first and screamed a warning to Tarzan and Taug. Then she fled past the fighters toward the opposite side of the clearing, fear for a moment claiming her. Nor can one censure her after the frightful ordeal from which she was still suffering.

Down upon them came the great apes. In a moment

Tarzan and Taug would be torn to shreds that would later form the *piece de resistance* of the savage orgy of a Dum-Dum. Teeka turned to glance back. She saw the impending fate of her defenders and there sprung to life in her savage bosom the spark of martyrdom, that some common forbear had transmitted alike to Teeka, the wild ape, and the glorious women of a higher order who have invited death for their men. With a shrill scream she ran toward the battlers who were rolling in a great mass at the foot of one of the huge boulders which dotted the grove; but what could she do? The knife she held she could not use to advantage because of her lesser strength. She had seen Tarzan throw missiles, and she had learned this with many other things from her childhood playmate. She sought for something to throw and at last her fingers touched upon the hard objects in the pouch that had been torn from the ape-man. Tearing the receptacle open, she gathered a handful of shiny cylinders — heavy for their size, they seemed to her, and good missiles. With all her strength she hurled them at the apes battling in front of the granite boulder.

The result surprised Teeka quite as much as it did the apes. There was a loud explosion, which deafened the fighters, and a puff of acrid smoke. Never before had one there heard such a frightful noise. Screaming with terror, the stranger bulls leaped to their feet and fled back toward the stamping ground of their tribe, while Taug and Tarzan slowly gathered themselves together and arose, lame and bleeding, to their feet. They, too, would have fled had they not seen Teeka standing there before them, the knife and the pocket pouch in her hands.

"What was it?" asked Tarzan.

Teeka shook her head. "I hurled these at the stranger bulls," and she held forth another handful of the shiny metal cylinders with the dull gray, cone-shaped ends.

Tarzan looked at them and scratched his head.

"What are they?" asked Taug.

"I do not know," said Tarzan. "I found them."

The little monkey with the gray beard halted among the trees a mile away and huddled, terrified, against a branch. He did not know that the dead father of Tarzan of the Apes, reaching back out of the past across a span of twenty years, had saved his son's life.

Nor did Tarzan, Lord Greystoke, know it either.

A Jungle Joke

TIME SELDOM HUNG heavily upon Tarzan's
hands. Even where there is sameness there cannot be
monotony if most of the sameness consists in dodging
death first in one form and then in another; or in
inflicting death upon others. There is a spice to such
an existence; but even this Tarzan of the Apes varied
in activities of his own invention.

He was full grown now, with the grace of a Greek
god and the thews of a bull, and, by all the tenets of
apedom, should have been sullen, morose, and brood-
ing; but he was not. His spirits seemed not to age at
all — he was still a playful child, much to the discomfiture of his fellow-apes. They could not understand
him or his ways, for with maturity they quickly forgot
their youth and its pastimes.

Nor could Tarzan quite understand them. It seemed
strange to him that a few moons since, he had roped
Taug about an ankle and dragged him screaming
through the tall jungle grasses, and then rolled and

tumbled in good-natured mimic battle when the young ape had freed himself, and that today when he had come up behind the same Taug and pulled him over backward upon the turf, instead of the playful young ape, a great, snarling beast had whirled and leaped for his throat.

Easily Tarzan eluded the charge and quickly Taug's anger vanished, though it was not replaced with playfulness; yet the ape-man realized that Taug was not amused nor was he amusing. The big bull ape seemed to have lost whatever sense of humor he once may have possessed. With a grunt of disappointment, young Lord Greystoke turned to other fields of endeavor. A strand of black hair fell across one eye. He brushed it aside with the palm of a hand and a toss of his head. It suggested something to do, so he sought his quiver which lay cached in the hollow bole of a lightning-riven tree. Removing the arrows he turned the quiver upside down, emptying upon the ground the contents of its bottom — his few treasures. Among them was a flat bit of stone and a shell which he had picked up from the beach near his father's cabin.

With great care he rubbed the edge of the shell back and forth upon the flat stone until the soft edge was quite fine and sharp. He worked much as a barber does who hones a razor, and with every evidence of similar practice; but his proficiency was the result of years of painstaking effort. Unaided he had worked out a method of his own for putting an edge upon the shell — he even tested it with the ball of his thumb — and when it met with his approval he grasped a wisp of hair which fell across his eyes, grasped it between the thumb and first finger of his left hand and sawed upon it with the sharpened shell until it was severed. All around his head he went until his black shock was rudely bobbed with a ragged bang in front. For the appearance of it he cared nothing; but in the matter of safety and comfort it meant everything. A lock of hair falling in one's eyes at the wrong moment might mean all the difference between life and death, while straggly strands, hanging down one's back were most uncomfortable, especially when wet with dew or rain or perspiration.

As Tarzan labored at his tonsorial task, his active mind was busy with many things. He recalled his recent battle with Bolgani, the gorilla, the wounds of which were but just healed. He pondered the strange sleep adventures of his first dreams, and he smiled at the painful outcome of his last practical joke upon the tribe, when, dressed in the hide of Numa, the lion, he had come roaring upon them, only to be leaped upon and almost killed by the great bulls whom he had taught how to defend themselves from an attack of their ancient enemy.

His hair lopped off to his entire satisfaction, and seeing no possibility of pleasure in the company of the tribe, Tarzan swung leisurely into the trees and set off in the direction of his cabin; but when part way there his attention was attracted by a strong scent spoor coming from the north. It was the scent of the Gomangani.

Curiosity, that best-developed, common heritage of man and ape, always prompted Tarzan to investigate where the Gomangani were concerned. There was that about them which aroused his imagination. Possibly it was because of the diversity of their activities and interests. The apes lived to eat and sleep and propagate. The same was true of all the other denizens of the jungle, save the Gomangani.

These black fellows danced and sang, scratched around in the earth from which they had cleared the trees and under-brush; they watched things grow, and when they had ripened, they cut them down and put them in straw-thatched huts. They made bows and spears and arrows, poison, cooking pots, things of metal to wear around their arms and legs. If it hadn't been for their black faces, their hideously disfigured features, and the fact that one of them had slain Kala, Tarzan might have wished to be one of them. At least he sometimes thought so, but always at the thought there rose within him a strange revulsion of feeling, which he could not interpret or understand — he simply knew that he hated the Gomangani, and that he would rather be Histah, the snake, than one of these.

But their ways were interesting, and Tarzan never tired of spying upon them. and from them he learned much more than he realized, though always his principal thought was of some new way in which he could render their lives miserable. The baiting of the blacks was Tarzan's chief divertissement.

Tarzan realized now that the blacks were very near and that there were many of them, so he went silently and with great caution. Noiselessly he moved through the lush grasses of the open spaces, and where the forest was dense, swung from one swaying branch to another, or leaped lightly over tangled masses of fallen trees where there was no way through the lower terraces, and the ground was choked and impassable.

And so presently he came within sight of the black warriors of Mbonga, the chief. They were engaged in a pursuit with which Tarzan was more or less familiar, having watched them at it upon other occasions. They were placing and baiting a trap for Numa, the lion. In a cage upon wheels they were tying a kid, so fastening it that when Numa seized the unfortunate creature, the door of the cage would drop behind him, making him a prisoner.

These things the blacks had learned in their old home, before they escaped through the untracked jungle to their new village. Formerly they had dwelt in the Belgian Congo until the cruelties of their heartless oppressors had driven them to seek the safety of unexplored solitudes beyond the boundaries of Leopold's domain.

In their old life they often had trapped animals for the agents of European dealers, and had learned from them certain tricks, such as this one, which permitted them to capture even Numa without injuring him, and to transport him in safety and with comparative ease to their village.

No longer was there a white market for their savage wares; but there was still a sufficient incentive for the taking of Numa — alive. First was the necessity for ridding the jungle of man-eaters, and it was only after depredations by these grim and terrible scourges that a lion hunt was organized. Secondarily was the excuse for an orgy of celebration was the hunt successful, and the fact that such fetes were rendered doubly pleasurable by the presence of a live creature that might be put to death by torture.

Tarzan had witnessed these cruel rites in the past. Being himself more savage than the savage warriors of the Gomangani, he was not so shocked by the cruelty of them as he should have been, yet they did shock him. He could not understand the strange feeling of revulsion which possessed him at such times. He had no love for Numa, the lion, yet he bristled with rage when the blacks inflicted upon his enemy such indignities and cruelties as only the mind of the one creature molded in the image of God can conceive.

Upon two occasions he had freed Numa from the trap before the blacks had returned to discover the success or failure of their venture. He would do the same today — that he decided immediately he realized the nature of their intentions.

Leaving the trap in the center of a broad elephant trail near the drinking hole, the warriors turned back toward their village. On the morrow they would come again. Tarzan looked after them, upon his lips an unconscious sneer — the heritage of unguessed caste. He saw them file along the broad trail, beneath the overhanging verdure of leafy branch and looped and festooned creepers, brushing ebon shoulders against gorgeous blooms which inscrutable Nature has seen fit to lavish most profusely farthest from the eye of man.

As Tarzan watched, through narrowed lids, the last of the warriors disappear beyond a turn in the trail, his expression altered to the urge of a newborn thought. A slow, grim smile touched his lips. He looked down upon the frightened, bleating kid, advertising, in its fear and its innocence, its presence and its helplessness.

Dropping to the ground, Tarzan approached the trap and entered. Without disturbing the fiber cord, which was adjusted to drop the door at the proper time, he loosened the living bait, tucked it under an arm and stepped out of the cage.

With his hunting knife he quieted the frightened animal, severing its jugular; then he dragged it, bleeding, along the trail down to the drinking hole, the half smile persisting upon his ordinarily grave face. At the water's edge the ape-man stooped and with hunting knife and quick strong fingers deftly removed the dead kid's viscera. Scraping a hole in the mud, he buried these parts which he did not eat, and swinging the body to his shoulder took to the trees.

For a short distance he pursued his way in the wake of the black warriors, coming down presently to bury the meat of his kill where it would be safe from the depredations of Dango, the hyena, or the other meat-eating beasts and birds of the jungle. He was hungry. Had he been all beast he would have eaten; but his man-mind could entertain urges even more potent than those of the belly, and now he was concerned with an idea which kept a smile upon his lips and his eyes sparkling in anticipation. An idea, it was, which permitted him to forget that he was hungry.

The meat safely cached, Tarzan trotted along the elephant trail after the Gomangani. Two or three miles from the cage he overtook them and then he swung into the trees and followed above and behind them — waiting his chance.

Among the blacks was Rabba Kega, the witch-doctor. Tarzan hated them all; but Rabba Kega he especially hated. As the blacks filed along the winding path, Rabba Kega, being lazy, dropped behind. This Tarzan noted, and it filled him with satisfaction — his being radiated a grim and terrible content. Like an angel of death he hovered above the unsuspecting black.

Rabba Kega, knowing that the village was but a short distance ahead, sat down to rest. Rest well, O Rabba Kega! It is thy last opportunity.

Tarzan crept stealthily among the branches of the tree above the well-fed, self-satisfied witch-doctor. He made no noise that the dull ears of man could hear above the soughing of the gentle jungle breeze among the undulating foliage of the upper terraces, and when he came close above the black man he halted, well concealed by leafy branch and heavy creeper.

Rabba Kega sat with his back against the bole of a tree, facing Tarzan. The position was not such as the waiting beast of prey desired, and so, with the infinite patience of the wild hunter, the ape-man crouched motionless and silent as a graven image until the fruit should be ripe for the plucking. A poisonous insect buzzed angrily out of space. It loitered, circling, close to Tarzan's face. The ape-man saw and recognized it. The virus of its sting spelled death for lesser things than he — for him it would mean days of anguish. He did not move. His glittering eyes remained fixed upon Rabba Kega after acknowledging the presence of the winged torture by a single glance. He heard and followed the movements of the insect with his keen ears, and then he felt it alight upon his forehead. No muscle twitched, for the muscles of such as he are the servants of the brain. Down across his face crept the horrid thing — over nose and lips and chin. Upon his throat it paused, and turning, retraced its steps. Tarzan watched Rabba Kega. Now not even his eyes moved. So motionless he crouched that only death might counterpart his movelessness. The insect crawled upward over the nut-brown cheek and stopped with its antennae brushing the lashes of his lower lid. You or I would have started back, closing our eyes and striking at the thing; but you and I are the slaves, not the masters of our nerves. Had the thing crawled upon the eyeball of the ape-man, it is believable that he could yet have remained wide-eyed and rigid; but it did not. For a moment it loitered there close to the lower lid, then it rose and buzzed away.

Down toward Rabba Kega it buzzed and the black man heard it, saw it, struck at it, and was stung upon the cheek before he killed it. Then he rose with a howl of pain and anger, and as he turned up the trail toward the village of Mbonga, the chief, his broad, black back was exposed to the silent thing waiting above him.

And as Rabba Kega turned, a lithe figure shot outward and downward from the tree above upon his broad shoulders. The impact of the springing creature carried Rabba Kega to the ground. He felt strong jaws close upon his neck, and when he tried to scream, steel fingers throttled his throat. The powerful black warrior struggled to free himself; but he was as a child in the grip of his adversary.

Presently Tarzan released his grip upon the other's throat; but each time that Rabba Kega essayed a scream, the cruel fingers choked him painfully. At last the warrior desisted. Then Tarzan half rose and kneeled upon his victim's back, and when Rabba Kega struggled to arise, the ape-man pushed his face down into the dirt of the trail. With a bit of the rope that had secured the kid, Tarzan made Rabba Kega's wrists secure behind his back, then he rose and jerked his prisoner to his feet, faced him back along the trail and pushed him on ahead.

Not until he came to his feet did Rabba Kega obtain a square look at his assailant. When he saw that it was the white devil-god his heart sank within him and his knees trembled; but as he walked along the trail ahead of his captor and was neither injured nor molested his spirits slowly rose, so that he took heart again. Possibly the devil-god did not intend to kill him after all. Had he not had little Tibo in his power for days without harming him, and had he not spared Mo-maya, Tibo's mother, when he easily might have slain her?

And then they came upon the cage which Rabba Kega, with the other black warriors of the village of Mbonga, the chief, had placed and baited for Numa. Rabba Kega saw that the bait was gone, though there was no lion within the cage, nor was the door dropped. He saw and he was filled with wonder not unmixed with apprehension. It entered his dull brain that in some way this combination of circumstances had a connection with his presence there as the prisoner of the white devil-god.

Nor was he wrong. Tarzan pushed him roughly into the cage, and in another moment Rabba Kega understood. Cold sweat broke from every pore of his body — he trembled as with ague — for the ape-man was binding him securely in the very spot the kid had previously occupied. The witch-doctor pleaded, first for his life, and then for a death less cruel; but he might as well have saved his pleas for Numa, since already they were directed toward a wild beast who understood no word of what he said.

But his constant jabbering not only annoyed Tarzan,

who worked in silence, but suggested that later the black might raise his voice in cries for succor, so he stepped out of the cage, gathered a handful of grass and a small stick and returning, jammed the grass into Rabba Kega's mouth, laid the stick crosswise between his teeth and fastened it there with the thong from Rabba Kega's loin cloth. Now could the witch-doctor but roll his eyes and sweat. Thus Tarzan left him.

The ape-man went first to the spot where he had cached the body of the kid. Digging it up, he ascended into a tree and proceeded to satisfy his hunger. What remained he again buried; then he swung away through the trees to the water hole, and going to the spot where fresh, cold water bubbled from between two rocks, he drank deeply. The other beasts might wade in and drink stagnant water; but not Tarzan of the Apes. In such matters he was fastidious. From his hands he washed every trace of the repugnant scent of the Gomangani, and from his face the blood of the kid. Rising, he stretched himself not unlike some huge, lazy cat, climbed into a near-by tree and fell asleep.

When he awoke it was dark, though a faint luminosity still tinged the western heavens. A lion moaned and coughed as it strode through the jungle toward water. It was approaching the drinking hole. Tarzan grinned sleepily, changed his position and fell asleep again.

When the blacks of Mbonga, the chief, reached their village they discovered that Rabba Kega was not among them. When several hours had elapsed they decided that something had happened to him, and it was the hope of the majority of the tribe that whatever had happened to him might prove fatal. They did not love the witch-doctor. Love and fear seldom are playmates; but a warrior is a warrior, and so Mbonga organized a searching party. That his own grief was not unassuagable might have been gathered from the fact that he remained at home and went to sleep. The young warriors whom he sent out remained steadfast to their purpose for fully half an hour, when, unfortunately for Rabba Kega — upon so slight a thing may the fate of a man rest — a honey bird attracted the attention of the searchers and led them off for the delicious store it previously had marked down for betrayal, and Rabba Kega's doom was sealed.

When the searchers returned empty handed, Mbonga was wroth; but when he saw the great store of honey they brought with them his rage subsided. Already Tubuto, young, agile and evil-minded, with face hideously painted, was practicing the black art upon a sick infant in the fond hope of succeeding to the office and perquisites of Rabba Kega. Tonight the women of the old witch-doctor would moan and howl. Tomorrow he would be forgotten. Such is life, such is fame, such is power — in the center of the world's highest civilization, or in the depths of the black, primeval jungle. Always, everywhere, man is man, nor has he altered greatly beneath his veneer since he scurried into a hole between two rocks to escape the tyrannosaurus six million years ago.

The morning following the disappearance of Rabba Kega, the warriors set out with Mbonga, the chief, to examine the trap they had set for Numa. Long before they reached the cage, they heard the roaring of a great lion and guessed that they had made a successful bag, so it was with shouts of joy that they approached the spot where they should find their captive.

Yes! There he was, a great, magnificent specimen — a huge, black-maned lion. The warriors were frantic with delight. They leaped into the air and uttered savage cries — hoarse victory cries, and then they came closer, and the cries died upon their lips, and their eyes went wide so that the whites showed all around their irises, and their pendulous lower lips drooped with their drooping jaws. They drew back in terror at the sight within the cage — the mauled and mutilated corpse of what had, yesterday, been Rabba Kega, the witch-doctor.

The captured lion had been too angry and frightened to feed upon the body of his kill; but he had vented upon it much of his rage, until it was a frightful thing to behold.

From his perch in a near-by tree Tarzan of the Apes, Lord Greystoke, looked down upon the black warriors and grinned. Once again his self-pride in his ability as a practical joker asserted itself. It had lain dormant for some time following the painful mauling he had received that time he leaped among the apes of Kerchak clothed in the skin of Numa; but this joke was a decided success.

After a few moments of terror, the blacks came closer to the cage, rage taking the place of fear — rage and curiosity. How had Rabba Kega happened to be in the cage? Where was the kid? There was no sign nor remnant of the original bait. They looked closely and they saw, to their horror, that the corpse of their erstwhile fellow was bound with the very cord with which they had secured the kid. Who could have done this thing? They looked at one another.

Tubuto was the first to speak. He had come hopefully out with the expedition that morning. Somewhere he might find evidence of the death of Rabba Kega. Now he had found it, and he was the first to find an explanation.

"The white devil-god," he whispered. "It is the work of the white devil-god!"

No one contradicted Tubuto, for, indeed, who else could it have been but the great, hairless ape they all so feared? And so their hatred of Tarzan increased again with an increased fear of him. And Tarzan sat in his tree and hugged himself.

No one there felt sorrow because of the death of

Rabba Kega; but each of the blacks experienced a personal fear of the ingenious mind which might discover for any of them a death equally horrible to that which the witch-doctor had suffered. It was a subdued and thoughtful company which dragged the captive lion along the broad elephant path back to the village of Mbonga, the chief.

And it was with a sigh of relief that they finally rolled it into the village and closed the gates behind them. Each had experienced the sensation of being spied upon from the moment they left the spot where the trap had been set, though none had seen or heard aught to give tangible food to his fears.

At the sight of the body within the cage with the lion, the women and children of the village set up a most frightful lamentation, working themselves into a joyous hysteria which far transcended the happy misery derived by their more civilized prototypes who make a business of dividing their time between the movies and the neighborhood funerals of friends and strangers — especially strangers.

From a tree overhanging the palisade, Tarzan watched all that passed within the village. He saw the frenzied women tantalizing the great lion with sticks and stones. The cruelty of the blacks toward a captive always induced in Tarzan a feeling of angry contempt for the Gomangani. Had he attempted to analyze this feeling he would have found it difficult, for during all his life he had been accustomed to sights of suffering and cruelty. He, himself, was cruel. All the beasts of the jungle were cruel; but the cruelty of the blacks was of a different order. It was the cruelty of wanton torture of the helpless, while the cruelty of Tarzan and the other beasts was the cruelty of necessity or of passion.

Perhaps, had he known it, he might have credited this feeling of repugnance at the sight of unnecessary suffering to heredity — to the germ of British love of fair play which had been bequeathed to him by his father and his mother; but, of course, he did not know, since he still believed that his mother had been Kala, the great ape.

And just in proportion as his anger rose against the Gomangani his savage sympathy went out to Numa, the lion, for, though Numa was his lifetime enemy, there was neither bitterness nor contempt in Tarzan's sentiments toward him. In the ape-man's mind, therefore, the determination formed to thwart the blacks and liberate the lion; but he must accomplish this in some way which would cause the Gomangani the greatest chagrin and discomfiture.

As he squatted there watching the proceeding beneath him, he saw the warriors seize upon the cage once more and drag it between two huts. Tarzan knew that it would remain there now until evening, and that the blacks were planning a feast and orgy in celebration of their capture. When he saw that two warriors were placed beside the cage, and that these drove off the women and children and young men who would have eventually tortured Numa to death, he knew that the lion would be safe until he was needed for the evening's entertainment, when he would be more cruelly and scientifically tortured for the edification of the entire tribe.

Now Tarzan preferred to bait the blacks in as theatric a manner as his fertile imagination could evolve. He had some half-formed conception of their superstitious fears and of their especial dread of night, and so he decided to wait until darkness fell and the blacks partially worked to hysteria by their dancing and religious rites before he took any steps toward the freeing of Numa. In the meantime, he hoped, an idea adequate to the possibilities of the various factors at hand would occur to him. Nor was it long before one did.

He had swung off through the jungle to search for

food when the plan came to him. At first it made him smile a little and then look dubious, for he still retained a vivid memory of the dire results that had followed the carrying out of a very wonderful idea along almost identical lines, yet he did not abandon his intention, and a moment later, food temporarily forgotten, he was swinging through the middle terraces in rapid flight toward the stamping ground of the tribe of Ker-chak, the great ape.

As was his wont, he alighted in the midst of the little band without announcing his approach save by a hideous scream just as he sprang from a branch above them. Fortunate are the apes of Kerchak that their kind is not subject to heart failure, for the methods of Tarzan subjected them to one severe shock after another, nor could they ever accustom themselves to the ape-man's peculiar style of humor.

Now, when they saw who it was they merely snarled and grumbled angrily for a moment and then resumed their feeding or their napping which he had interrupted, and he, having had his little joke, made his way to the hollow tree where he kept his treasures hid from the inquisitive eyes and fingers of his fellows and the mischievous little manus. Here he withdrew a closely rolled hide — the hide of Numa with the head on; a clever bit of primitive curing and mounting, which had once been the property of the witch-doctor, Rabba Kega, until Tarzan had stolen it from the village.

With this he made his way back through the jungle toward the village of the blacks, stopping to hunt and feed upon the way, and, in the afternoon, even napping for an hour, so that it was already dusk when he entered the great tree which overhung the palisade and gave him a view of the entire village. He saw that Numa was still alive and that the guards were even dozing beside the cage. A lion is no great novelty to a black man in the lion country, and the first keen edge of their desire to worry the brute having worn off, the villagers paid little or no attention to the great cat, preferring now to await the grand event of the night.

Nor was it long after dark before the festivities commenced. To the beating of tom-toms, a lone warrior, crouched half doubled, leaped into the firelight in the center of a great circle of other warriors, behind whom stood or squatted the women and the children. The dancer was painted and armed for the hunt and his movements and gestures suggested the search for the spoor of game. Bending low, sometimes resting for a moment on one knee, he searched the ground for signs of the quarry; again he poised, statuesque, listening. The warrior was young and lithe and graceful; he was full-muscled and arrow-straight. The firelight glistened upon his ebon body and brought out into bold relief the grotesque designs painted upon his face, breasts, and abdomen.

Presently he bent low to the earth, then leaped high in air. Every line of face and body showed that he had struck the scent. Immediately he leaped toward the circle of warriors about him, telling them of his find and summoning them to the hunt. It was all in pantomime; but so truly done that even Tarzan could follow it all to the least detail.

He saw the other warriors grasp their hunting spears and leap to their feet to join in the graceful, stealthy "stalking dance." It was very interesting; but Tarzan realized that if he was to carry his design to a successful conclusion he must act quickly. He had seen these dances before and knew that after the stalk would come the game at bay and then the kill, during which Numa would be surrounded by warriors, and unapproachable.

With the lion's skin under one arm the ape-man dropped to the ground in the dense shadows beneath the tree and then circled behind the huts until he came out directly in the rear of the cage, in which Numa paced nervously to and fro. The cage was now unguarded, the two warriors having left it to take their places among the other dancers.

Behind the cage Tarzan adjusted the lion's skin about him, just as he had upon that memorable occasion when the apes of Kerchak, failing to pierce his disguise, had all but slain him. Then, on hands and knees, he crept forward, emerged from between the two huts and stood a few paces back of the dusky audience, whose whole attention was centered upon the dancers before them.

Tarzan saw that the blacks had now worked themselves to a proper pitch of nervous excitement to be ripe for the lion. In a moment the ring of spectators would break at a point nearest the caged lion and the victim would be rolled into the center of the circle. It was for this moment that Tarzan waited.

At last it came. A signal was given by Mbonga, the chief, at which the women and children immediately in front of Tarzan rose and moved to one side, leaving a broad path opening toward the caged lion. At the same instant Tarzan gave voice to the low, couching roar of an angry lion and slunk slowly forward through the open lane toward the frenzied dancers.

A woman saw him first and screamed. Instantly there was a panic in the immediate vicinity of the ape-man. The strong light from the fire fell full upon the lion head and the blacks leaped to the conclusion, as Tarzan had known they would, that their captive had escaped his cage.

With another roar, Tarzan moved forward. The dancing warriors paused but an instant. They had been hunting a lion securely housed within a strong cage, and now that he was at liberty among them, an entirely different aspect was placed upon the matter. Their nerves were not attuned to this emergency. The women

and children already had fled to the questionable safety
of the nearest huts, and the warriors were not long in
following their example, so that presently Tarzan was
left in sole possession of the village street.

But not for long. Nor did he wish to be left thus
long alone. It would not comport with his scheme.
Presently a head peered forth from a near-by hut, and
then another and another until a score or more of
warriors were looking out upon him, waiting for his
next move — waiting for the lion to charge or to
attempt to escape from the village.

Their spears were ready in their hands against either
a charge or a bolt for freedom, and then the lion rose
erect upon its hind legs, the tawny skin dropped from
it and there stood revealed before them in the firelight
the straight young figure of the white devil-god.

For an instant the blacks were too astonished to act.
They feared this apparition fully as much as they did
Numa, yet they would gladly have slain the thing could
they quickly enough have gathered together their wits;
but fear and superstition and a natural mental density
held them paralyzed while the ape-man stooped and
gathered up the lion skin. They saw him turn then and
walk back into the shadows at the far end of the village.
Not until then did they gain courage to pursue him,
and when they had come in force, with brandished
spears and loud war cries, the quarry was gone.

Not an instant did Tarzan pause in the tree. Throwing the skin over a branch he leaped again into the
village upon the opposite side of the great bole, and
diving into the shadow of a hut, ran quickly to where
lay the caged lion. Springing to the top of the cage he
pulled upon the cord which raised the door, and a
moment later a great lion in the prime of his strength
and vigor leaped out into the village.

The warriors, returning from a futile search for Tarzan, saw him step into the firelight. Ah! there was the

devil-god again, up to his old trick. Did he think he could twice fool the men of Mbonga, the chief, the same way in so short a time? They would show him! For long they had waited for such an opportunity to rid themselves forever of this fearsome jungle demon. As one they rushed forward with raised spears.

The women and the children came from the huts to witness the slaying of the devil-god. The lion turned blazing eyes upon them and then swung about toward the advancing warriors.

With shouts of savage joy and triumph they came toward him, menacing him with their spears. The devil-god was theirs!

And then, with a frightful roar, Numa, the lion, charged.

The men of Mbonga, the chief, met Numa with ready spears and screams of raillery. In a solid mass of muscled ebony they waited the coming of the devil-god; yet beneath their brave exteriors lurked a haunting fear that all might not be quite well with them — that this strange creature could yet prove invulnerable to their weapons and inflict upon them full punishment for their effrontery. The charging lion was all too lifelike — they saw that in the brief instant of the charge; but beneath the tawny hide they knew was hid the soft flesh of the white man, and how could that withstand the assault of many war spears?

In their forefront stood a huge young warrior in the full arrogance of his might and his youth. Afraid? Not he! He laughed as Numa bore down upon him; he laughed and couched his spear, setting the point for the broad breast. And then the lion was upon him. A great paw swept away the heavy war spear, splintering it as the hand of man might splinter a dry twig.

Down went the black, his skull crushed by another blow. And then the lion was in the midst of the warriors, clawing and tearing to right and left. Not for long did they stand their ground; but a dozen men were mauled before the others made good their escape from those frightful talons and gleaming fangs.

In terror the villagers fled hither and thither. No hut seemed a sufficiently secure asylum with Numa ranging within the palisade. From one to another fled the frightened blacks, while in the center of the village Numa stood glaring and growling above his kills.

At last a tribesman flung wide the gates of the village and sought safety amid the branches of the forest trees beyond. Like sheep his fellows followed him, until the lion and his dead remained alone in the village.

From the nearer trees the men of Mbonga saw the lion lower his great head and seize one of his victims by the shoulder and then with slow and stately tread move down the village street past the open gates and on into the jungle. They saw and shuddered, and from another tree Tarzan of the Apes saw and smiled.

A full hour elapsed after the lion had disappeared with his feast before the blacks ventured down from the trees and returned to their village. Wide eyes rolled from side to side, and naked flesh contracted more to the chill of fear than to the chill of the jungle night.

"It was he all the time," murmured one. "It was the devil-god."

"He changed himself from a lion to a man, and back again into a lion," whispered another.

"And he dragged Mweeza into the forest and is eating him," said a third, shuddering.

"We are no longer safe here," wailed a fourth. "Let us take our belongings and search for another village site far from the haunts of the wicked devil-god."

But with morning came renewed courage, so that the experiences of the preceding evening had little other effect than to increase their fear of Tarzan and strengthen their belief in his supernatural origin.

And thus waxed the fame and the power of the

ape-man in the mysterious haunts of the savage jungle where he ranged, mightiest of beasts because of the man-mind which directed his giant muscles and his flawless courage.

Tarzan Rescues the Moon

*T*HE MOON SHONE down out of a cloudless sky
— a huge, swollen moon that seemed so close to earth
that one might wonder that she did not brush the
crooning tree tops. It was night, and Tarzan was abroad
in the jungle — Tarzan, the ape-man; mighty fighter,
mighty hunter. Why he swung through the dark shadows of the somber forest he could not have told you.
It was not that he was hungry — he had fed well this
day, and in a safe cache were the remains of his kill,
ready against the coming of a new appetite. Perhaps it
was the very joy of living that urged him from his
arboreal couch to pit his muscles and his senses against
the jungle night, and then, too, Tarzan always was
goaded by an intense desire to know.

The jungle which is presided over by Kudu, the sun,
is a very different jungle from that of Goro, the moon.
The diurnal jungle has its own aspect — its own lights
and shades, its own birds, its own blooms, its own
beasts; its noises are the noises of the day. The lights
and shades of the nocturnal jungle are as different as
one might imagine the lights and shades of another
world to differ from those of our world; its beasts, its

blooms, and its birds are not those of the jungle of
Kudu, the sun.

Because of these differences Tarzan loved to investigate the jungle by night. Not only was the life another
life; but it was richer in numbers and in romance; it
was richer in dangers, too, and to Tarzan of the Apes
danger was the spice of life. And the noises of the
jungle night — the roar of the lion, the scream of the
leopard, the hideous laughter of Dango, the hyena,
were music to the ears of the ape-man.

The soft padding of unseen feet, the rustling of leaves
and grasses to the passage of fierce beasts, the sheen of
opalesque eyes flaming through the dark, the million
sounds which proclaimed the teeming life that one
might hear and scent, though seldom see, constituted
the appeal of the nocturnal jungle to Tarzan.

Tonight he had swung a wide circle — toward the east
first and then toward the south, and now he was
rounding back again into the north. His eyes, his ears
and his keen nostrils were ever on the alert. Mingled
with the sounds he knew, there were strange sounds —
weird sounds which he never heard until after Kudu
had sought his lair below the far edge of the big
water-sounds which belonged to Goro, the moon —
and to the mysterious period of Goro's supremacy.
These sounds often caused Tarzan profound speculation. They baffled him because he thought that he
knew his jungle so well that there could be nothing
within it unfamiliar to him. Sometimes he thought
that as colors and forms appeared to differ by night
from their familiar daylight aspects, so sounds altered
with the passage of Kudu and the coming of Goro, and
these thoughts roused within his brain a vague conjec-
ture that perhaps Goro and Kudu influenced these
changes. And what more natural that eventually he
came to attribute to the sun and the moon personali-
ties as real as his own? The sun was a living creature

and ruled the day. The moon, endowed with brains and miraculous powers, ruled the night.

Thus functioned the untrained man-mind groping through the dark night of ignorance for an explanation of the things he could not touch or smell or hear and of the great, unknown powers of nature which he could not see.

As Tarzan swung north again upon his wide circle the scent of the Gomangani came to his nostrils, mixed with the acrid odor of wood smoke. The ape-man moved quickly in the direction from which the scent was borne down to him upon the gentle night wind. Presently the ruddy sheen of a great fire filtered through the foliage to him ahead, and when Tarzan came to a halt in the trees near it, he saw a party of half a dozen black warriors huddled close to the blaze. It was evidently a hunting party from the village of Mbonga, the chief, caught out in the jungle after dark. In a rude circle about them they had constructed a thorn boma which, with the aid of the fire, they apparently hoped would discourage the advances of the larger carnivora.

That hope was not conviction was evidenced by the very palpable terror in which they crouched, wide-eyed and trembling, for already Numa and Sabor were moaning through the jungle toward them. There were other creatures, too, in the shadows beyond the fire-light. Tarzan could see their yellow eyes flaming there. The blacks saw them and shivered. Then one arose and grasping a burning branch from the fire hurled it at the eyes, which immediately disappeared. The black sat down again. Tarzan watched and saw that it was several minutes before the eyes began to reappear in twos and fours.

Then came Numa, the lion, and Sabor, his mate. The other eyes scattered to right and left before the menacing growls of the great cats, and then the huge orbs of the man-eaters flamed alone out of the darkness. Some of the blacks threw themselves upon their faces and moaned; but he who before had hurled the burning branch now hurled another straight at the faces of the hungry lions, and they, too, disappeared as had the lesser lights before them. Tarzan was much interested. He saw a new reason for the nightly fires maintained by the blacks — a reason in addition to those connected with warmth and light and cooking. The beasts of the jungle feared fire, and so fire was, in a measure, a protection from them. Tarzan himself knew a certain awe of fire. Once he had, in investigating an abandoned fire in the village of the blacks, picked up a live coal. Since then he had maintained a respectful distance from such fires as he had seen. One experience had sufficed.

For a few minutes after the black hurled the firebrand no eyes appeared, though Tarzan could hear the soft padding of feet all about him. Then flashed once more the twin fire spots that marked the return of the lord of the jungle and a moment later, upon a slightly lower level, there appeared those of Sabor, his mate.

For some time they remained fixed and unwavering — a constellation of fierce stars in the jungle night — then the male lion advanced slowly toward the boma, where all but a single black still crouched in trembling terror. When this lone guardian saw that Numa was again approaching, he threw another firebrand, and, as before, Numa retreated and with him Sabor, the lioness; but not so far, this time, nor for so long. Almost instantly they turned and began circling the boma, their eyes turning constantly toward the firelight, while low, throaty growls evidenced their increasing displeasure. Beyond the lions glowed the flaming eyes of the lesser satellites, until the black jungle was shot all around the black men's camp with little spots of fire.

Again and again the black warrior hurled his puny brands at the two big cats; but Tarzan noticed that Numa paid little or no attention to them after the first few retreats. The ape-man knew by Numa's voice that the lion was hungry and surmised that he had made up his mind to feed upon a Gomangani; but would he dare a closer approach to the dreaded flames?

Even as the thought was passing in Tarzan's mind, Numa stopped his restless pacing and faced the boma. For a moment he stood motionless, except for the quick, nervous up-curving of his tail, then he walked deliberately forward, while Sabor moved restlessly to and fro where he had left her. The black man called to his comrades that the lion was coming, but they were too far gone in fear to do more than huddle closer together and moan more loudly than before.

Seizing a blazing branch the man cast it straight into the face of the lion. There was an angry roar, followed by a swift charge. With a single bound the savage beast cleared the boma wall as, with almost equal agility, the warrior cleared it upon the opposite side and, chancing the dangers lurking in the darkness, bolted for the nearest tree.

Numa was out of the boma almost as soon as he was inside it; but as he went back over the low thorn wall, he took a screaming Negro with him. Dragging his victim along the ground he walked back toward Sabor, the lioness, who joined him, and the two continued into the blackness, their savage growls mingling with the piercing shrieks of the doomed and terrified man.

At a little distance from the blaze the lions halted, there ensued a short succession of unusually vicious growls and roars, during which the cries and moans of the black man ceased — forever.

Presently Numa reappeared in the firelight. He made a second trip into the boma and the former grisly tragedy was reenacted with another howling victim.

Tarzan rose and stretched lazily. The entertainment was beginning to bore him. He yawned and turned upon his way toward the clearing where the tribe would be sleeping in the encircling trees.

Yet even when he had found his familiar crotch and curled himself for slumber, he felt no desire to sleep. For a long time he lay awake thinking and dreaming. He looked up into the heavens and watched the moon and the stars. He wondered what they were and what power kept them from falling. His was an inquisitive mind. Always he had been full of questions concerning all that passed around him; but there never had been one to answer his questions. In childhood he had wanted to *know,* and, denied almost all knowledge, he still, in manhood, was filled with the great, unsatisfied curiosity of a child.

He was never quite content merely to perceive that things happened — he desired to know *why* they happened. He wanted to know what made things go. The secret of life interested him immensely. The miracle of death he could not quite fathom. Upon innumerable occasions he had investigated the internal mechanism of his kills, and once or twice he had opened the chest cavity of victims in time to see the heart still pumping.

He had learned from experience that a knife thrust through this organ brought immediate death nine times out of ten, while he might stab an antagonist innumerable times in other places without even disabling him. And so he had come to think of the heart, or, as he called it, "the red thing that breathes," as the seat and origin of life.

The brain and its functionings he did not comprehend at all. That his sense perceptions were transmitted to his brain and there translated, classified, and labeled was something quite beyond him. He thought that his fingers knew when they touched something, that his eyes knew when they saw, his ears when they heard, his nose when it scented.

He considered his throat, epidermis, and the hairs of his head as the three principal seats of emotion. When Kala had been slain a peculiar choking sensation had possessed his throat; contact with Histah, the snake, imparted an unpleasant sensation to the skin of his whole body; while the approach of an enemy made the hairs on his scalp stand erect.

Imagine, if you can, a child filled with the wonders of nature, bursting with queries and surrounded only by beasts of the jungle to whom his questionings were as strange as Sanskrit would have been. If he asked Gunto what made it rain, the big old ape would but gaze at him in dumb astonishment for an instant and then return to his interesting and edifying search for fleas; and when he questioned Mumga, who was very old and should have been very wise, but wasn't, as to the reason for the closing of certain flowers after Kudu had deserted the sky, and the opening of others during the night, he was surprised to discover that Mumga had never noticed these interesting facts, though she could tell to an inch just where the fattest grub worm should be hiding.

To Tarzan these things were wonders. They appealed to his intellect and to his imagination. He saw the flowers close and open; he saw certain blooms which turned their faces always toward the sun; he saw leaves which moved when there was no breeze; he saw vines crawl like living things up the boles and over the branches of great trees; and to Tarzan of the Apes the flowers and the vines and the trees were living creatures. He often talked to them, as he talked to Goro, the moon, and Kudu, the sun, and always was he disappointed that they did not reply. He asked them questions; but they could not answer, though he knew that the whispering of the leaves was the language of the leaves — they talked with one another.

The wind he attributed to the trees and grasses. He thought that they swayed themselves to and fro, creating the wind. In no other way could he account for this phenomenon. The rain he finally attributed to the stars, the moon, and the sun; but his hypothesis was entirely unlovely and unpoetical.

Tonight as Tarzan lay thinking, there sprang to his fertile imagination an explanation of the stars and the moon. He became quite excited about it. Taug was sleeping in a near-by crotch. Tarzan swung over beside him.

"Taug!" he cried. Instantly the great bull was awake and bristling, sensing danger from the nocturnal summons. "Look, Taug!" exclaimed Tarzan, pointing toward the stars. "See the eyes of Numa and Sabor, of Sheeta and Dango. They wait around Goro to leap in upon him for their kill. See the eyes and the nose and the mouth of Goro. And the light that shines upon his face is the light of the great fire he has built to frighten away Numa and Sabor and Dango and Sheeta.

"All about him are the eyes, Taug, you can see them! But they do not come very close to the fire — there are few eyes close to Goro. They fear the fire! It is the fire that saves Goro from Numa. Do you see them, Taug? Some night Numa will be very hungry and very angry — then he will leap over the thorn bushes which encircle Goro and we will have no more light after Kudu seeks his lair — the night will be black with the blackness that comes when Goro is lazy and sleeps late into the night, or when he wanders through the skies by day, forgetting the jungle and its people."

Taug looked stupidly at the heavens and then at Tarzan. A meteor fell, blazing a flaming way through the sky.

"Look!" cried Tarzan. "Goro has thrown a burning branch at Numa."

Taug grumbled. "Numa is down below," he said.

"Numa does not hunt above the trees." But he looked curiously and a little fearfully at the bright stars above him, as though he saw them for the first time, and doubtless it was the first time that Taug ever had seen the stars, though they had been in the sky above him every night of his life. To Taug they were as the gorgeous jungle blooms — he could not eat them and so he ignored them.

Taug fidgeted and was nervous. For a long time he lay sleepless, watching the stars — the flaming eyes of the beasts of prey surrounding Goro, the moon — Goro, by whose light the apes danced to the beating of their earthen drums. If Goro should be eaten by Numa there could be no more Dum-Dums. Taug was overwhelmed by the thought. He glanced at Tarzan half fearfully. Why was his friend so different from the others of the tribe? No one else whom Taug ever had known had had such queer thoughts as Tarzan. The ape scratched his head and wondered, dimly, if Tarzan was a safe companion, and then he recalled slowly, and by a laborious mental process, that Tarzan had served him better than any other of the apes, even the strong and wise bulls of the tribe.

Tarzan it was who had freed him from the blacks at the very time that Taug had thought Tarzan wanted Teeka. It was Tarzan who had saved Taug's little balu from death. It was Tarzan who had conceived and carried out the plan to pursue Teeka's abductor and rescue the stolen one. Tarzan had fought and bled in Taug's service so many times that Taug, although only a brutal ape, had had impressed upon his mind a fierce loyalty which nothing now could swerve — his friendship for Tarzan had become a habit, a tradition almost, which would endure while Taug endured. He never showed any outward demonstration of affection — he growled at Tarzan as he growled at the other bulls who came too close while he was feeding — but he would have died for Tarzan. He knew it and Tarzan knew it; but of such things apes do not speak — their vocabulary, for the finer instincts, consisting more of actions than words. But now Taug was worried, and he fell asleep again still thinking of the strange words of his fellow.

The following day he thought of them again, and without any intention of disloyalty he mentioned to Gunto what Tarzan had suggested about the eyes surrounding Goro, and the possibility that sooner or later Numa would charge the moon and devour him. To the apes all large things in nature are male, and so Goro, being the largest creature in the heavens by night, was, to them, a bull.

Gunto bit a sliver from a horny finger and recalled the fact that Tarzan had once said that the trees talked to one another, and Gozan recounted having seen the ape-man dancing alone in the moonlight with Sheeta, the panther. They did not know that Tarzan had roped the savage beast and tied him to a tree before he came to earth and leaped about before the rearing cat, to tantalize him.

Others told of seeing Tarzan ride upon the back of Tantor, the elephant; of his bringing the black boy, Tibo, to the tribe, and of mysterious things with which he communed in the strange lair by the sea. They had never understood his books, and after he had shown them to one or two of the tribe and discovered that even the pictures carried no impression to their brains, he had desisted.

"Tarzan is not an ape," said Gunto. "He will bring Numa to eat us, as he is bringing him to eat Goro. We should kill him."

Immediately Taug bristled. Kill Tarzan! "First you will kill Taug," he said, and lumbered away to search for food.

But others joined the plotters. They thought of many

things which Tarzan had done — things which apes did not do and could not understand. Again Gunto voiced the opinion that the Tarmangani, the white ape, should be slain, and the others, filled with terror about the stories they had heard, and thinking Tarzan was planning to slay Goro, greeted the proposal with growls of accord.

Among them was Teeka, listening with all her ears; but her voice was not raised in furtherance of the plan. Instead she bristled, showing her fangs, and afterward she went away in search of Tarzan; but she could not find him, as he was roaming far afield in search of meat. She found Taug, though, and told him what the others were planning, and the great bull stamped upon the ground and roared. His bloodshot eyes blazed with wrath, his upper lip curled up to expose his fighting fangs, and the hair upon his spine stood erect, and then a rodent scurried across the open and Taug sprang to seize it. In an instant he seemed to have forgotten his rage against the enemies of his friend; but such is the mind of an ape.

Several miles away Tarzan of the Apes lolled upon the broad head of Tantor, the elephant. He scratched beneath the great ears with the point of a sharp stick, and he talked to the huge pachyderm of everything which filled his black-thatched head. Little, or nothing, of what he said did Tantor understand; but Tantor is a good listener. Swaying from side to side he stood there enjoying the companionship of his friend, the friend he loved, and absorbing the delicious sensations of the scratching.

Numa, the lion, caught the scent of man, and warily stalked it until he came within sight of his prey upon the head of the mighty tusker; then he turned, growling and muttering, away in search of more propitious hunting grounds.

The elephant caught the scent of the lion, borne to

him by an eddying breeze, and lifting his trunk trumpeted loudly. Tarzan stretched back luxuriously, lying supine at full length along the rough hide. Flies swarmed about his face; but with a leafy branch torn from a tree he lazily brushed them away.

"Tantor," he said, "it is good to be alive. It is good to lie in the cool shadows. It is good to look upon the green trees and the bright colors of the flowers — upon everything which Bulamutumumo has put here for us. He is very good to us, Tantor; He has given you tender leaves and bark, and rich grasses to eat; to me He has given Bara and Horta and Pisah, the fruits and the nuts and the roots. He provides for each the food that each likes best. All that He asks is that we be strong enough or cunning enough to go forth and take it. Yes, Tantor, it is good to live. I should hate to die."

Tantor made a little sound in his throat and curled his trunk upward that he might caress the ape-man's cheek with the finger at its tip.

"Tantor," said Tarzan presently, "turn and feed in the direction of the tribe of Kerchak, the great ape, that Tarzan may ride home upon your head without walking."

The tusker turned and moved slowly off along a broad, tree-arched trail, pausing occasionally to pluck a tender branch, or strip the edible bark from an adjacent tree. Tarzan sprawled face downward upon the beast's head and back, his legs hanging on either side, his head supported by his open palms, his elbows resting on the broad cranium. And thus they made their leisurely way toward the gathering place of the tribe.

Just before they arrived at the clearing from the north there reached it from the south another figure — that of a well-knit black warrior, who stepped cautiously through the jungle, every sense upon the alert against the many dangers which might lurk anywhere along the way. Yet he passed beneath the southernmost sentry that was posted in a great tree commanding the trail from the south. The ape permitted the Gomangani to pass unmolested, for he saw that he was alone; but the moment that the warrior had entered the clearing a loud "Kreeg-ah!" rang out from behind him, immediately followed by a chorus of replies from different directions, as the great bulls crashed through the trees in answer to the summons of their fellow.

The black man halted at the first cry and looked about him. He could see nothing, but he knew the voice of the hairy tree men whom he and his kind feared, not alone because of the strength and ferocity of the savage beings, but as well through a superstitious terror engendered by the man-like appearance of the apes.

But Bulabantu was no coward. He heard the apes all about him; he knew that escape was probably impossible, so he stood his ground, his spear ready in his hand and a war cry trembling on his lips. He would sell his life dearly, would Bulabantu, under-chief of the village of Mbonga, the chief.

Tarzan and Tantor were but a short distance away when the first cry of the sentry rang out through the quiet jungle. Like a flash the ape-man leaped from the elephant's back to a near-by tree and was swinging rapidly in the direction of the clearing before the echoes of the first "Kreeg-ah" had died away. When he arrived he saw a dozen bulls circling a single Gomangani. With a blood-curdling scream Tarzan sprang to the attack. He hated the blacks even more than did the apes, and here was an opportunity for a kill in the open. What had the Gomangani done? Had he slain one of the tribe?

Tarzan asked the nearest ape. No, the Gomangani had harmed none. Gozan, being on watch, had seen him coming through the forest and had warned the tribe — that was all. The ape-man pushed through the circle of bulls, none of which as yet had worked himself into sufficient frenzy for a charge, and came where he had a full and close view of the black. He recognized the man instantly. Only the night before he had seen him facing the eyes in the dark, while his fellows groveled in the dirt at his feet, too terrified even to defend themselves. Here was a brave man, and Tarzan had deep admiration for bravery. Even his hatred of the blacks was not so strong a passion as his love of courage. He would have joyed in battling with a black warrior at almost any time; but this one he did not wish to kill — he felt, vaguely, that the man had earned his life by his brave defense of it on the preceding night, nor did he fancy the odds that were pitted against the lone warrior.

He turned to the apes. "Go back to your feeding," he said, "and let this Gomangani go his way in peace. He has not harmed us, and last night I saw him fighting Numa and Sabor with fire, alone in the jungle. He is brave. Why should we kill one who is brave and who has not attacked us? Let him go."

The apes growled. They were displeased. "Kill the Gomangani!" cried one.

"Yes." roared another, "kill the Gomangani and the Tarmangani as well."

"Kill the white ape!" screamed Gozan, "he is no ape at all; but a Gomangani with his skin off."

"Kill Tarzan!" bellowed Gunto. "Kill! Kill! Kill!"

The bulls were now indeed working themselves into the frenzy of slaughter; but against Tarzan rather than the black man. A shaggy form charged through them, hurling those it came in contact with to one side as a strong man might scatter children. It was Taug — great, savage Taug.

"Who says 'kill Tarzan'?" he demanded. "Who kills Tarzan must kill Taug, too. Who can kill Taug? Taug will tear your insides from you and feed them to Dango."

"We can kill you all," replied Gunto. "There are many of us and few of you," and he was right. Tarzan knew that he was right. Taug knew it; but neither would admit such a possibility. It is not the way of bull apes.

"I am Tarzan," cried the ape-man. "I am Tarzan. Mighty hunter; mighty fighter. In all the jungle none so great as Tarzan."

Then, one by one, the opposing bulls recounted their virtues and their prowess. And all the time the combatants came closer and closer to one another. Thus do the bulls work themselves to the proper pitch before engaging in battle.

Gunto came, stiff-legged, close to Tarzan and sniffed at him, with bared fangs. Tarzan rumbled forth a low, menacing \growl. They might repeat these tactics a dozen times; but sooner or later one bull would close with another and then the whole hideous pack would be tearing and rending at their prey.

Bulabantu, the black man, had stood wide-eyed in wonder from the moment he had seen Tarzan approaching through the apes. He had heard much of this devil-god who ran with the hairy tree people; but never before had he seen him in full daylight. He knew him well enough from the description of those who had seen him and from the glimpses he had had of the marauder upon several occasions when the ape-man had entered the village of Mbonga, the chief, by night, in the perpetration of one of his numerous ghastly jokes.

Bulabantu could not, of course, understand anything which passed between Tarzan and the apes; but he saw that the ape-man and one of the larger bulls were in argument with the others. He saw that these two were standing with their back toward him and between him and the balance of the tribe, and he guessed, though it seemed improbable, that they might be defending him. He knew that Tarzan had once spared the life of Mbonga, the chief, and that he had succored Tibo, and Tibo's mother, Momaya. So it was not impossible that he would help Bulabantu; but how he could accomplish it Bulabantu could not guess; nor as a matter of fact could Tarzan, for the odds against him were too great.

Gunto and the others were slowly forcing Tarzan and Taug back toward Bulabantu. The ape-man thought of his words with Tantor just a short time before: "Yes, Tantor, it is good to live. I should hate to die." And now he knew that he was about to die, for the temper of the great bulls was mounting rapidly against him. Always had many of them hated him, and all were suspicious of him. They knew he was different. Tarzan knew it too; but he was glad that he was — he was a MAN; that he had learned from his picture-books, and he was very proud of the distinction. Presently, though, he would be a dead man.

Gunto was preparing to charge. Tarzan knew the signs. He knew that the balance of the bulls would charge with Gunto. Then it would soon be over. Something moved among the verdure at the opposite side of the clearing. Tarzan saw it just as Gunto, with the terrifying cry of a challenging ape, sprang forward. Tarzan voiced a peculiar call and then crouched to meet the assault. Taug crouched, too, and Bulabantu, assured now that these two were fighting upon his side, couched his spear and sprang between them to receive the first charge of the enemy.

Simultaneously a huge bulk broke into the clearing from the jungle behind the charging bulls. The trumpeting of a mad tusker rose shrill above the cries of the anthropoids, as Tantor, the elephant, dashed swiftly across the clearing to the aid of his friend.

Gunto never closed upon the ape-man, nor did a

fang enter flesh upon either side. The terrific reverbera-
tion of Tantor's challenge sent the bulls scurrying to
the trees, jabbering and scolding. Taug raced off with
them. Only Tarzan and Bulabantu remained. The latter
stood his ground because he saw that the devil-god did
not run, and because the black had the courage to face
a certain and horrible death beside one who had quite
evidently dared death for him.

But it was a surprised Gomangani who saw the
mighty elephant come to a sudden halt in front of the
ape-man and caress him with his long, sinuous trunk.

Tarzan turned toward the black man. "Go!" he said
in the language of the apes, and pointed in the direction of the village of Mbonga. Bulabantu understood
the gesture, if not the word, nor did he lose time in
obeying. Tarzan stood watching him until he had
disappeared. He knew that the apes would not follow.
Then he said to the elephant: "Pick me up!" and the
tusker swung him lightly to his head.

"Tarzan goes to his lair by the big water," shouted
the ape-man to the apes in the trees. "All of you are
more foolish than Manu, except Taug and Teeka. Taug
and Teeka may come to see Tarzan; but the others must
keep away. Tarzan is done with the tribe of Kerchak."

He prodded Tantor with a calloused toe and the big
beast swung off across the clearing, the apes watching
them until they were swallowed up by the jungle.

Before the night fell Taug killed Gunto, picking a
quarrel with him over his attack upon Tarzan.

For a moon the tribe saw nothing of Tarzan of the
Apes. Many of them probably never gave him a
thought; but there were those who missed him more
than Tarzan imagined. Taug and Teeka often wished
that he was back, and Taug determined a dozen times
to go and visit Tarzan in his seaside lair; but first one
thing and then another interfered.

One night when Taug lay sleepless looking up at the

starry heavens he recalled the strange things that Tarzan once had suggested to him — that the bright spots were the eyes of the meat-eaters waiting in the dark of the jungle sky to leap upon Goro, the moon, and devour him. The more he thought about this matter the more perturbed he became.

And then a strange thing happened. Even as Taug looked at Goro, he saw a portion of one edge disappear, precisely as though something was gnawing upon it. Larger and larger became the hole in the side of Goro. With a scream, Taug leaped to his feet. His frenzied "Kreeg-ahs!" brought the terrified tribe screaming and chattering toward him.

"Look!" cried Taug, pointing at the moon. "Look! It is as Tarzan said. Numa has sprung through the fires and is devouring Goro. You called Tarzan names and drove him from the tribe; now see how wise he was. Let one of you who hated Tarzan go to Goro's aid. See the eyes in the dark jungle all about Goro. He is in danger and none can help him — none except Tarzan. Soon Goro will be devoured by Numa and we shall have no more light after Kudu seeks his lair. How shall we dance the Dum-Dum without the light of Goro?"

The apes trembled and whimpered. Any manifestation of the powers of nature always filled them with terror, for they could not understand.

"Go and bring Tarzan," cried one, and then they all took up the cry of "Tarzan!" "Bring Tarzan!" "He will save Goro." But who was to travel the dark jungle by night to fetch him?

"I will go," volunteered Taug, and an instant later he was off through the Stygian gloom toward the little land-locked harbor by the sea.

And as the tribe waited they watched the slow devouring of the moon. Already Numa had eaten out a great semicircular piece. At that rate Goro would be entirely gone before Kudu came again. The apes trembled at the thought of perpetual darkness by night. They could not sleep. Restlessly they moved here and there among the branches of trees, watching Numa of the skies at his deadly feast, and listening for the coming of Taug with Tarzan.

Goro was nearly gone when the apes heard the sounds of the approach through the trees of the two they awaited, and presently Tarzan, followed by Taug, swung into a nearby tree.

The ape-man wasted no time in idle words. In his hand was his long bow and at his back hung a quiver full of arrows, poisoned arrows that he had stolen from the village of the blacks; just as he had stolen the bow. Up into a great tree he clambered, higher and higher until he stood swaying upon a small limb which bent low beneath his weight. Here he had a clear and unobstructed view of the heavens. He saw Goro and the inroads which the hungry Numa had made into his shining surface.

Raising his face to the moon, Tarzan shrilled forth his hideous challenge. Faintly and from afar came the roar of an answering lion. The apes shivered. Numa of the skies had answered Tarzan.

Then the ape-man fitted an arrow to his bow, and drawing the shaft far back, aimed its point at the heart of Numa where he lay in the heavens devouring Goro. There was a loud twang as the released bolt shot into the dark heavens. Again and again did Tarzan of the Apes launch his arrows at Numa, and all the while the apes of the tribe of Kerchak huddled together in terror.

At last came a cry from Taug. "Look! Look!" he screamed. "Numa is killed. Tarzan has killed Numa. See! Goro is emerging from the belly of Numa," and, sure enough, the moon was gradually emerging from whatever had devoured her, whether it was Numa, the lion, or the shadow of the earth; but were you to try to convince an ape of the tribe of Kerchak that it was aught but Numa who so nearly devoured Goro that night, or that another than Tarzan preserved the brilliant god of their savage and mysterious rites from a frightful death, you would have difficulty — and a fight on your hands.

And so Tarzan of the Apes came back to the tribe of Ker-chak, and in his coming he took a long stride toward the kingship, which he ultimately won, for now the apes looked up to him as a superior being.

In all the tribe there was but one who was at all skeptical about the plausibility of Tarzan's remarkable rescue of Goro, and that one, strange as it may seem, was Tarzan of the Apes.

CPSIA information can be obtained
at www.ICGtesting.com
Printed in the USA
LVHW031609050320
649104LV00002B/289

[4]